COLD BLOOD

Newsreader Devon Bliss was murdered in the prime of her life, and the police and tabloid press are convinced that loner Graham Scobie is guilty. The eminent defence lawyer Sir John Hathaway persuades the court that the evidence is circumstantial and Scobie walks away a free man. When Hathaway becomes the target of vandalism and threats in his retirement, Superintendent Gregory Summers is called in to investigate. Graham Scobie has recently moved to the area, but why should he threaten the man who saved him from prison – and why is tabloid journalist Reuben ap Morgan suddenly sniffing around?

COLD BLOOD

COLD BLOOD

by

Susan Kelly

Magna Large Print Books
Long Preston, North Yorkshire,
BD23 4ND, England.

British Library Cataloguing in Publication Data.

Kelly, Susan
   Cold blood.

A catalogue record of this book is
available from the British Library

   ISBN   0-7505-2200-3

First published in Great Britain in 2003 by Allison & Busby Ltd.

The right of Susan Kelly to be identified as the author of this
work has been asserted by her in accordance with the
Copyright, Designs and Patents Act, 1988

Published in Large Print 2004 by arrangement with
Allison & Busby Ltd.

Magna Large Print is an imprint of Library Magna Books Ltd.

Printed and bound in Great Britain by
T.J. (International) Ltd., Cornwall, PL28 8RW

Prologue

Not guilty.

All but one of the daily newspapers carried that headline on the morning of Friday March 9th, with or without an exclamation mark, depending on how exclamatory the paper's tone, in general, tended to be. Only *The Times,* preferring to distinguish itself from its more melodramatic rivals, eschewed the obvious with:

'Bliss accused in surprise acquittal.'

They carried similar front-page photographs of Graham Scobie, punching the air in triumph as he left the Central Criminal Court in Old Bailey a free man, oblivious to the thin spring rain that was falling upon him. He had been offered a quiet exit through the back but had elected to walk down the broad front steps, braving the mingled cheers and boos of the damp crowd of spectators.

Booing predominated by a ratio of about eight to one.

A number of tight-lipped police officers followed at a distance, alert for trouble, but the only sign of civil unrest was an ill-aimed egg which spattered harmlessly against a pillar. The derelict marksman – a middle-aged man in a blue, green and purple anorak – ran off with a nervous giggle when one of the constables moved a menacing step in his direction.

It seemed that Scobie had no friends or relatives to escort him to freedom and champagne. He was, as the newspapers had made clear at the time of his arrest, a loner: a plain, short, tubby man with few social skills; an orphan who had never been married. So sure had those same newspapers been of his guilt and his inevitable conviction since the morning the police had found him in Devon Bliss's back garden with her blood on his hands, that none of them had bid for his story on acquittal.

No limo with darkened windows waited to whisk him to a secret hideaway.

Scobie ignored the cameras and microphones that were thrust in his face, making no answer to the questions thrown at him. He walked straight through the crowd which parted before him, since it could think of nothing else to do, leaving the reporters wrong-footed. He turned right up Old Bailey at a brisk walk and disappeared round the corner where Newgate prison had once stood.

The press pack, recovering from their surprise, surged after him, but he was gone. The police officers glanced at each other, shrugged and headed back to their station.

Graham Scobie was no longer their problem.

Sir John Hathaway QC, leading counsel for the defence and the man who had single-handedly secured Scobie's acquittal, waited a few minutes before making his own way down the stone steps, also turning down the offer of a more private exit. He told the waiting reporters courteously but succinctly that British Justice had once again triumphed that day: the prosecution case – mere circumstance and speculation – being caught out in its flimsiness.

The crowd booed, if anything, more loudly as he departed at a measured pace, walking west down Ludgate Hill towards Aldwych.

The broadsheets carried his picture too that Friday morning. He looked composed, not unpleased with himself, in what was to prove his last case.

Not that anybody needed to read Friday's papers to know that the man accused of the shocking murder of television newsreader Devon Bliss had been acquitted, to the dismay and disgust of the Metropolitan police and the Crown Prosecution Service. It had been the lead story on every radio and television news bulletin from eleven o'clock on Thursday morning, less than ten minutes after the jury returned and delivered their verdict.

They had been deliberating for eight days by then and, with the Easter recess looming, the judge had been prepared to accept a majority verdict of at least ten to two. Eleven of them had ruled the day, one elderly woman sitting in grimfaced dissension with her arms folded, as the foreman said the two words that, in her opinion, put a psychotic killer back on the streets.

At home in the Berkshire village of Kintbury, Superintendent Gregory Summers saw the details on an extended early evening news broadcast, watching with sympathy as Devon's former colleagues maintained a professional demeanour over this fresh blow, their mouths grim, their eyes sad. Nothing would bring their golden Devon back, but to know that the bastard who had stabbed her twenty-three times in her own back garden was paying the greatest penalty that the law could exact would have been some meagre consolation.

The TV companies had been preparing one-hour specials on the case since the arrest of Scobie the previous July, convinced, like the newspapers, of his guilt, waiting only for the foreman of the jury to say that one word – Guilty – which would give them the green light to rearrange their schedules and pull in a peak time audience

10

with the gruesome details.

Those specials would now be shelved indefinitely.

Greg watched as a spokesman from the Metropolitan police – a well-dressed chief inspector with a neat haircut, seen-it-all eyes and a manner that spoke professional media training – stated baldly that, although the case would, of course, remain open, they were not looking for anyone else in connection with the crime.

'The operation was scaled down at the time of Graham Scobie's arrest,' he said, 'and will not be reactivated.'

He added in a neutral tone that the prosecution did not have the luxury of appeal that was afforded the defence. You didn't have to be a copper to understand what that meant: Scobie is as guilty as a fox caught in the hen coop with blood and feathers stuck to his muzzle, and the jury should have their sodding heads examined.

If only they had had the blood and the feathers, mused Greg, who had taken a mild professional interest in the case, if only there had been any hard evidence at all. So, Scobie had dozens of pictures of Devon Bliss on his bedroom wall in Catford, hundreds more in a series of scrapbooks meticulously annotated with place and date. Devon Bliss had been in her prime at thirty, blonde and shapely with a smile as wide as an Exmoor sky. All over the country boys of nine and old men of ninety cherished her image. So, Scobie had written her fan letters at the rate of one or two a week; she had many such admirers and the letters themselves bore no word of threat. So, the only girlfriend he'd ever had came forward to say that he was weird and obsessive and that that was why she'd ditched him after a month.

It was not given to every man to love and be loved. To be unloved – even unlovable – did not make you a murderer.

It was while Gregory Summers was watching his London colleague in full flow that John Hathaway got back to Middle Temple and let himself in at the door of Chapel Court, the chambers of which he had been head for the past eight years, and into the deserted clerk's room. It was late – already six hours since he had left the Bailey – and most of his colleagues had given up the wait, saving their back-slapping and champagne-quaffing for the morning. The telephone was ringing. He hesitated then picked it up.

'Chapel Court.'

A male voice said, 'You can tell John Hathaway he's a dead man.'

'I'll be sure to pass the message on, madam.'

He hung up. The phone immediately rang again but he ignored it. He cleared his pigeon hole into his briefcase without so much as glancing at its contents and left the room as swiftly as he had come. As he made his way to his office on the first floor, only one door stood open, awaiting his footfall.

A bass voice boomed. 'John?'

He sighed – he had been hoping to put it off for one more day – but composed his face into a smile as he stopped in the doorway.

'Reggie.'

'At last! Nice bit of work.'

Typical English understatement. 'Thank you.'

'Been out celebrating?'

'Something like that.'

He went into the room and sank wearily onto the client's chair on his side of Reginald Westfield's portentous desk. Hathaway was a man of middling height and slender build, pale of face, not physically impressive, although his modulated tenor carried well in court. His old friend was a barn of a man, almost six and a half feet tall, who had always eaten his share of dinners at the Inns of Court. His florid face with its three ruddy chins beamed now, rejoicing in the reflected glory of his colleague's triumph.

Junior members of chambers called them Laurel and Hardy when they weren't listening, or pretending not to be.

'You really put Chapel Court on the map today,' Reginald said fondly. 'But tell me something, John – did Lady Justice wince up on her roof when she heard the verdict?'

'Now, now, Reggie.'

'Or did she just wish she was blindfolded, the way everyone seems to think she is, when you put a crazed murderer back on the streets?'

'My client was innocent. Eleven good persons and true said so.'

'And one sensible woman said not. What's that graffiti in the Bailey lavatories? – "I'm being tried by twelve people who were too stupid to get out of doing jury service".'

'I'm glad I caught you, in fact,' Hathaway lied, ignoring his friend's raillery, 'since I wanted you to be the first to know ... that that was my last case.'

'Hah!' Westfield sprang up and thrust open his graceful, oak-fronted cupboard with a vigour that made the hinges flinch, producing a bottle of best malt whisky and two crystal highball glasses which he'd got free with his petrol. 'So the call has come at last.'

'The call?' Hathaway waved away the proffered bottle.

'From the Lord Chancellor's office, of course.' Westfield poured himself a generous measure. 'You're going over to the other side at last – Mr Justice Hathaway.' He raised his glass. 'Your Lordship's very good health!' He downed the smoky brown liquid in one gulp, coughed and refilled.

His friend laughed. 'The bench? You must be joking. I could have become a judge years ago if that had been my ambition. No, I'm retiring. Pure and simple.'

Westfield was puzzled. 'Going into politics? Haven't you left it a bit late?'

'Reggie, watch my lips. *I am retiring.*'

'But you're only fifty-eight, John. Good God, you've got years left in you. Maxwell Mason over in Lamb Buildings is still going strong at seventy-two.'

'Years which I intend to devote to my wife and family since I am not, like Maxwell Mason, an ugly old queen whom nobody loves.'

'After today's triumph every lost cause in the country will be after you to represent them, at premium rates.' Seeing the un-persuaded look on his colleague's face, Westfield asked, 'Charity work? Is that it?'

'Reg...' John Hathaway wasn't a particularly patient man and his old friend was already up against the limit of his tolerance. 'I'm getting out of the rat race. I was waiting only for the verdict in this case – a better swan song than I could have dared to hope for, admittedly. The house in London is up for sale. We're going to live permanently in the country.'

'Your place near Newbury?'

'It's at Lambourn, as you know. I shall read all those books I never have time for and potter about the garden, maybe write my memoirs, while India concentrates on her beloved horses. And with Olivia coming to live with us ... I don't know why you look so dumbfounded.'

'Here's another fine mess you've gotten me into, Ollie.'

'Stanley. *You're* Ollie. I don't know what you mean. This is your big chance. Who'll be head of chambers now if not you? The prima donna has broken her leg and the understudy is going out and will come back a star.'

'It's just,' Reginald said slowly as it was finally brought home to him that his friend wasn't joking, 'that the bar has been your life for thirty-five years.'

'All good things come to an end.'

Reuben ap Morgan was sitting in a similar position to John Hathaway, although he was leaning forward on the desk of his editor, Jackson Deans, his leather-clad elbows planted firmly on the scuffed wooden top. Unlike Hathaway, he had accepted his host's offer of a drink and was sipping blended whisky from a paper cup, which he clutched in both hands as if he thought it might escape – which it might, since Jack was notoriously mean with his booze.

'That's a turn up for the book,' said Deans, who favoured cliché, as did his newspaper, the *Daily Outlook*. It made the readers feel more secure. He was old by tabloid-editor standards where only the young could take the strain: fifty-two and looking every day of it, with hair which, though still copious, was uncompromisingly white, worn long around a wrinkled forehead and pouchy cheeks, no spare flesh to iron out his features.

Hamster face, his secretary called him and he had the same beady-eyed look that that rodent generally has before it turns and sinks its teeth into its owner's hand.

He had ruled the *Outlook* for more than twenty years, something of a record in the uncertain business of daily news. This was his kingdom and he was at home on his throne. Now he leaned back in his chair, put his feet up on his desk and fondled his own paper cup like his best beloved. It contained twice as much whisky as the one cradled by ap Morgan.

'Who'd have thought it,' Reuben agreed neutrally.

His birth had been registered in Aberystwyth thirty-seven years previously as plain Reuben Morgan, but he'd assumed the ap on moving to London and the *Outlook* eight years back, thought it gave his by-line

17

distinction, although a particularly dim girlfriend had once remarked that it was an unusual middle name. He could have gone with his mother's lineage and called himself Reuben ben Morgan but that would have confused the dim girlfriend into a fit.

The mixture of Welsh and Jewish blood-lines in him was a felicitous one, bestowing thick black curls and dark eyes, a skin more olive than sallow, a body that resisted the thickening waistline of time, irregular meals and strong drink. He turned women's heads, literally as well as metaphorically.

'I mean, it was a foregone conclusion,' Deans persisted, 'or so we thought.'

The newspaper had been certain of Scobie's guilt and made sure, within the confines of the laws of contempt and libel, that its readers knew it. Reuben had been on the Bliss case since the morning when Devon's fit young body – many a viewer's onanistic fantasy – had been lifted, dew-soaked, from the rear lawn of her house in Blackheath.

Soaked in dew and saturated in blood, Reuben thought. He had seen the body after the post mortem, wangling an illicit viewing from one of the local bobbies. He was good with bobbies, even the uncorrupt ones, knew how to get round them, especially the women. Good with bobbies but not so good with bodies, he thought, smiling faintly at

18

his own joke. He had stumbled out of the morgue that afternoon and deposited his lunch in a neat and steaming heap on the pavement.

'I don't know what you're bloody smiling at,' Deans snarled.

'Nothing, boss.'

'This is a disaster. We can't use half the material we've been gathering for the big post-trial splash.'

We? Reuben thought. He liked *we.*

'Bloody John Hathaway's made us look like fools.'

'Made the police look fools more like,' Reuben demurred.

'Well, it's not over yet–'

'Oh, I think it is, Jack.'

Deans swung his legs down from the desk and banged on it. 'Not as far as I'm concerned. I want you to stay on the case, Reuben, keep on Scobie's tail.'

'There are laws against harassment,' the younger man protested.

'Then don't break them. I'm not asking you to *stalk* the guy. Keep an eye on him, see where he goes, who he associates with. Maybe dig up some fresh evidence.'

'You can't be tried twice for the same crime,' Reuben pointed out. 'They call it double jeopardy.'

'Yeah! And what sort of a bloody stupid law is that?' Deans paused, thinking. 'You never know, he might try it again.'

The young Welshman raised his eyebrows. 'And I shall be on hand with my trusty laptop to stop him?'

'Or if you *did* turn up some new evidence, we could start a crusade to change the law about double jeopardy.' His eyes were afire with enthusiasm.

'There has been some talk in government circles of scrapping it,' Reuben admitted.

'There you go then! Can't let the bloody Labour party take all the credit, can we?' Like most London dailies, the *Outlook* was fiercely right-wing, as was its editor. 'Ages since we had a good crusade, a *people's* crusade... Well?'

'Well?'

'Why are you still here?'

'I'm not. I'm an optical illusion.' Reuben drained his paper cup, pitched it into the waste paper basket and left.

Deans retrieved the cup and rinsed it out in the filthy sink in the corner of his office. *Waste not, want not,* he thought, delighted by the appositeness of the phrase, the way it encapsulated, in only four words, the sentiment he wanted to convey.

He wouldn't hear a word said against cliché.

A 'Real IRA' bomb attack in Croydon, speedily followed by one in Enfield, kept

20

Reuben occupied for the next few weeks. Then he had to run home to Wales for grandfather Ginsberg's funeral – eighty-three years old and still swimming in Cardigan Bay every morning till the very last one – after which the trail had gone cold.

So it wasn't until August that he caught up with Graham Scobie, by which time Sir John Hathaway and his wife, Lady India, had sold their London house and were settled permanently in the charming racing village of Lambourn, not far from Newbury, where Superintendent Gregory Summers was head of CID.

Chapter One

Gregory Summers relieved his guest of his herringbone jacket and flung it unceremoniously over the newel post at the foot of the stairs.

'Glass of wine?' he suggested, heading for the kitchen.

'Not for me thanks, sir. I don't drink alcohol.'

To Greg, a policeman who didn't drink alcohol was synonymous with an alcoholic. They came in two forms: the ones who'd been to AA and who announced proudly 'I am an alcoholic' and the ones who didn't.

DCI Lomax didn't say it.

'I think there's some apple and mango juice in the fridge,' Greg offered.

'Sounds good.'

Lomax followed his host into the kitchen at the back of the house and his tall figure loomed while Greg poured a tumbler of juice for him and a wine glass of Chardonnay for himself. Otherwise the fridge was pretty much bare, as he had thought, and he was glad that he'd phoned ahead for a Chinese.

His new chief inspector, Alex Lomax, had

transferred about three weeks earlier from the Devon and Cornwall police. Greg had half expected him to manifest a West Country burr, but he sounded much like everyone else these days: a cross between working class London and a BBC presenter.

He blamed *EastEnders*.

A single man of forty-six, the new DCI was in a bed and breakfast until he got his bearings and Greg had issued the invitation on the spur of the moment that afternoon, partly because he wanted to get to know his new colleague and partly because he felt sorry for him, all alone in a strange town. Now he stood sipping his wine as neither of them spoke, hoping the Chinese takeaway wasn't on a go-slow tonight.

'I'm not,' Lomax said after a while.

'Sorry?'

'An alcoholic.'

'Thought never crossed my mind.'

Greg had never met a man who looked so much like a ferret, with his long thin face and small black eyes. Hair which had once been chestnut but was now faded was receding at the front, adding to the length of pale flesh poking out above a white collar and a maroon knitted tie. High-arched eyebrows gave him a permanently startled look. He looked as if he might recently have lost weight, since his clothes hung loose on him and, more than once, Greg saw him hitch up the waistband of his trousers, as if the gesture had become habitual. Not so much tall, dark and handsome, he thought, as tall and handsome in the dark.

Ferrets were useful, he reminded himself, handy for flushing out burrows. Rabbits, criminals.

'Come from a long line of them, though,' the man went on, 'which is why I made the decision not to take that first drink thirty years ago.'

Greg said heartily, 'Good for you.' He had no desire to hear the whole squalid story but a strong feeling that he was going to.

Lomax gazed moodily into his glass of vivid orange liquid without drinking any. 'All those years watching my dad come home from the pub – or be dragged home, more like, too drunk to stand.'

'Was he violent?' Greg asked nervously.

'No. One blessing. Hard to be violent when you're too pissed to stay upright. He died when I was fifteen.'

'Oh dear.'

'On his way back from the pub one snowy winter's night. Whoever'd been told to see him safely home left him at the end of our road, thinking he couldn't come to much harm over those last few yards. He fell over in a side alley and couldn't get up again. Died quietly of hypothermia.'

'Oh dear.'

'They say it's not a bad way to go.'

'I've heard that.' Like anyone had come back to tell.

'Your systems slow down and you feel kind of muzzy, or so they say, then you lose consciousness and everything stops. Eventually. He was Glaswegian,' he added, leaving Greg to wonder if this was germane. 'Never really settled down south. Maybe that was part of it.' He knocked back his juice with surprising suddenness. 'Cheers!'

'Must have been hard keeping off the bottle all these years,' Greg ventured, refilling both their glasses.

'The teenage years were the worse, of course,' Lomax said. 'Peer pressure. Made to feel that you're not a real man. "Just one won't hurt". But, as they say in AA, "One's not enough and a thousand's too many".'

'I think it may be the other way round,' Greg suggested.

'Eh?'

'Most people would agree that one's not enough and everybody thinks a thousand's too many, with the possible exception of the late Oliver Reed.'

Lomax thought about it, then laughed. 'Oh, yeah! *One's too many and a thousand's not enough.* Of course. Wonder how many years I've been getting that wrong. What an idiot. Thanks.'

'My pleasure.'

'My kid sister – Bridget – she gave in to the pressure, to the "one won't hurt".'

'And what happened to her?' Greg was forced to ask, since it would seem plain rude not to.

'Oh, nothing too out of the way – lives in a council flat in Tiverton, unemployable, three kids by three different fathers, though they're pretty much grown up now, spends her spare pennies on drink, and some that aren't spare too. I send her a few quid from time to time. Don't know if I should. She only spends it on booze.'

'Oh dear,' Greg said helplessly.

'Tell you the truth the main reason I applied for this transfer was to put a bit of distance between myself and Bridget. These past few years, she's expected me to be at her beck and call, dropping everything to rush over when she phones. It'll do her good to stand on her own two feet for a change. Is Mrs Summers joining us?' Lomax asked suddenly. 'There *is* a Mrs Summers?'

'Yes there is,' Greg said truthfully, since Angie, his son's widow, was a Mrs Summers, just not Mrs Gregory Summers. 'I'm afraid she's out at a lecture tonight, won't be back till late. Bachelor evening.'

The Death of the Id: he really hoped she wasn't going to tell him about it when she got home.

'Only you can learn a lot about people

26

from their partners,' Lomax said.

Greg was glad of the change of subject. 'Indeed.'

'Some men marry the most frightful women. Know what I mean?' Greg nodded, safe in the knowledge that Lomax was unlikely ever to meet his frightful ex-wife, Diane. 'Makes you question their judgment on everything,' the DCI went on, 'if they can't get something as fundamental as that right.'

'Good point and Angie isn't at all frightful.'

'Dear me no! Never meant to suggest such a thing. Sure she's charming. I never married, of course. Didn't want to pass on those bad genes.'

'Oh dear.' No change of subject after all.

'Haven't quite given the idea up entirely, mind, now that I'm older. Nice woman my own age, maybe, done the kids thing, menopausal or had a hysterectomy.'

'... Right.'

'Though policemen don't exactly make the best husbands,' Lomax concluded.

'That's true.'

'How does Mrs Summers cope?'

'Angie's very independent.'

'Yes, that's the best way, when they make separate lives for themselves, lectures and so forth. Trouble is that, then, when you retire, they're so used to going it alone that they get fed up having you under their feet all the time and that's when they bugger off.'

Greg was running mentally over the array of sharp objects that the kitchen afforded, wondering which of them would be most effective for cutting his own throat. He'd just settled on a vicious vegetable knife – small but should do the trick with a good hard wrist action – when the front doorbell rang.

'Oh, Thank god!' he said, then added hastily, 'I'm starving. How 'bout you?'

Greg was in a bad mood the following morning, partly because Angie had given him a blow-by-blow account of the lecture when she got home, but mostly because he had a hangover. He had drunk more of the Chardonnay than he had intended during the several days that the previous evening had lasted, finishing the second half of the bottle under the openly disapproving eye of Alex Lomax who seemed always on the point of saying 'Don't you think you've had enough?' before bowing to the privileges of rank.

They had remained 'Lomax' and 'Sir' to each other all evening, with greater informality neither offered nor presumed.

The annoying thing was that Lomax was obviously a damn good copper. Greg, suspicious of his glowing references, had telephoned his counterpart in Plymouth to check that they weren't just desperate to get rid of the man, but Detective Superintendent Burnip had been adamant that Greg had robbed him of a treasure.

'Doesn't mind doing the leg work, see,' he had said – and he did have a West Country accent, a voice made gruff by a lifetime of best Wessex cider – 'never moans about the boring stuff or the paperwork. Plodding, maybe, but thorough and effective. Excellent clear-up rate. Good collection of informers.'

Not that Lomax's snitches would be any use to him up here. He would have to begin again with the local low-life. Since most meetings with informants took place in pubs to the lubrication of alcohol, a teetotaller started at a clear disadvantage, but the DCI obviously managed somehow.

'I'm getting my bearings,' he'd said last night, 'spending my free time driving round the area, stopping at pubs and cafés, getting into conversation with as many people as possible.'

Making them suicidal, Greg thought.

'I drink ginger ale and people assume it's Scotch and ginger,' the DCI explained. 'No one trusts a teetotaller.'

'He's not been ill, has he?' Greg asked Burnip as an afterthought. 'He looks as if he's lost weight recently.' Many a first-rate copper had proved next to useless after a breakdown.

'Well, the best of us could do with losing a few pounds,' the man said, 'and that's what Alex did, I guess.' Greg wondered, after hanging up, if he had been deliberately evasive.

His team seemed to have taken to the new man, adopting him as a pet or mascot. Both his constables – George 'The Bubble' Nicolaides and Andy Whittaker – had pronounced him 'a good bloke' and even Sergeant Barbara Carey, who had been investigating the antics of a pair of con artists with him, had described him as 'quite entertaining'.

'It's like taking a peculiarly sad blood-hound for a walk,' she explained when he queried this.

All of which annoyed Greg. He felt like an outsider in the gang, the kid who gets picked on. And he was the leader of the gang. It was *his* gang.

So it was that, for the first time in over a year, Greg had a second in command to whom he could safely leave the day-to-day work of Newbury CID. Which was all very well but it left him with nothing but internal politics and policy documents to occupy his mind and those had never been his favourite aspects of policing.

He was working on a report on the manpower crisis that was looming in the Thames Valley as officers, complaining of the high cost of living in this prosperous part of England, were resigning *en masse* and heading for cheaper locations in the North, West and Wales. If things continued at this rate they would be twenty-five percent under strength in a couple of years time, leaving the muggers, rapists and murderers of Berkshire to go about their unlawful business more or less undisturbed.

Greg had no solution to this problem – short of doubling everyone's wages, including his own – but then nor did anyone else.

He was delighted, therefore, when his secretary, Susan Habib, who was apparently satisfied with her pay, told him that the Chief Superintendent would like to see him at his earliest convenience.

Chief Superintendent James Barkiss was standing at the open window of his office when Greg arrived, looking out over the flourishing market town of Newbury. Greg joined him.

Barkiss was a short man, barely making the regulation height that had been in force for police recruitment twenty-five years ago, and was now settling into the slight portliness of early middle age which necessitated a larger size of uniform every five years.

'Looks peaceful, doesn't it?' he remarked.

Greg examined the constant flow of traffic

round the nearby roundabout and the comings and goings at the Sainsbury supermarket opposite. A spell of hot weather had recently settled over southern England, with the afternoon temperature in the high twenties, and both men were in shirtsleeves. He could see exhaust fumes shimmering upwards in the sunlight.

'More like bustling,' he said.

'All quiet on the crime front, though?'

'Fairly,' Greg said cautiously. 'With it being August and the holiday season it's prime time for burglaries.' Every burglar welcomed a hot snap as it meant windows thrown open and often forgotten in the haste to leave the house.

'And DCI Lomax?' Barkiss said. 'How's he shaping up?'

'Early days...'

'It would be nice if we could hang on to this one before we start getting a reputation as the place where chief inspectors come to...'

'To die?' Greg suggested.

'To destroy their careers!'

Greg, who had been through three DCIs in little more than a year, offered a mild objection. 'Megan Davies left for personal reasons.'

'Yes. Yes. No one's saying it's your fault,' Barkiss said, in the tone of voice that implied the exact opposite. 'Had a phone

32

call this morning,' he said, finally getting to the point. 'Slight acquaintance called John Hathaway. Got a problem he'd like help with.'

Greg thought about it. 'I seem to know the name.'

'If I say *Sir* John Hathaway QC?'

'The Devon Bliss case?'

'Exactly.'

On the roundabout a lorry attempting to speed off towards the M4 had a near miss with a car heading for the station and a hooting competition ensued.

'He doesn't live round here, does he?' Greg asked.

'He's recently retired–'

'Resting on his laurels?'

'Presumably. Settled in his country cottage in Lambourn. I say cottage...'

'More like a mansion?'

'I haven't been there but I don't suppose it's a two-up-two-down, no.'

'So what's his problem?'

'Claims he's being harassed. You mentioned the Bliss murder. That was his last case before he retired, went out with a splash. Plenty of people say that justice was made a mockery of that day, that Hathaway's eloquence put a deranged murderer back on the streets...'

Both car and lorry were now stationery and the drivers had got out: a large man

33

with tattoos in tracksuit bottoms and singlet; a tall thin man in suit trousers and a short-sleeved shirt, his jacket hung neatly on a peg in the back of his car. Oddly, he too had a tattoo, a snake curling up his left arm. Fists were being shaken, the red serpent and a green mermaid flexing aggressively at each other.

More horns joined in the chorus as other drivers found themselves trapped behind the feuding pair.

'It's this hot weather,' Barkiss commented placidly. 'Road rage.'

'He's defended some pretty high-profile cases over the years,' Greg mused.

'And prosecuted a fair few, come to that,' Barkiss added. 'Put some very nasty people behind bars.'

'Is he under any form of police protection?'

'Not now he's retired. I got a courtesy call when he came to live in the area full time.'

'What form is this harassment taking?' Greg queried, raising his voice above the din as his colleague reached up to close the double-glazed window, smothering the sound as with a blanket.

'Graffiti sprayed on his car. Weed killer dumped on his lawn. His granddaughter's puppy found hanged from a tree.'

Greg winced. 'That's vicious. The dog, I mean. Especially a child's puppy.'

'Cruel,' Barkiss agreed.

Greg noticed dispassionately that the roundabout was now close to gridlock. He wouldn't feel so indifferent if it was still gridlocked when he wanted to go out in his car.

'And Hathaway thinks it's connected to the Bliss case?' he asked. 'Some relative of the dead girl's, or another fan, with a grudge against him?'

Two uniformed officers, making their way back to the station, were intervening in the logjam of cars, remonstrating with the tattooed drivers who got sullenly back behind their steering wheels and pulled to one side to continue their row more conveniently. The constables restored the roundabout to its normal chaos in two minutes flat.

'That's the bizarre thing,' Barkiss said slowly. 'He thinks that he's being harassed by the accused, Graham Scobie, the very man you'd think had the most cause to be grateful to him.'

Chapter Two

Lambourn was a village apart. It lived by, with and for horses. And not any old horses, either, not working horses or children's ponies, not much-loved pets. Racehorses ruled Lambourn: neurotic, skinny beasts with legs two yards long that covered the grassy acres of Lambourn Downs at thirty miles an hour and made it look like a morning stroll.

Everybody in the village talked of them all day long, probably dreamed of them at night. If you had no interest in matters equine and couldn't tell your five-to-two on from your thirteen-to-eight against then you had no place here, no lawful business.

All of which gave Lambourn a community spirit usually lacking in such large villages in the twenty-first century.

The Hathaways' 'country cottage', on the outskirts of the village off a narrow lane leading vaguely in the direction of Wantage, was not what Gregory Summers had been expecting. He'd envisaged something Georgian and stately, set in its own parkland. Ascot House dated from some time between the wars and was mock-Tudor in style, white with fake black beams.

Standing in a garden of no more than half an acre, it was almost suburban with its ordered shrubs and neat flower beds. It looked well cared-for, though, recently painted, which made Greg feel guilty as he'd still done nothing about sprucing up his own increasingly shabby house.

He made a swift resolution to phone round for quotes this weekend.

The metal gate into the drive was shut and he decided to leave his car on the road rather than get out, open it, drive in and shut it behind him. The gate opened easily on well-oiled hinges and his footsteps were silent on the brick path that led up to the front door. Musing on his own mute approach, he noticed that there was no sign of a burglar alarm.

He raised his hand to the bell but the door was already opening, so it seemed that his arrival had not been as cat-like as he had imagined. A woman's voice said, 'Super-intendent Summers, I presume?'

'Lady Hathaway?'

He held out his hand. She grabbed it in her strong fist and pumped it up and down, almost dragging him in through the door. He saw a middle-aged woman who could never have been handsome but who looked capable and sensible and good. He liked her at once. She was wearing loose cotton trousers and a short top which revealed a tanned midriff as firm as that of a girl half her age. She wore her abundant blonde hair caught back in a blue ribbon and he noticed that her feet were bare.

'It's technically Lady India,' she said, ushering him into an octagonal hallway with parquet flooring and stained-glass flowers on the windows. She grinned, showing excellent teeth. 'I wouldn't mention it but people get unaccountably embarrassed if they find out later that they've been "getting it wrong". Why don't you call me Indie? Everyone does.'

It suited her, he thought. Independent Indie. He would have to avoid calling her anything now as he could hardly invite her to call him Gregory when he was here on police business: most unprofessional.

'Is that Mr Summers?' John Hathaway, looking thin and pale compared to his wife's almost aggressive good health, emerged from the back of the house to deliver a lawyer's handshake – firm and reassuring but held very slightly too long. He had dark hair tinged with grey and eyes the colour of chestnuts. He was wearing corduroy trousers, the colour of sludge and with the seat worn smooth and shiny, and a green and white checked shirt. 'Thank you so much for coming.'

'Coffee,' India announced and left without

waiting for a reply.

'Come through to the study.' Hathaway steered Greg with a hand on his arm through an open door to their left into a pleasant room with views over a small lily pond at the side of the house. The desk was tucked away in a dark corner as if it was no longer much needed, although Greg saw that the computer on it was switched on, an array of Windows icons filling the cloudy sky of its background, or 'wallpaper' as he'd recently been instructed to call it.

'Writing my memoirs,' Hathaway murmured modestly. 'Slow work.'

Two leather armchairs stood either side of an empty grate and Greg and his host sat without ceremony. He found his eyes drawn to a coat of arms above the mantelpiece. It was not the hotch-potch of gaudy flowers and mythical animals that drew his eye so much as the motto:

Plus Jamais Rien.

Which Greg's 'A' level French (failed) told him translated as something along the lines of *Nothing, ever more, ever again.*

'Indie's family,' Hathaway said, following his eye. 'The Nethermores.'

'The motto ... isn't it a bit?'

'Negative?' he suggested. 'Depressing? Nihilistic?'

'Um, yes.'

'All of those,' Sir John said cheerfully.

'Basically, it's a play on words, of course: Nethermore – nevermore. Do you see? Actually, the Nethermores are the most down-to-earth and unneurotic bunch of people you could hope to meet.'

'So...' Greg began, settling into his chair. 'You think you're the victim of some sort of vendetta, I understand.'

'At first I thought it was an act of mindless vandalism,' Hathaway said, 'if that isn't a tautology.' He took a notebook from the breast pocket of his shirt. 'When I realised that it was something more concerted than that, I started keeping a record of dates. It began a couple of weeks ago, on the 15th of July, with paint being sprayed on the car.'

'Your car?' He had observed two cars in the drive: a Range Rover with a towing bar and a spanking new silver Aston Martin. Neither looked any the worse for wear.

'Indie's car to be precise. The Rover.'

'Bloody lucky it wasn't John's precious Aston Martin.'

India's voice came from behind and above them as she swept into the room and, before either man could move a muscle to help, had pulled a low table deftly from the window bay to the fireside and deposited a tarnished metal tray on it, holding two unmatching mugs of coffee and a chipped saucer with four Bourbon biscuits.

'Otherwise,' she concluded ominously,

'the world would have come to an end. Talk about mid-life crisis! I mean–' she looked to Greg for support '– a car's just a car. Right? A to B, preferably in one piece.'

Greg thought it politic not to answer – you should never come between husband and wife unless one of them was criminally assaulting the other – and smiled politely.

'Yes, well,' Sir John said. He looked fondly at his wife's retreating back and sipped his coffee. 'Indie's not bothered about material things. Grew up surrounded by Meissen and Chippendale at Nethermore Hall. Her father had a nice Gainsborough.' His eyes took on a far-away look. 'A *very* nice Gainsborough, which was taken by the state in lieu of death duties when the old man died. Now we have to go to the National Gallery if we want to look at it. "Stuff", Indie calls it. "Just *stuff*". All right for some.'

Greg had done a little research into John Hathaway and had learned that he'd hardly been born with a silver spoon in his mouth. The son of a grocer from Manchester, his fine brain had won him a scholarship to the famous grammar school and, later, one to Cambridge where he'd gained a first. He'd swiftly made a name for himself at the bar and married the daughter of an earl, although Greg's antennae told him it had been a love match and not another step on the road to advancement.

He sipped his coffee which he diagnosed as instant and nibbled at the edge of a stale Bourbon, wondering if it would be beyond the pale to render it edible by dunking it. 'What did the graffiti say?'

'What?' Hathaway was startled out of a reverie. 'Oh, it said "Die".'

'Short but not very sweet.'

'Indeed.'

'And you called the police?'

'Naturally, if only for insurance purposes. They agreed with my own view that it was just malice, bored kids lashing out at someone more privileged. We got the car resprayed and thought no more about it, until–' he consulted his notebook again '–the 27th, when we awoke to find that someone had used weedkiller to burn graffiti into the back lawn in letters two feet high. "You will die". More loquacious this time.'

'My God!'

'Yes. Not what you really want to see when you look out of your bedroom window first thing in the morning.'

'Can I take a look?'

'You can see where it was but we've had it returfed.'

They'd not wasted time, Greg thought, on either occasion, in erasing the damage and, with it, any forensic evidence. Unsurprising but annoying. He liked Hathaway, though not with the instinctive warmth that his wife had inspired. He sensed beneath that mild exterior the arrogance of a man who knew himself cleverer than the herd, the certainty of rightness that would not be gainsaid.

The older man was speaking again. 'Then the worse thing happened just four days ago. Olivia, our granddaughter, found her puppy hanged from the apple tree at the bottom of the garden, strung up with a bit of twine. That was when I decided to call Chief Superintendent Barkiss.'

'How horrible. There's no better friend than a faithful dog.'

'You have one?'

'A West Highland Terrier, I ... inherited her a few months ago and now I can't imagine life without her.'

Sir John's eyes took on a haunted look and his hand cupped his mouth, muffling his words. 'I shall never forget her face as she walked into the kitchen with the strangled dog in her arms: the bewilderment; the incomprehension. She didn't say a word for the rest of the day. Just put him in his basket by the Aga as if he needed a warm after a romp in the rain, sat down at the kitchen table and laid her head on her arms and wept.' Hathaway lowered his own head as if he were trying himself to blink back tears.

'She's how old?' Greg asked gently.

'Eight.'

'She lives with you?'

'Yes.'

'Her parents...?'

'Mmm? Oh, no. No tragedy. Nothing like that. My son Richard is in the Diplomatic Corps, still junior – chief bootlicker, as he calls it. He was stationed in Rome until six months ago, which was fine, but then he was moved to Moscow. Neither he nor Melissa, my daughter-in-law, was happy about Liv being there. Apart from the wretchedness of the climate, it's become a lawless place these last few years.'

'So I hear.'

'Gangs roaming the streets in open warfare, fighting over territory for drugs and prostitution.' He paused, thoughtful. 'Why on earth did they have to seize on all the *worst* aspects of Capitalism when they gave up Communism when, whatever the faults of our system, there is much that is good and noble?'

'I've wondered that myself.'

'Anyway, it was agreed that Olivia would come and live with me and Indie for the time being. She's young for boarding school and, with me retiring, we've got plenty of time for her. She's a great kid. We adore her. We got her the puppy as soon as she arrived. She hadn't been allowed to have one in Rome, what with quarantine problems, and we thought it'd help, so she wouldn't miss her parents so much. It was a funny little mongrel – mess of colours and an odd shape: big body but short legs, as if a Dalmatian had mated with a Yorkshire terrier – but she was adamant she didn't want anything smarter. She called it Pizza.'

'What did you do with the body?' Greg asked.

'Buried it at the bottom of the garden.' Hathaway looked hard at him. 'You don't want it dug up? Only I'm afraid that'll set Liv off again.'

'Not at the moment. I'll take a look at the tree where it was found hanging, though, and the ligature, if you have it.' He hesitated. 'The Chief Superintendent intimated that you knew who was behind this.'

Hathaway sighed and ran a hand over his face as if trying to wash away some blemish. 'I'm reluctant to point the finger. I don't know! Maybe the man's suffered enough.'

'You think Graham Scobie's harassing you,' Greg persisted.

'It's just a hunch. I wish I hadn't mentioned it to Mr Barkiss now. But it seems so odd otherwise, him turning up like that, in Lambourn.'

'He's not a local man?'

'God, no! He comes from Catford in south-east London, not far from Devon Bliss's house in Blackheath – though a world away socially and financially, of course. You didn't follow the trial?'

'Not in detail,' Greg admitted. 'I had my own murder case to solve back in March.'

'Scobie worked for some of Devon's neighbours as a jobbing gardener,' Hathaway explained. He paused, struck by a thought. 'I never met her when she was alive and yet I've fallen into the habit of calling her by her first name as if she was my oldest friend.'

'Appearing on TV does that to people,' Greg said.

'It was her real name, you know. Only it sounds like something you'd make up, doesn't it? Devon Bliss. Anyway, the body had been lying in the garden all night and was found by her driver when he came to collect her at nine a.m. to take her to the studio for the one o'clock news.

'He got no reply at the front door and wandered round to the back. He screamed his head off when he saw her corpse – practically hysterical – and Scobie came running from a couple of doors down to see what all the noise was about. He attempted some sort of resuscitation. He wasn't trained in first aid and Devon had clearly been dead for hours but it's not an unnatural reaction. That was how he came to have her dried blood on his hands and clothes, of course, which the prosecution tried to make something of.'

'And the murder weapon was never found, was it?'

'No. A six-inch smooth blade, narrow, like a stiletto, or so the pathologist said. That remains a mystery.'

'But Scobie didn't murder Devon,' Greg said, 'according to the jury.'

'But that doesn't make him a nice man, Mr Summers. Sadly. To be frank, he's pretty creepy. He has few social skills, no friends, and it's not altogether surprising that the police set him up for that murder.' Observing Greg's face as it solidified into hostile iceberg, he amended quickly, 'What I mean is that the police made the mistake they did.'

'I see.' Greg decided to let it go. 'And he's here, in Lambourn?'

'I ran into him in the High Street one morning, about a month ago. You could have knocked me down with a feather, as they say.'

'It's not surprising that he wanted to get away, perhaps, to start afresh.'

'But why here? Isn't that a bit of a coincidence?'

'A bit,' Greg admitted.

'I don't believe in coincidence.'

Coincidences did happen, of course, although often there was some logical explanation. Greg recalled a school trip to the Sussex coast when he was fifteen. The history master had explained that the Battle of Hastings had not taken place at Hastings at all but at the town of Battle some miles inland and Jeff James, the class thicko, had piped up, 'That's quite a coincidence, isn't it, sir?'

He said, 'What I don't understand, Sir John, is why he should feel any animosity towards you. Surely he must see you as his saviour – if anything – his *hero.*'

'It doesn't make much sense,' Hathaway agreed, 'but Scobie is an odd little man, as I said, and sometimes people fixate on their heroes, then get angry because they can't live up to their fantasies.'

That was true, Greg thought, it was the archetypal stalking scenario. It was probably why Devon Bliss had met her horrible death: because some man who fantasised himself in love with her couldn't bear not to have that love requited, couldn't stand to see her out with her string of glamorous boyfriends – soap actors, pop stars, models, premier-league footballers – and decided that if he couldn't have her then nobody would.

The threat was not always physical or emotional. There had been a recent case where the snubbed fan of a world-famous sportsman turned over his comprehensive archive to the authorities to prove that his former idol had not been resident in low-tax Monaco quite as often as he'd claimed, leaving him to face millions of Euros in back taxes and fines, even the threat of imprisonment.

Hell had no fury like a fan scorned.

'Do you know where Scobie is living?' he asked.

'No. I was almost too stunned to speak to him, let alone ask him questions.'

'Might he have felt slighted?'

Hathaway said slowly, 'Possibly.'

And that might be enough: something as small as that could turn hero worship into hatred.

'He rang me,' Sir John said, 'a few days later. We're in the phone book, so nothing sinister about that. He asked if I knew of any gardening work he might do locally since that was where his experience lay. I think he was intimating that he might do my garden but it isn't huge and quite low-maintenance and I like to do it myself, now that I've plenty of time on my hands. I let him down lightly but I suppose that might have looked like a snub too.'

It couldn't be easy for him to find work, Greg thought, not if people knew who he was. Even if he had been acquitted, why would anyone take that risk?

'I'd rather you didn't let him know of my suspicions,' Hathaway added. 'As I say, it's little more than a gut feeling and I've learned not to trust those.'

So had Greg; so had anyone who'd reached middle age intact, if they had any sense.

'Okay.' Greg felt in his pocket and

produced his business card. 'There's very little I can do at the moment, anyway. The most important thing is for you to contact me if anything new happens, then don't touch it, whatever it is, till I can get a forensic team out here. Meantime, I'll set about finding out where Scobie's living and if we can get some evidence then we might be able to lock him up for a while.'

Scobie's fingerprints would have been destroyed on his acquittal; that was the rule, or had been till recently. Some police forces had started keeping prints and DNA samples on acquittal, only to have the action challenged in the courts. Every detective in the country was awaiting the judge's ruling with interest.

He decided to explore alternative theories. 'Have you been threatened before?'

'I've put a few nasty people away over the years, of course. Plenty of them shouted abuse at me from the dock after sentencing but nothing much came of it. The only one that gave me cause for concern was the gangland leader, Eddie Machin – remember him?'

'I certainly do. What was that – mid eighties?'

'1987. Psychotic, of course, but the jury wouldn't accept that he was mentally ill and he went down for life with a recommendation of thirty years. He was quietly transferred to Broadmoor three years later and I have it on good authority that he'll die there. He said he'd see me in my grave and there was something about him that made me believe him.' Hathaway gave a small shudder. 'Something in the eyes. I had police protection for six months but nothing untoward happened and I was glad when it was finally stood down. It was getting wearying.'

'Empty threats?'

'I think that, with Eddie banged up, someone else took over his "businesses" and they weren't interested in taking revenge for Eddie, probably grateful to me for clearing him out of the way, if anything.'

'Is there anybody who might be upset by your memoirs?'

'I doubt it. Tell you the truth, it's more of a hobby than anything. I haven't got a publisher fixed up. Who wants to read the tedious anecdotes of a retired barrister?'

Greg couldn't imagine but then he couldn't imagine who wanted to read the tedious anecdotes of retired cabinet ministers; and yet they all got half-million pound advances, serialisation in a serious Sunday newspaper and a guaranteed place on the best-seller list. Funny he'd never met anyone who admitted to reading this stuff.

'You and I come up against some pretty awful people in our lines of work, Mr

Summers,' Hathaway said, '–serial killers, rapists, child murderers – and half the time we watch them walk away unpunished or be released from jail after a few pitiful years.'

It was a conversation Greg had had a thousand times and he didn't feel like having it again. He said, 'Do you keep weapons in the house?'

'Indie keeps a shotgun which she uses occasionally on visits to Nethermore Hall, when her brother invites her down in the season. I wouldn't know which way round to hold it, but she's not a bad shot. We keep it locked in the gun cupboard, naturally.'

Which was just as it should be. Greg placed his empty coffee cup on the tray and rose. 'Can I see the tree?'

Hathaway led the way through the kitchen into the back garden, passing an outhouse and a log store where piles of neatly chopped firewood sat waiting for winter and their rightful destiny. Several yards of clipped lawn led slightly downhill into a small orchard where Sir John pointed to an apple tree, old and bushy, dull on this day in early August with its blossom over and its apples no more than green swellings. He reached up and tapped his fingers on a branch that stood about seven feet off the ground, running straight and knotty.

'There's not even a mark,' he said. 'The poor creature wasn't heavy.'

Greg, having ascertained the truth of this, stood looking round the grounds. Although the garden was modest, a stile in the far corner led into an adjacent field or paddock a good acre in size. He could see India there, her cotton trousers tucked into Wellington boots, with a girl of about eight in jodhpurs and a hacking jacket, a pretty little thing with her grandfather's black hair flowing from under her riding hat.

'I take it that's Olivia,' he said.

'That's her,' Hathaway said with justifiable pride.

They stood by the stile for a moment, watching the child. She was mounted on a bay pony with a white blaze and four white socks and was carrying out some complicated dressage manoeuvres under the fond but not uncritical eye of her grandmother and another woman. As she turned at the end of the paddock, she noticed the two men watching and brought the pony to a halt, waving eagerly. Greg saw Hathaway's pale face flush with love for her as he waved back.

He envied him, he who would never have a grandchild.

India walked across to join them. 'Examining the scene of the crime?' she asked in a low voice.

'Yes,' Greg said rather abruptly. He was looking intently at the other woman as she took the pony by the bridle and began to offer advice to the little girl. She had an ethereal beauty that made him think of a fairy or an elf, hair so blonde as to be almost silver. He couldn't make out her eyes at this distance but they must be blue. Or green, or grey. She was wearing jeans tucked into scuffed riding boots and a v-necked T-shirt the same colour as the sky. Early twenties, he thought. He did not consider himself susceptible to feminine beauty, in general, but he felt startled by this girl, wrong footed.

India was watching him with amusement. 'That's Grace,' she said, 'and she's young enough to be your daughter.'

So was Angie for that matter. He collected himself and gave her the look that said 'I'm sure I don't know what you mean' which only amused her more. 'I was just thinking,' he said with dignity, 'that it would be easy to get into the garden from that field.'

'Yes,' Indie agreed gravely. 'It would.'

'So, where are your nearest neighbours?' Greg asked briskly. 'I passed a row of cottages a little way back...'

'Yes,' Hathaway said. 'We're the last house in the village so those are the nearest dwellings. It's a row of old almshouses, four of them.'

'Do you know who lives there?'

It was India who answered him. 'The two in the middle are weekend cottages and the people only come down about once a month, shocking waste when there are so many homeless–'

Her husband gave a slightly theatrical cough, a tool he must often have used in court. 'This was a weekend cottage for years, darling.'

'Yes, but we came down *every* weekend,' she said impatiently, 'and other holidays and–' she turned to Greg for support '–barristers get loads of holidays, don't they? And I was here on my own sometimes during the flat season.' Seeing Greg's raised eyebrows she explained, 'I keep a racehorse in training in Lambourn, with Paddy Nash – Gnasher.'

'Your horse is called Gnasher?'

She barked out a laugh. 'That's what we call Paddy! No, the mare is Ranulf's Daughter. Don't ask me why. I didn't name her.' She gave him a sideways look. 'You a betting man, Mr Summers?'

'Not really.'

'Pity! She's running at Windsor in ten days time and I'd have advised you to back her. You can get fifteen-to-one ante-post.' She nodded at the silver-haired fairy. 'Grace is one of Paddy's lads and Ranulf's one of her charges. Paddy sometimes lets her help out with Liv as she's very patient, much patienter than I am.'

'The almshouses, darling,' Hathaway murmured, steering her back to the subject like a rambling witness in the box.

Apparently recognising the technique, India snapped, 'I'm not under cross examination, Johnny. Mr Summers asked about the horse.'

'No, he didn't.'

'Well ... he *looked* as if he wanted to know.' She scrutinised her husband with fond exasperation. 'Right! Almshouses. Girl called Molly Hawkins at the far end. I say *girl*, she's about thirty, works in London, something at the BBC, commutes every day, doesn't get home till at least ten most nights, just uses the place to sleep as far as I can make out. At this end there's a very quiet young man called Michael something. Parkinson?'

'Isn't he the TV chat-show man?' Hathaway asked.

'Okay. Patterson. Peterson... It could still be Parkinson: it's not like the telly man has a *monopoly* on the name. I bet there's a dustman in Newbury called John Hathaway, come to that.'

There might be, Greg thought, but it was a fair bet that his wife wasn't called India; only the upper classes named their daughters after odd bits of Empire.

'He's also about thirty,' India was saying. 'Works locally, something clerical, and doesn't seem to go out much or have many visitors. Not a lot to say for himself but

56

entirely harmless. He's the only one who can truly be said to be a full-time resident so he might have noticed something.'

'I'll see if he's in,' Greg said.

He shook hands once more with India and she went back to her granddaughter, leaving her husband to see him out.

'Extraordinary, isn't she?' Sir John remarked as they made their way back to the house.

'Lady India?'

'Well, she is too, obviously, but I meant Grey – Grace.'

'Oh.' There seemed no point in denying it, in pretending that he hadn't noticed. 'She's lovely.'

'Brain like a rabbit, though. Still, you can't have everything.'

'There's just one thing,' Greg said, as Hathaway opened the gate for him. 'What makes you so sure that it's you and not Lady India who's the target of this harassment? It was her car, after all, that was vandalised and not yours.'

Sir John looked startled. 'It never crossed my mind! Indie? She hasn't an enemy in the world.'

Chapter Three

Greg left his car where it was and walked the two hundred yards to the almshouses. The lane had no pavement so he kept to the right, facing oncoming traffic, of which there was none.

After fifty yards he took off his suit jacket and hooked it over his shoulder by his thumb, feeling the sweat clammy in his armpits despite a liberal application of deodorant after his shower that morning.

By the time he reached the row of houses, he felt he could do with a swim, but in Lambourn only the horses had swimming pools.

They were narrow dwellings, so narrow that Greg felt as if he could stretch out his arms and touch the boundaries with his fingertips. It had been assumed that the requirements of those needing charity were modest. Each had a door and one window on the ground floor and a larger window above.

One up, one down, he thought, with a galley kitchen tacked on at the back and a tiny bathroom shoe-horned in sometime in the twentieth century. Cosy, though, and well cared-for, each with its window box as it fronted the road on the edge of the village. Large plots suggested long, thin gardens where the poor of the parish could grow vegetables and keep chickens.

A plaque told him that the terrace had been built in 1775. The houses were probably now 'much sought after'.

He knocked on the first door where the window box sported marigolds, but Michael Parkinson, Patterson or Peterson was not in and nor, it seemed, were any of his neighbours – not the miniature roses, nor either set of wilting geraniums.

Greg walked slowly back to his car, resolving to return that evening. He drove home. Bored with the news on Radio Four, he flipped stations at random. A mournful piece of music was coming to an end on Radio Three and the announcer said in a respectful tone, 'That was part of Mahler's *Kindertotenlieder:* Songs for dead children.'

Not in the mood for anything so gloomy, he tried again. Tammy Winette was singing; he let her; she was off, once again, apparently, with her suitcase in her hand, running away down River Road.

By the time he reached Great Shefford, he was joining in the choruses.

Joy Reynolds was not one of nature's barmaids. She had been perfectly happy with her clerical job at the building society in Greenford in West London, but then Eric had been made redundant and had hailed it as the opportunity he'd been waiting for; with his pay-off and the sale of their modest 1930s semi for what seemed like a ridiculous sum he could realise his lifelong dream of running a pub somewhere in the country.

Grateful only that premature retirement had not sent her husband spiralling into one of his depressions, Joy had meekly accepted the loss of her home and friends and found herself, a short three months later, serving behind the bar of the Jolly Fisherman in Lambourn and putting a brave face on it.

The Fisherman was not the most central pub in the village but it occupied a nice spot near the river with a big car park. The previous owner had let the place get a bit run down and there was plenty of scope to improve profits. Soon business was brisk, although stable lads were not well paid, and they increased their income by sporadically letting the three spare bedrooms on the first floor.

After a year in the village, Joy was popular with the locals, as she had a naturally friendly disposition and was pretty in the slightly plump, girl-next-door kind of way that most ordinary men found unthreatening. The more philosophical of them occasionally speculated amongst themselves as to why a live wire like Joy had ever hooked up with a miserable git like Eric Reynolds but, as was usual with such conversations, no conclusion was ever reached.

By his standards, Eric seemed happy in his new life which meant that Joy was content. His latest plan was to upgrade their bar meals to a better class of restauration and, to this end, he'd borrowed what seemed to his wife like an eye-poppingly large amount of money from the bank, invested in an enormous cold store and was busily redecorating the function room at the back to turn it into the Fisherman's Rest.

It would mean a lot more work for Joy but she'd been promised extra staff as soon as they could afford it.

Although they kept the front door of the Fisherman's open all afternoon, the lunch-time drinkers were gone by three and it was rare for even passing trade to arrive before six-thirty, so Joy was immersed in her bookkeeping in the back room, keeping the finances straight for Mike, the accountant, when she heard the door open and a man's voice call out to ask if there was anyone there.

Smoothing her russet curls tidy, she emerged into the bar and offered her best smile. It wasn't hard; the man before her was decidedly handsome – slender and dark, nothing like Eric and just how she liked them – about her own age, which was thirty-eight, though dressed younger in tight jeans and black leather jacket.

'What can I get you, sir?'

'I'm told you let rooms.'

Welsh, she thought, hearing his voice, the residue of the lilt he had vainly fought to discard. She had taken him for a Londoner by his clothes. 'Oh, yes,' she said. 'Is it just for yourself?' He nodded. 'I have a nice single overlooking the garden.'

'A double might be better,' he suggested. 'I need room to spread out, to do a bit of work.' He waved a small case at her which she recognised as the housing of a laptop computer.

'Work?' she queried.

'I'm a journalist,' he said readily.

As she led the way up the stairs to the double room at the front, she called over her shoulder, 'Racing journalist, is it, sir?'

'General news,' he replied.

'Not expecting any excitement here, are you?'

'Nothing like that,' he laughed.

'Only nothing ever happens in Lambourn. Trust me.'

She threw open the door ahead of them and he surveyed the square room beyond. The carpet was hideous in the usual English hotel manner – random brown squiggles on a startling blue background, as if a herd of small rodents had been electrocuted on it – but the walls were a restful cream and the bed looked large and comfortable.

He advanced and placed his hands on the counterpane, feeling the firm springs yield.

There was a polished oak wardrobe and a table in the window with two upright chairs. The curtains were unobtrusive and the ceilings high. A portable TV stood on a movable bracket opposite the bed, its black plastic remote tidy on top. There was a sink in the corner and an electric kettle on a tray on the floor under it, along with two cups, some tea bags, sachets of instant coffee, sugar and powdered milk.

'Bathroom's right next door,' Joy explained, 'and we have no other guests at the moment so you'd have it to yourself. My husband and I are on the top floor with our own facilities.'

When he didn't speak, she said, 'It's forty pounds a night.' She added apologetically, 'I mean, it *is* a double...'

'Fine. I'll take it.'

'How many nights is it for?'

'Oh! I don't know. Can I stay indefinitely? Pay by the week.' He felt in the inside pocket of his jacket. 'In advance, naturally, in cash.'

'That will be fine,' she said. 'If you're taking it weekly then we can even manage a small discount. Shall we say two hundred and fifty pounds a week, including breakfast?'

'That sounds perfect.'

He put his laptop down on the table to take possession and removed a roll of fifty-pound notes from his pocket, peeling off five of them and handing them over without counting them twice. Joy stuffed them in the pocket of her denim mini skirt, also without counting them.

'Well, I hope you'll be very comfortable, Mr...?'

'Ap Morgan,' he said, 'but my friends call me Reuben. Mrs...?'

'Joy,' she supplied. 'Joy Reynolds.'

They smiled at each other like old friends. He had a sweet, open smile and she was suddenly aware of being alone in a bedroom with a fanciable man. The bed seemed to grow larger as she stared at it, to loom and to beckon.

'I'll leave you to settle in,' she said hastily, and withdrew.

She remembered one of the drawbacks to her working in the bar.

Eric Reynolds was a very jealous man.

When Greg arrived back at the almshouses early that evening, he realised that he still didn't know for sure the name of the young man he had come to see. He rapped on the narrow door nonetheless and was answered immediately.

'Mr Parkinson?' he hazarded.

'Patterson.' The man seemed wary. 'Michael Patterson.'

'Patterson. Of course.' He held up his warrant card and identified himself by rank and name. The young man backed away before him, his blue eyes startled. Greg took this as invitation and followed him in.

He found himself in a dark space, more like a corridor than a room, although it filled the ground floor of the house. At the far end he could make out a compact kitchen, separated from the living area by a breakfast bar – a modern addition, clearly, in yellowing pine. A staircase rose steeply before him, with a wooden banister, starkly new, its treads old bare boards that had been painted cream.

The householder bent and switched on a lamp which stood on a table beside a two-seater sofa, the only seating that the room afforded. Greg saw him more clearly now: a man of about thirty, six feet tall and very lean. His hair was a dirty blond colour, collar length about a pale face.

Nondescript was the word that sprang into his mind. He thought that he might have seen Patterson before, however, but then he had lived in Newbury all his life and seen many people and maybe the young man just had 'one of those faces'.

He was wearing a grey suit and white shirt and held a blue tie in his right hand. Following Greg's eye, he folded the tie neatly and laid it on the table under the lamp.

'Just this minute got in from work,' he said. His fingers twitched up and released the top button of his shirt, looking immediately more relaxed. 'I'm an accountant,' he added. 'Freelance mostly. Checking the books of small businesses locally.'

'Really,' Greg said politely. People who volunteered information unasked usually made him suspicious and Patterson did not strike him as the chatty type but he seemed harmless enough.

'Yes, don't like being cooped up in the same place all the time – offices, confined spaces.' He drew in a deep breath as if he realised he was talking too much and was forcing himself to stop. He gestured to the sofa. 'Do sit.'

'Thanks.' Greg settled himself without ceremony. 'This shouldn't take long, sir. I'm hoping you can help me with some enquiries.'

Michael Patterson let slip a slight smile, as people so often did at this formula, taking it no doubt for the euphemism it often was. He sat carefully at the other end of the sofa, turned slightly to one side so that he could look at Greg. He was pressed up against the arm, maximising the distance between them, as if ensuring that there should be no physical contact, his legs stiff, his bare wrist almost white against the green tweed fabric.

'It's about your neighbours,' Greg explained.

'Neighbours?'

'The Hathaways.'

'Sir John and Lady India?' It was as if all the tension had been stripped from his body. 'I thought you meant one of the other people in the terrace. It's a good two or three hundred yards to the Hathaways' place.'

'But you're their nearest neighbour,' Greg pointed out.

He considered this. 'I suppose I must be. I hadn't really thought.'

'And you know them, to speak to.'

'To say "Good morning" to,' he agreed. 'They're always civil, especially her.' He smiled properly for the first time. 'I like her.'

'Me too.'

'But they're hardly on my Christmas card list. Until recently they only came down at weekends. I mean, we don't socialise.' He added simply, 'He's one of the country's top barristers – or was – and her brother's a lord or something.'

'Still, you might notice any disturbance at night, cars passing your house. You sleep at the front?'

'Yes. What is this about please?'

There was no reason not to explain, to enlist his help as fully as possible. 'The Hathaways have been subjected to some unpleasant acts of vandalism these last couple of weeks.'

'You're kidding!'

'Hardly,' Greg said.

'No, I just meant... Who would do such a thing? And why?'

'Hard to say at the moment. Could be bored kids just looking for trouble. Could be something nastier.'

'Do you have dates?'

Greg recited the dates of the incidents from memory. Patterson rose and fetched a diary from a writing desk that had been crammed under the stairs. He stood leafing through the pages. 'I was in all those evenings and nights but I heard nothing out of the way.'

'Are you usually here at night?'

He hesitated for just a second. 'Yes.' He pressed the diary to his lips, nibbling a hard corner in thought.

'There can't be much traffic,' Greg said, 'not on a country lane like this. People wanting to get to Wantage would take the main road, the B4001.'

Patterson said slowly, 'But the person responsible wouldn't necessarily have come up the road, would they, or by car?'

'Where else?'

'Across the fields from the village, or from one of the neighbouring villages – Eastbury, East Garston. There's a whole network of footpaths. It's not difficult to slip about at night without being seen. You can get from Lambourn to the paddock behind Ascot House in a few minutes along the bridle-way.'

He laid the diary down again and turned on Greg his gentle, slightly empty smile, as Greg envisaged this young man slipping about the byways of Lambourn after dark, an idea which disturbed him for some reason. He said, 'Well, I'd be grateful if you would keep your eyes and ears open – an informal neighbourhood watch, if you like.'

The front door opened as he spoke, startling him. A third party erupted into the room, saw him and said, 'Oh!'

It was Grace, the 'lad', clutching a white paper bag to her chest from which issued the smell of fish and chips with too much vinegar. He stood up in automatic tribute to beauty. Close up, she was older than he had thought: late rather than early twenties.

She looked at him through narrow eyes. 'Saw you this after,' she said with a note of accusation, as if she suspected him of following her. 'At Ascot House.'

'Quite right, Miss...'

'Rutherford,' Patterson supplied. He emerged from under the stairs and kissed her gently on the cheek. 'Hello, Grey.' His voice was tender.

'All right, Mike?'

Greg, deciding that he was superfluous, left them to their supper. So there was, after all, a perfectly innocent explanation of Patterson's remark about the bridleway; no doubt Grace used it all the time.

No accounting for female taste, he thought as he walked back to his car, if this young goddess could share her chips with the colourless accountant. And now he knew why Patterson had hesitated when asked if he always slept there: no doubt he sometimes slept at her place.

Lucky bastard.

Chapter Four

For Greg to be summoned to the Chief Super's office twice in one week was rare enough to raise Susan Habib's eyebrows when the phone call came. The Chief understood that his job was to run the station and he left the actual solving of crime in the capable hands of his head of CID.

Mrs Asquith, the Chief's secretary, was coldly polite, as ever. Could the Superintendent spare Mr Barkiss a few minutes as soon as possible?

'I'm on my way,' Greg told her.

It was five past four and he found Barkiss sipping tea out of a dainty cup with pink rosebuds. The Chief gestured him to a seat and said, 'Tea?'

'I won't say no. I've been at my desk all day.'

Which was somehow more tiring and thirst-provoking than rushing around the streets of Newbury.

Barkiss fetched a second cup from his private cabinet and poured, leaving Greg to help himself to milk and sugar. They sipped for a while. Greg noticed that a new photograph had joined the gallery on the

71

wall, obvious in its gilded frame, taking pride of place next to the one that showed Barkiss as the cox of his school rowing team.

In it, the Chief Super was shaking hands with the Queen during her recent visit to Newbury as part of her golden jubilee tour. He was beaming in full dress uniform while she wore a large purple hat and a frown. The celluloid Barkiss looked mightily pleased with himself and Greg, who hadn't been invited to meet Her Majesty, thought spitefully that he liked standing next to her because she made him look tall.

'I've been reading your report on the Hathaway business,' Barkiss said, interrupting Greg's thoughts. 'Something or nothing?'

'Hard to say at this stage. There's no forensic from the attacks so far and I've asked Sir John to let me know at once if there are any fresh occurrences. Meanwhile, I've tracked down Graham Scobie who's renting a room in Eastbury, not two miles from Lambourn.'

'That's damn close. Been to see him?'

'Not yet. The man's recently been acquitted of a major crime. I don't want to go in for anything that'll have him shouting police harassment. Besides, Sir John's back-peddling a bit – says it was just a hunch and that there's nothing in it – so I'm not placing too much store by it at the expense of other lines of enquiry.'

Barkiss leafed through the pages of A4 on his desk that was Greg's summing up of the case so far. 'About this neighbour of the Hathaways – man called Michael Patterson.'

'What about him?'

'Is he a suspect?'

'Not at all, just a possible witness.'

'To what exactly?'

Greg shrugged. 'To the vandalism. You know the drill, Jim: leg work, knocking on doors, asking questions. Routine.'

'But he says that he saw and heard nothing on any of the days in question. It'd be much better to keep an eye on Scobie, surely, or on the Hathaway property, maybe even mount a discreet surveillance.'

'That would be expensive.' Greg looked at his superior officer in surprise. It wasn't at all like Jim Barkiss to attempt to interfere in this way. He spread his hands wide. 'I may need to talk to Patterson again.'

'I'd rather you didn't,' Barkiss said. 'I'd rather you kept him out of the investigation and, especially, out of the papers.' He poured himself another cup of tea and settled back in his chair, waiting for the inevitable objections.

All Greg said was, 'Why?'

'Can't say. Sorry. Call it a favour to me.'

Greg leaned forward, his elbow on the desk, his chin on his fist, his mind working overtime. The Chief's face was bland and gave nothing away. 'Is he an undercover policeman?' he asked finally. 'If so, he's very convincing since he's a mouse of a man, but I find it odd that I wasn't told.'

'There are, I believe, six people in this country who know who Michael Patterson is, so you're in good company.'

'Some sort of witness protection?' Greg hazarded. 'I thought that his face looked vaguely familiar, now you come to mention it.'

Barkiss said quietly, 'Don't go there, Gregory. We've worked together a long time with what I hope is mutual respect and I'm asking you to trust me on this one.'

Greg drained his cup, his thirst not satisfied by the dainty china's meagre offerings, his curiosity, if anything, aroused by his boss's even more meagre words.

He brought Patterson into his mind: a man of about thirty, fair hair with a widow's peak at the front, blue eyes, nondescript features; tallish, thinnish, nothing to get hold of there; a grey suit and white shirt, blue tie, black shoes.

If he was working undercover then he'd been chosen well to blend into the background.

And yet he had seen that face before, he knew it now – a long time ago, certainly, perhaps fifteen years, when Patterson could have been no more than a boy.

He mentally brought the hairline forward, stripped a few dry lines from the skin, dressed him in jeans and a sweatshirt.

The Queen glared down at him as he scrutinised the mental image.

Now he knew where he had seen the man before, although his face then had been fatter, as well as frightened and slightly startled: on the front page of every newspaper in the country some sixteen years ago.

'My God,' he said softly. 'Ian Callaghan.'

And then there were seven.

Ian Callaghan had been fourteen years old at the time, though young for his age, as everyone agreed, including the psychiatrist who gave evidence at his trial.

He'd been an ordinary, middle-class boy, an only child, his father a biology lecturer at Sheffield University, his mother a former secondary-school teacher, now a full time home maker. Ian's world had fallen apart at the age of twelve when his father had come home one day and announced that he was leaving. He'd fallen in love with one of his graduate students, a love that could not be denied.

'This doesn't mean that I don't love you, Ian,' he had explained to his son. 'I shall always love you, no matter what.'

He'd moved out of the comfortable, four-bedroomed detached house that had been the family home for eleven years, for as long as Ian's memory went back, and set up home with Silvie in a flat near the university.

Ian's mother became very depressed for a while, coping only with the help of her doctor's extensive pharmacopoeia and by immersing herself in her painting, but gradually began to piece her life together again and resumed her career with more gusto and commitment than she had brought to it the first time round.

Ian spent two weekends a month with his father and stepmother, a morose presence in their burgeoning partnership. His school work suffered and his teachers said in exasperation that he had stopped trying. He skipped classes and spent his days hanging round the shopping precinct with a gang of bigger boys who mildly bullied him.

His relationship with his mother deteriorated; he resented the fact that she had accepted the situation and moved on, unwilling to do likewise.

When Ian was thirteen, his father told him that he would soon no longer be an only child, that Silvie was expecting his brother or sister. The boy took the news without comment although his eyes dwelled on the woman's growing belly with something like fear.

In the event, it was twins – beautiful,

golden-haired girls whom they named Rose and Lily.

'Like a pair of Edwardian housemaids,' Ian's mother snorted on hearing the news.

The flat seemed small now and they bought a cottage in a village a few miles from Sheffield, with a green where cricket was played, a pub and a post office cum general stores. There was a compact back bedroom which was designated as Ian's and decorated with football posters of Sheffield Wednesday although he had switched to supporting United, unable to bear the memories of Saturday afternoons spent watching The Owls at Hillsborough with his father in the happy days.

One Saturday night after supper, Silvie, who had hardly been out of the house since the birth of the twins three months earlier, suggested a trip to the pub. It was barely two hundred yards and Ian was old enough to be left in charge – the responsibility would do him good. In an emergency, he could run for them.

They spent the entire evening at the pub, rolling out only at closing time, engrossed in a trivia quiz, a grudge match against the next village, feeling themselves accepted by the villagers at last. Ian was already in bed when they got home and Silvie went to look in on the twins while Gerry made them both a cup of tea.

He ran upstairs when he heard her screams. He took one look at the cold and silent bodies of his baby daughters and called the police. He told them to bring an ambulance too as Silvie was vomiting with hysteria and shock and a pain that could never be soothed.

A double cot death was unheard of and, having established that there was no carbon-monoxide build-up from a faulty heater, no pair of infant sniffles that might have turned rapidly to meningitis, the police questioned Gerry minutely, turning their attention to Silvie once she was calm enough to respond. It had been Silvie, after all, who had gone to take a last look at her darlings before leaving for the pub; both parents were agreed on that, not seeing how damaging such an admission might be to her, which, to the experienced inspector in charge of the case, spoke volumes for her innocence.

'You didn't fix up a babysitter?' she asked and Silvie explained that her puny stepson was in fact fourteen and almost grown up.

The medical examiner dealt brusquely, almost rudely, with the inspector's concerns about the purple and red bruises on the babies' bodies, on the fleshy parts of their shoulders and minuscule buttocks. 'Livor mortis,' he explained, 'where the blood stops flowing and settles in the lowest part. You must have seen it in human corpses.'

'Not to the same extent,' Inspector Leavis demurred.

'It's more noticeable in a baby. That's all. Certainly not a sign of parental abuse.'

It wasn't until the following afternoon that they arrested Ian. The post mortem proved that both girls had been stifled with a pillow, their tiny lungs and airways choked with fibres, and, while forensic science had a long way to go back in the mid eighties when even DNA testing was not routine, there was enough evidence to question the boy on.

He was a minor and could not be interviewed without a responsible adult present. His father was too busy comforting his distraught wife and his mother too stunned to be effective so they got him a social worker. The woman sat slightly apart from the boy all through the hours in the interview room and tried not to look appalled.

Ian rapidly confessed to smothering the twins as the inspector struggled to understand his crime. Had they been crying? Was that it? He had been trying to stop them crying, hadn't he, and, having no experience of babies, had made a terrible mistake?

No. Ian shook his head vehemently. He had known what he was doing. It had been the only means at his disposal, he explained – cold-blooded, dry-eyed – to bring home to his father how deeply he felt the betrayal of his leaving home, deserting his mother and himself, and bringing these two squalling, dribbling cuckoos into the nest.

'He didn't understand. This was the only way I could make him understand.' He kept saying, 'But they'll be all right, won't they? I mean, they'll be fine when they wake up?'

On the tapes experienced police officers could be heard saying in confusion, 'But they're not going to wake up, son. Your sisters are dead.' They were used to equivocation and denial, but this was new.

Despite his confession, the boy was persuaded by his lawyers to plead not guilty when the case came to court. The prosecution claimed that his apparent belief that his half sisters were not really dead was merely a cynical ploy to gain the sympathy of the court.

He looked small in the juvenile court, in his school uniform: grey slacks and blue blazer, white shirt and maroon tie. He sat looking round the room, dispassionately examining the spectators, the officers of the court, the jury, his hands folded neatly in his lap.

People queued all night for the trial, which lasted eight days.

The psychiatrist who had interviewed him at length while he was awaiting trial described him as a typical teenager, struggling with the upheavals of puberty. He had been displaying symptoms of a low-grade depression following the divorce, which was commonplace in this age of broken families and which only time could heal.

He was of above average intelligence, as you might expect from the son of two graduates, but nothing extraordinary. His schoolwork had been satisfactory until the recent deterioration. The man even described him as 'normal', a term which psychiatrists tended to avoid, and could offer no explanation for this sudden act of outrage.

'Is there any evidence that he heard voices?' the Prosecution asked.

'I could find no signs of schizophrenic tendencies.'

'In short, he was perfectly sane when he carried out this act?'

'That would seem to be the case.'

Ian did not go into the witness box in his own defence. His barrister decided that his composure could only count against him as he had showed no sign of remorse at any time during the four months between arrest and trial. The case had come to trial more swiftly than if Ian had been an adult accused of murder – an act of mercy towards a mere boy.

All through the proceedings Ian was Child

C but, after the jury had delivered their inevitable guilty verdict, the judge ordered that Ian's name be released 'in the public interest', although it also identified his tragic father and stepmother. The newspapers didn't need telling twice. They named him and published the photographs of his bewildered face and called him an unnatural monster who should never be released back into decent society.

The judge's decision, announced a few days later, that Ian should serve a minimum of eight years was greeted with derision and fury. With a general election looming, the Home Secretary swiftly raised the tariff to fifteen years and proclaimed his party the guardian of law and order.

Ian found that his father had been lying when he said that he would always love him, no matter what. All paternal love had died on that dreadful night, along with his baby sisters.

Once the trial was over, Gerry Callaghan accepted a job lecturing in Philadelphia and he and Silvie left England, never to return. They split up soon after the emigration – driven apart by the grief that should have riven them together – and Silvie committed suicide by jumping off the Benjamin Franklin bridge into the Delaware six months later.

Leaving Ian with three deaths on his conscience.

His mother moved away, changed her name, distancing herself from the scandal and the blatant hatred of strangers. If anyone asked, she told them she had no children, had never been bothered about it, that breeding was an overrated hobby.

'I rely absolutely on your discretion in this, Greg.'

'You can.'

'You must tell no one. No pillow talk.'

It was the first time that Jim Barkiss had admitted, however obliquely, to knowing about the relationship between him and Angie. Greg let the moment pass and said, 'I didn't know he'd been released.'

'Four years ago, after he'd served twelve years of the fifteen-year tariff imposed at the time. The Home Office managed to keep it quiet. I think people had largely forgotten the case, what with the babies' parents not being around to agitate for his continued detention. He got a good education in juvenile custody – better than he'd have got on the outside, most likely, smaller classes, for a start – and did an Open University degree in prison.

'They gave him a new identity, naturally, and he's qualified as an accountant. He lives very quietly and reports regularly to his probation officer. He told her of your visit and she rang me this morning, nervous of any publicity. Some people have a good eye for faces, even after all these years. If the press start swarming round Lambourn ... anything could happen.'

'And you've known he was on our patch these four years?'

'Somebody had to know and I'm the senior officer covering the Lambourn area.'

'And is he safe?' Greg asked bluntly.

'One hundred percent – or so the psychiatrists say. The circumstances in which he killed were special, even unique.'

'But it means that he has it in him to do it,' Greg said, 'to *murder.*'

Barkiss spread his hands wide, almost a parody of Greg's earlier gesture. 'He was a model prisoner and has lived an exemplary life since his release.'

'What if he wants to marry?' Greg persevered. 'What if he has children of his own?'

'Why should he harm them?'

'He might get jealous!' Greg said.

He remembered the day his then wife Diane had brought the baby Frederick – although he didn't yet have a name – home from the maternity ward. Not normally a demonstrative woman, she had been besotted by this tiny pink hairless creature and Greg, simultaneously proud and terrified, had felt marginalised and, yes, jealous.

The feeling had soon passed, of course,

but then he wasn't a convicted child murderer.

Barkiss was talking. 'Children of his own would hardly bring on the same feelings of resentment as his half sisters did but ... well, we could debate this all day but I don't think there's much point.'

'There's a girlfriend, one of the stable lasses. I've seen her.'

'If and when the time comes he will be encouraged to tell her the truth but it has to be at a time of his choosing. So! Will you let him alone?'

Greg thought about it. 'Unless he's really crucial to the investigation, in which case I shall keep him anonymous.'

'Make sure you're the only one who speaks to him, in that case,' Barkiss said. 'I want him kept tightly under wraps so don't go sending Lomax along to interview him, or Barbara. Agreed?'

'Agreed. I shall keep personal charge of the Hathaway case.'

Greg went to leave but turned back in the doorway. 'I take it the court has placed an absolute embargo on the media revealing his new identity.'

'Actually, no,' Barkiss said. 'The case doesn't seem to have stayed in the public consciousness as much as some others and the court decided a new identity was all the protection he needed. Which makes it all the more vital that you keep this to yourself. It only needs one irresponsible reporter sniffing round, out to make a name for himself...'

Greg found himself musing over the Callaghan case. Why had it been largely forgotten where other child murders were routinely dredged up? Usually the victim's family made sure that their child's grisly fate stayed in the public eye but this time the victim's father had been the perpetrator's father too, which no doubt explained it.

There had been enough kerfuffle at the time of the crime, though, and all through the trial. Some right-wing commentators had blamed the father for the tragedy and Linda Linton, controversial and outspoken columnist on the *Daily Outlook*, had openly stated that he had been justly punished for betraying his first wife and family – for adultery, which the Bible deemed a capital offence.

Her remarks had provoked a public outcry and demands that she be sacked. The circulation of the *Outlook* had risen twenty percent overnight and Miss Linton had received a handsome bonus from a grateful Jackson Deans.

Chapter Five

'One large – sorry *tall* – cappuccino with extra shot,' Lomax said, placing the mug in question on the table in front of his colleague, 'and one hazelnut latte for yours truly. I'm sure life was simpler when you just ordered coffee.'

'And it tasted like warm mud?'

'There were drawbacks,' he admitted.

Barbara spooned up some froth and licked it sensuously, savouring the powdered chocolate. 'Thanks, sir. Just what I needed.'

'Call me Alex.'

'Thanks, Alex.' She was grateful both for the coffee and for the lack of formality. Calling people 'sir' was as natural as breathing to a police officer and you soon forgot how odd it was in the twenty-first century, although nowhere near as odd as calling a woman 'ma'am' like a character out of one of the BBC's frequent costume dramas.

She didn't fancy herself in a bonnet and stays. Detective Sergeant Barbara Carey was a thoroughly modern young woman, dressed for comfort in khaki trousers with matching T-shirt under a black silk jacket.

She didn't encumber herself with a bag but wore the items she was likely to need – including a pair of handcuffs – strapped to her belt in the small of her back. She could walk twenty miles in her leather lace-ups without one blister to show for it.

Her dark hair was short, framing delicate features which were free of make-up and pretty only off duty. Tiny gold ear studs and a good watch were her only jewellery.

Alex Lomax sank into the seat opposite her with a small sigh. He had never been comfortable with his name. The second name was almost, but not quite, an anagram of the first and people tended to repeat it slowly – A-lex Lo-max – as if afraid that they might trip over their own tongues. He had tried being Al for a while but it hadn't caught on. Sandy made him feel like a beach. Xander was too pretentious. Alexander Lomax was his father and the less said about him the better.

They both sipped in silence for two minutes, sating their thirst.

'I fear we're going to be seeing the inside of rather a lot of cafés over the next few days,' Barbara said finally.

'Well, I can think of a lot of worse places.'

'Something tells me this is going to be a long haul, though.'

'Rome wasn't burned in a day,' Lomax said, 'and give me an investigation where you spend a lot of time in cafés any day.'

'Or the pub,' Barbara said.

'Alcohol is not the answer,' he said, rather sententiously.

'But sometimes it helps you forget the question,' Barbara murmured.

They were investigating a string of crimes that had been committed in the area over the past few weeks, mostly in Newbury itself. It was a simple enough scam, a cross between a mugging and a con trick. A woman's bag was snatched in the street by a young man who ran off, only to be stopped when a middle-aged woman hurled her shopping bag into his running feet, sending him sprawling. The boy then leaped up, spitting curses at her, and hobbled off, leaving the purloined bag on the ground.

The woman returned the bag to its owner and comforted her, modestly accepting her thanks. After a moment, she suggested that they adjourn to the nearest café to compose themselves after their ordeal, fortify themselves with tea. The rescuer – she was variously Sally, Molly, Shirley, something safe and reassuring – pumped the victim for details of herself, her name and where she lived, whether there was anyone waiting for at home who would be able to care for her should shock take its toll later.

She also insisted on paying for their tea and cakes, just would not take no for an answer. The reason for this became clear when the victim reached home, or her car, or the bus stop and found everything of value gone from her bag, including her house keys.

By the time she got home, various small but valuable items – mostly jewellery and cash – had gone from the house too.

Barbara had been able to find no record of a similar sting. It was an audacious crime since the victim saw the woman clearly over a period of at least half an hour, and yet each victim had given a different description. DC Andy Whittaker's theory that they were dealing with a mistress of disguise seemed melodramatic. As Gregory Summers pointed out, disguise was much easier for a woman than a man: she had only to change the style or colour of her hair, adjust her make-up, or switch from flowery dress to jeans and T-shirt to look completely different.

'I've decided to call it the Good Samaritan con,' Alex remarked after a few minutes. 'What do you think?'

'Not bad.' Barbara drained her mug and licked away the foam moustache. 'That's half the battle, after all, having a name for it.' He gave her a sardonic look and she grinned back at him. She was sitting with her back to the wall and a clear view of the café. She murmured, 'Bit of a lull at the counter. Let's see what the staff have to say.'

They walked over and Barbara showed her warrant card to a young woman seven or eight years her junior, introducing herself and her colleague. 'Were you working Friday afternoon?' she asked. 'Around two-thirty, three o'clock?'

They were in luck. 'Yeah, I was here,' the girl said. 'I do nine till five-thirty, Monday through Saturday.'

'And you are?'

'Julie Bassett,' she said readily. 'What's it about?'

'I was wondering if you saw two women in here around that time. One was in her early fifties, grey hair, fair skin, wearing a blue dress and white cardigan. She may have seemed a bit agitated. Upset. The other woman would have been comforting her.'

The description was of the latest victim, Mrs Kathy Potts, who had said repeatedly that her husband would kill her when he got home and found his silver cups missing.

'Darts champion at the Flying Horse seven years on the trot,' she'd sniffed as Barbara and Alex examined the empty display cabinet. 'Bought that special – best mahogany. He'll go spare.'

There had been no fingerprints, not even ones that had a right to be there, but then Mrs Potts was a dedicated polisher of furniture.

Julie was thinking. 'It gets that busy,' she said doubtfully. 'And there are always pairs of women in during the day, mostly middle-aged. One or two lots I recognise as regulars but otherwise...'

She shrugged. Barbara knew what she meant. When you were twenty-one, middle-aged people all looked the same; they were of no interest. In the same way the girl's eyes slid over the DCI without noticing him since he was way too old to be boyfriend material, it being a well-known fact to Julie's generation that nobody over the age of forty did it, or if they did then it was just too gross to think about.

Alex spoke. 'It's likely that the upset woman took a seat and the other one came to the counter to order for them both.'

'Hang on!' Julie said, and Barbara looked at her new boss with respect. 'Hey, yeah. And they both had tea which is odd because–' she gestured at the hissing cappuccino machine '– that's not really what this place is about. Right?'

'Nothing like a nice hot cup of tea for a shock,' Alex murmured to Barbara, 'like when you've just been mugged. So you got a good look at the other woman?' he asked the waitress. 'The one who came to the counter.'

Julie subsided again. 'I didn't really pay much mind. She was ... ordinary.'

Which was exactly what Mrs Potts had

92

said. Ordinary. Nice. Sympathetic. Can't believe she did such a thing.

'Try, Julie,' Alex said with his sweetest smile.

She closed her eyes, making an effort. 'She was wearing a dress and a cardigan, just like the other woman. I mean, that's what half the middle-aged women in town wear in summer. It's what my mum wears.' Barbara was prepared to bet that Julie's mum wasn't much over forty, which hardly qualified as middle-aged these days. 'Big bag. Not a handbag, a shopping bag.' Her eyes popped open and she blinked at the sudden daylight. 'That's all. Sorry.'

'Long hair? Short hair?' Alex said. 'Height?'

She shook her head. 'Sorry.'

'Would you be able to work with a police artist to do a picture?'

'Oh, no! I couldn't. No way! Sorry. I'd be hopeless.'

The girl looked quite panic stricken and Alex left it. The door swung open at that moment and four men burst in, noisy, burly, wanting coffee and wanting it now. They were all in their twenties and Barbara saw Julie straighten her back and instinctively push out her meagre chest at the sight of them, ready for the mating ritual. She gave her her card. 'If you remember anything else or see her again, give me a call. Especially if you see her again.' Julie promptly pocketed the card and, Barbara surmised, equally promptly forgot about it.

'What now?' Alex said.

'There's a place round the corner it might be worth taking a look at,' Barbara said. 'More down-market, hot tea and lots of it. You never know – we might catch the Good Samaritan in the act.'

'Yeah. Right. That's gonna happen. I bet you do the lottery every week as well, don't you?'

'You've got to have a dream...'

As they left the café they stood on the canal bridge for a moment, watching the water shimmer in the sunlight. Barbara said, 'So, Alex, what do you think of Newbury?'

After a pause Lomax said, 'It's no different from any other market town in Britain these days. Look...' He gestured along the shopping precinct to their right, glancing up. 'There are fine Georgian buildings all along this street but then you look at ground level and they've been eviscerated to put in plate glass shop fronts and offices.'

Barbara, who had never noticed the graceful Georgian rooftops in all her years in Newbury, was silenced as she looked at the *eviscerated* buildings with new eyes.

Soon Alex continued. 'Countryside's not bad, mind, though Devon – that's God's own country.'

'Why d'you leave then?'

'Personal reasons.' He abruptly changed the subject. 'I'm getting my bearings, moving out into the surrounding villages now.'

'Any thoughts about where you might live?'

'I've accepted an offer on my house in Plymouth. I can hardly believe the prices round here, though. How's an honest man supposed to live?'

'Tell me about it.'

'Went to Hungerford last night. Can't afford to live there.'

'It's a pretty little town,' Barbara said.

'I had a look at the memorial. I don't suppose you were here at the time of the massacre. It's hard to believe when it seems so peaceful. What was it – ten years ago?'

'Fifteen,' Barbara said. 'I was still at school, the other side of London. Mr Summers was there that day but he doesn't like to talk about it. Maybe when he knows you better...'

'You don't forget a trauma like that,' Alex said. 'I know.'

Graham Scobie sat at the corner table in a cramped café in the Market Place. He always chose the corner furthest from the entrance, if possible; in fact, he had been known to walk straight out of a café if no such table was available. He sat with his back to the wall. That way no one could sneak up on him from behind. It meant that his face was visible but he kept his head lowered.

It was only just after ten and the café was quiet: too late for breakfasts, too early for elevenses. It was the sort of old-fashioned place that he preferred to the swanky coffee bars with their confusing menus and teeth-breaking *biscotti* that seemed to have sprung up on every street corner. More of a caff than a café. Cheaper too and he had not been able to find work since the trial. Not that cash was really a problem but frugality was a lifetime's habit.

The waitress gave him time to settle and read the menu then clipped across to him on her high heels, her indifferent mouth bent in an automatic and meaningless smile. He could hear her coming and felt his pulse rate rise at her approach. He had never been good at talking to women, especially young ones. He sucked in a deep breath.

She said, 'Help you?'

It came out too abruptly. 'Pot of tea.' He didn't meet her eye. 'Double poached egg on toast.' He wanted to say 'please' like a normal person, but it caught somewhere between the will and the execution.

'Coming right up.'

He looked up then and watched her go, her pert backside wiggling inside her nylon uniform. Two middle-aged women came in and installed themselves at the table in the window with what seemed like unnecessary bustle. They might be sisters, he thought, or even mother and daughter; it was hard to tell. One stood up again to remove her cardigan, hanging it on the back of her chair and taking a leisurely look round the room as she did so. Her eyes didn't linger on his corner but he hastily buried his head in the menu anyway.

'There you go.' The waitress placed an oblong plate in front of him. The toast was too pale, as usual, ejected prematurely from the toaster, but they had not been mean with the butter, which gathered in melted pools. The eggs were perfectly round and the whites wobbled with the momentum of their journey from the kitchen. She unloaded a metal teapot from her tray with the teabag still in it, then a mug and some tiny cartons of UHT milk. Too much bloody trouble to buy fresh milk and pour it into a jug, he thought sourly.

A sugar dispenser already stood on the table, along with a ketchup bottle, like a giant plastic tomato.

'Enjoy,' the girl added, without much hope. Ugly little man, she thought, too ignorant to say please and thank you.

Scobie stirred the tea, then poured it onto the thin pretend milk in the mug. He tipped up the sugar dispenser once and, carefully, twice. Once didn't dispense enough, twice too much. He stirred the final mixture and sipped. It was hot and it was wet. His landlady, Mrs Brakespear, always wanted him out of the house as soon as possible in the morning and, in the face of her banal conversation, he often found his mouth too dry to manage the mealy breakfast cereal she provided, the toast with margarine that tasted of car oil.

Behind him he heard the waitress whisper something confidential to her friend. The other woman laughed. It was a loud and frank laugh, clearly infectious since the two women in the window glanced over at them and smiled tentatively. He tensed, the giant plastic tomato poised over his poached eggs.

Were they laughing at him?

They were all laughing at him.

There was no one else here so they had to be laughing at him.

He couldn't bear it, this persecution. His pulse began to race again. He could feel his heart banging at the wall of his chest. He drained his tea, slammed three pound coins down on the table and left the café at something approaching a run.

The waitress glanced after him and shrugged as she went to clear the debris and wipe a soggy cloth across the formica. The two women did not even notice him go.

Safely round the corner he stopped to take his breath, his face ruddy. As he gasped in air a man paused and said, 'You all right, mate?'

'Yes! Leave me alone.'

'All right! I was trying to help. No need to be so bloody rude...' He went to move on, then hesitated. 'Here ... you're him, aren't you?' The man's face was close to his now, a sharp face with hard little eyes. 'You're that bloke who murdered Devon Bliss.'

'No! You're mistaken. I'm not him.'

He tried to move away but the man had seized him by the scruff of his T-shirt, his short nails dark with grease under Scobie's lowered eyes. He was taller than Scobie, older but stronger, and his grip was fierce. 'I never forget a face.'

A few passers-by had stopped to see what was going on and he raised his voice for their benefit.

'It's the bloke that killed our Devon.'

Interested parties rapidly gathered. A debate ensued as to whether he was indeed the accused man with one woman asserting in a no-nonsense tone that he bore no resemblance whatsoever.

'I didn't,' Scobie gasped. 'I was acquitted.'

'See!' the first man said in triumph. 'It *is* him. I told you.'

'All right! Break it up.' Barbara Carey forced her way easily through the crowd and knocked the man's hand away from Scobie's shirt with one quick blow. 'I'm a police officer. What's going on here?'

'This man assaulted me,' Scobie squeaked.

'He's the bastard that murdered Devon Bliss,' the man grumbled, 'and got away with it scot free. Bloody disgrace.'

The crowd murmured support.

'That John Hathaway should be bloody well hung,' the man added.

Barbara gave Scobie a quick but thorough scrutiny. She had recognised him now. 'Looks nothing like him,' she snapped, 'so I must ask you all to move along. Now!' As the crowd reluctantly dispersed she muttered, 'Get lost. Sharpish!' to Scobie, who ducked away towards the bus station.

'Not you, sir.' Alex Lomax, who had been watching Barbara's deft handling of the situation without feeling the need to interfere, laid a hand on the sleeve of the man who had first challenged Scobie as he made to move off. 'A word, if you please, down at the station.'

'Eh?' The man stared in disbelief. 'What am I supposed to have done? He's the murderer, not me.'

'It's just round the corner – only take a minute.'

Back in the café the two women were gathering their belongings.

'You sure you're all right, Beatrice?' the first one said. She was of medium height and build with blonde hair curling onto her shoulders, a style which her companion thought a little young for her.

In a dignified tone, she replied, 'I'm perfectly fine, Maisie. There was no harm done in the end.'

'But it's a shock all the same. Shock can do nasty things to people. And there's definitely no one at home to look after you?'

'No, but really, I'm quite all right. Please don't fuss. I still think we should have called the police, though. He'll try it again.'

The blonde clicked her tongue as a negative. 'It's not worth the aggro. They'll keep you hanging around the station for hours filling in forms, then they'll tell you they can't waste any manpower on it as there's no hope of solving it. Take my word for it; I got burgled last year.'

'How very unpleasant for you.'

'Wouldn't have bothered calling the police at all only the insurance company make you.'

'Still, the station is just the other side of the roundabout. I may call in there on my way home. It's my civic duty. Perhaps you can give me your full name and address in case the police want to interview you as a witness.'

The blonde bit her lip. 'I'll write it down

for you.'

The other woman picked up the bill and made to rummage in her handbag but 'Maisie' almost snatched the paper from her hand.

'I'll get this.'

'No. Let me.'

'Really.'

'The least I can do is stand you a cup of tea and an Eccles cake. You've been a real Good Samaritan. Perhaps you will get a reward, or one of those commendations the police give people for bravery.' Politely but firmly she extricated the bill from her companion's firm grip and there was a slight look of challenge in her intelligent eyes.

'Well if you insist.' The blonde shot to her feet. 'Is there a loo here? Be right back.' She headed for the rear of the café, passed the lavatory without stopping or looking round, and dived through the kitchens, ignoring a 'Can I help you?' from a surprised woman wielding a fish slice. She found herself in a service alley with a smelly skip half blocking the way.

Damn! she thought. Bloody woman. She had heard the word *police* too often for comfort in the past five minutes. She had her purse, of course, but it wasn't much to show for a morning's work. She threw her victim's keys into the skip out of sheer spite and moved quickly along the alleyway into the market place. There was some sort of fracas going on – two men shaping up for a fight, she thought – but she ignored them and shot round the corner into Carnegie Road where a shabby Ford Cortina waited on a double yellow line.

She wrenched open the passenger door. 'Drive,' she said.

'Where to?' The young man slid the car into gear. He was always described by witnesses to the attempted bag snatch as a teenager but, close up, he was in his early or even mid twenties, just dressed younger in baggy trousers with a sleeveless T-shirt, a woollen cap pulled low over his head. His bare arms were well muscled.

'Home,' she snapped. 'Anywhere.'

'No good?'

'Bloody woman wouldn't let me pay. Might just as well have saved time and let you make off with her bag.' She dug the stolen purse out of the oversized bag Julie Bassett had mentioned and riffled through the notes. 'Twenty, forty, sixty, and five.'

'Not so bad, Mum.' The young man grinned as he gunned the car onto the roundabout outside the police station. 'Remember that time we got three pounds 45 and an expired library ticket?'

'Yes, Brian,' she said grimly. 'I remember.'

Chapter Six

'"That John Hathaway should be bloody well hung,"' DCI Lomax quoted. 'And it's hanged, by the way, not hung.'

'Eh?' Peter Tilsley looked nervous and confused, fidgeting on his hard chair in the interview room. He had expressed no interest in talking to a solicitor, having a vague fear that this might cost him money, but was wondering self-pityingly how an ordinary morning had turned out so badly. He had been on his way to his job as an engineer for the bus company, same as usual, heading for the bus station in Market Street, and then he'd been abducted by aliens, or might as well have been.

The boss alien was talking again. Shabby-looking geezer, Peter thought disdainfully, clothes too big for him. Wanted to smarten hisself up a bit. Probably hadn't got the hang of human gear yet, used to a silver metal jump suit, gravity boots and a helmet over his little green head. He smiled to himself and felt a bit less afraid.

'Are you denying that you said those words?' Lomax was saying. 'I heard you clearly and so did Sergeant Carey.'

'Absolutely,' the female alien agreed. Barbara had not heard Tilsley's words, being too busy with the rest of the crowd, but she would back her DCI to the hilt so long as it didn't involve perjury or conspiracy to pervert the course of justice.

'So what if I did?' Tilsley folded his arms contentiously, clenching his buttocks as he wondered when the intrusive medical experiments would begin. He couldn't see anything in this dingy room that looked like a probe but he was taking evasive action anyway. 'It's a free country. I can say what I like.'

'Up to a point,' Alex said. 'Uttering threats can be against the law.'

'I dunno what you're on about, mate. I didn't threaten anyone.'

'Yet you think Sir John Hathaway should be executed?'

He shrugged. 'It's just talk. Don't mean it literally.'

'I should hope not.' The door of the interview room opened. Without seeming to look round Lomax said into the tape recorder, 'Detective Superintendent Summers enters the room at eleven-oh-five.'

Tilsley turned to Greg in appeal as he took a seat, understanding that he was the chief alien, the captain of this flying saucer. 'Look, there's been some sort of misunderstanding, Chief.'

Greg scrutinised the man, in no hurry to speak since silence was a potent weapon: late thirties, he thought, thick, dark hair with eyes to match, on the small side but with thick lashes and brows that almost met in the middle; heavy features, which to Greg's mind usually denoted a lack of intelligence although he had no proof to back up this prejudice; chinos and a T-shirt so glaringly white it could have starred in its own soap-powder ad; brown leather slip-ons rather than the ubiquitous trainers, expensive leather jacket in a different shade of brown.

Finally, he said, 'My understanding is that you were heard to threaten Sir John Hathaway publicly.'

'Not *threaten*. What is all this?'

Greg looked at him for a moment then said, 'Suppose I were to tell you that Sir John and his family have been subjected to a vicious and sustained campaign of vandalism and violence?'

'You what!' Peter Tilsley was panic stricken. 'I don't ... I mean, it's not as if they live round here even!'

'No? Guess again.'

'You mean ... you mean Hathaway lives in Newbury?'

'In the Newbury area.'

'I had no idea! Honestly. It's just the type of thing you say like when one of the kids breaks a plate and you say you'll bloody kill them...'

'All right.' Greg got up. 'We have his details, Chief Inspector?'

DCI Lomax nodded, making no move to end the interview. 'And guess what, sir? He lives just outside Lambourn.'

'Does he indeed?' Greg sat down again and Tilsley, who had thought for a moment that he was about to be returned safely to planet earth none the worse for his ordeal, emitted an audible sigh.

'I live in East Garston,' he said. 'What of it?'

'What's that – three miles from Lambourn?'

'More like four or five. Is that where Hathaway lives?'

'Can you tell me what you were doing on the night of the 15th July?' Greg asked. 'Or the 27th? Or August 1st?'

'Not offhand, no.'

Which was fair enough. Greg would have been hard pushed to say what he had been doing on those nights himself. His instinct told him that Tilsley was the harmless idiot he appeared to be – ignorant and belligerent, maybe, but no stringer-up of puppies. As he said, brutal threats were uttered as part of daily discourse, even to your nearest and dearest. Especially to them.

He got to his feet again. 'Let him go. We

know where to find him if we have any further questions.'

Jesus, Tilsley thought, talk about close encounters.

'That was probably a waste of time,' Alex said, as he followed Greg out of the interview room. 'Like he says, people say that sort of stuff. Mrs Potts kept saying her husband would kill her over getting his darts trophies stolen but I'm not about to offer her police protection.'

'Maybe we should be a bit less violent in our language,' Greg suggested.

'He's obviously just some prat, but I like to be thorough.'

'Fair enough,' Greg said.

'Sir.' Greg looked round. It was the uniformed inspector in charge of the 6a.m. to 2p.m. shift and he was speaking to Alex. 'Glad I caught you. We've had another of those con tricks pulled, in Pam's Café about three quarters of an hour ago, in the Market Place.'

'What!' Barbara said. 'We were on our way there when we ran into Scobie and his lynch mob.'

'So near and yet so far.' Greg patted her on the arm. 'You better get back there and talk to the staff.'

'Yeah, but I'm definitely buying a lottery ticket this Saturday.'

Greg thought of asking for clarification of

this obscure remark, but decided not to bother. Explanations were usually less interesting than mysteries.

'If previous experience is anything to go by,' Alex said with a sigh, 'they'll have seen and heard nothing at all out of the way.'

Greg said, 'Keep me informed of your progress.'

'Where did you say this chap Scobie is living now?' Alex asked.

'I'm not sure I did, did I?'

'I like to know where the villains are on my patch.'

Greg could think of no reason not to tell him, even if Scobie wasn't officially a villain. 'In a rented room in Eastbury.'

'Mrs Beatrice Pitcher,' Barbara mused as they sped along country roads towards the village of Crockham Woods. 'Victim number five – that we know about.'

'Big pitchers have small ears,' Alex said.

'I think it may be the other way round, guv.'

'Really? Makes no sense either way. I'll tell you what else makes no sense: "The child is father to the man". What the hell does that mean?'

'It means that if you're a rotten little bastard at four, you'll be a rotten big bastard at forty.'

'Oh? Thanks. That's a load off my mind.'

Barbara drew up in front of Rose Cottage, thinking that every village in Berkshire must have its Rose Cottage. This one fitted the bill better than most, though; not only was the front garden crammed with rose bushes but climbing varieties covered the front and sides.

'This is nice,' Alex said. 'Typically English: brotherhood and shepherd's pie.'

'Please tell me you do that on purpose.'

'What?'

'Never mind.'

They made their way up the path to the front door. Before they had a chance to knock, the door opened on a chain and a woman's voice, clear and assertive, said, 'Yes?'

'Mrs Pitcher? Sergeant Carey from Newbury CID. My colleague is Chief Inspector Lomax.'

She held up her warrant card to the narrow aperture. The woman took the bottom edge in firm fingers and examined it with care, her eyes flickering from the photograph to Barbara's face and back again.

'You'll understand if I make quite sure of your identity,' she said, 'in the circumstances.'

'Quite right, madam,' Lomax said.

Satisfied, she unchained the door and motioned them into the cool interior. Passing rapidly through the narrow hallway, they found themselves in a large room that took up most of the ground floor.

Barbara's practised eye took in polished wood floors with a few pretty rugs, two plain sofas at right angles to a grate filled with pine cones, one wall of overflowing bookshelves. The framed watercolours on the white walls were not of rural scenes but depicted busy urban sights – markets, museums, a busker. The kitchen was open-plan, very modern in black and chrome. Small windows gave onto a rear garden with, oddly, not a rose to be seen.

Music was playing, something classical and soothing. Barbara didn't know what it was but thought that she liked it.

'And it's *Miss* Pitcher,' the woman said. 'Spinster of this parish and proud of it.' She turned the music down. 'I hope you don't mind if I leave this playing; I find Brahms good for stress. Sit.'

They obeyed, squatting side by side on one of the sofas while Miss Pitcher took the other. She was a tall woman of about fifty, or so Barbara surmised. She had a trim figure and emphasised it by sitting up straight, her head erect. Her hair was short, grey and tidy. She wore black trousers and a yellow T-shirt which did not, as with most people, make her look sallow, since her unmade-up skin was well tanned. A pearl necklace hung around her neck and Barbara

111

noticed that, despite her pride in her maidenhood, she was wearing a wedding ring.

'So,' she said, taking easy charge. 'A Chief Inspector. I must confess I didn't expect such a response to a minor mugging; in fact, I expected hardly any interest from the constabulary at all. Would I be right in thinking that I am not the first to be taken in by this woman?'

'Very astute, Miss Pitcher,' Alex said, 'and you've got off comparatively lightly. Previous victims had their houses done over too.'

'Ah, yes. She took my house keys as well as my purse, this nimble-fingered felon, and I had, of course, been naive enough to tell her where I lived. Luckily, I leave a spare key with my neighbour in case of lock-outs.'

'You'd better get your locks changed,' Barbara said.

'The locksmith is calling later this afternoon. "Before close of play", as he put it. I haven't heard that expression for a while; I do like cricketing metaphors. I'm talking too much. I must be more shocked than I thought. How galling for me. I would offer to make tea but that would just look pathetic.'

'Can you tell us exactly what happened,' Alex said, suppressing a grin.

Her story did not differ. It seemed it was

only the woman's name and appearance that changed, not her modus operandi. She had been leaving the Kennet Centre, her handbag slung lightly over her arm, as usual, when a boy – 'A "green, unknowing youth", I thought him at the time, Dryden, you know' – had barged into her from behind. Turning to demand an apology she had been shocked to find the bag wrenched from her, but not too shocked to call out for help.

She had thought the woman brave to tackle the youngster while other bystanders watched in mild indifference, hurling her own large shopping bag under his feet, causing him to stumble and curse, drop the stolen bag and hobble away. 'I wonder,' she said, 'if she took my purse and keys at that point or later in the café. Either way one must admire such adroitness. Worthy of a magician.'

'Did you get a good look at the boy?' Alex asked.

'Fleeting but *boy* is perhaps not the right word. He was older than that: mid twenties.'

'Really?' Barbara looked at her in surprise. 'The previous victims have all spoken of a teenager.'

'I can believe that as he was dressed very young but I was a school mistress for thirty years, until my retirement last year, and I can tell the difference between an adolescent and a man.'

'Interesting,' Alex said. 'And possibly helpful.'

'You retired last year?' Barbara queried.

'Yes. I'm sixty-one.'

'Blimey!' Alex said.

'Thank you, Chief Inspector. I shall take that as a compliment.'

It was clear that Miss Pitcher was both more intelligent and more observant than their earlier victims and Alex felt a surge of optimism that she might prove their breakthrough. 'Do you think you could work with a police artist to do a likeness of this woman?' he asked.

'I can do better than that.' Beatrice Pitcher rose and went to a walnut desk in the corner. She took out a pad of drawing paper and some charcoal. 'History was my subject, but art was my passion.' She waved an arm at the pictures on the walls. 'This is my work.'

'They're really good,' Alex said, as if he meant it.

'I pride myself on my skill at portraiture too, despite the danger of falling into deadly sin. I shall draw her for you.'

As Miss Pitcher sketched, Barbara went to look out of the back window. The garden surprised her, but the older woman seemed full of surprises. In contrast to the traditional cottage feel out front, the back had been transformed into an Oriental garden. There was no grass, no shrubs or hedges, only gravel. Slightly off centre to the right was a bubbling water feature, a wooden bench beside it, very simple in design. To the left stood what Barbara was fairly sure was a magnolia tree, now bare; otherwise the eye was drawn to statuary rather than plants, abstract in the main and green-bronze in colour.

'I can't be doing with all that English-cottage stuff,' Miss Pitcher remarked without looking up from her task. 'Couldn't do much about the front, what with the house being called Rose Cottage – the prettiest-village-in-Berkshire committee would have had kittens – but I was damn well going to have what I wanted at the back. The magnolia blooms for only a few weeks each year but when it does it's beautiful enough to bring tears to the most jaundiced eye.'

'You have a lovely home,' Barbara said. 'Have you lived here long?'

'No, I came here on my retirement.'

'From far away?'

'The North,' she said vaguely. 'There.'

She passed her sketch to Alex and Barbara hastened to join them. She saw hair falling to the shoulders, which were broad for a woman, eyes set wide under unplucked brows. Little that could not be changed except the high cheekbones and those shoulders.

'Like the man,' Miss Pitcher said, 'she was not as young as she was dressed or painted.' She pointed. 'The neck is a giveaway. And the hair was certainly a wig. Eyebrows darker and eyes brown so probably not a real blonde.'

'So what would you put her age at?' Alex asked.

'Forty-five to fifty,' she said promptly.

'You grew suspicious?' Barbara said.

'I suppose I must have done, although trying not to look your age is hardly sinister. There was something about the way she asked a lot of questions without volunteering any information of her own. The art of conversation is very much give and take, I find. I am accustomed to ... to people evading questions, to the technique or art. Also, after so many years in the classroom, you get an instinct for when someone is trying to pull the wool over your eyes. I don't know what guardian angel told me not to let her pay in the café. She was adamant, but so was I.'

She glanced round the cottage. 'Not that there is much to steal, but I should have been sorry to lose my mother's pearl necklace and her wedding ring.' She fingered the necklace and Barbara saw what she meant about the neck. It also explained

116

the anomaly of the ring. 'You see that I'm wearing them now for safe-keeping. Absurd. They don't think of these things, that an item may be worth far more to its owner than they can get from their "fence".'

She turned back to her sketch pad. 'I shall do the man for you, though it will be less precise.'

Alex gave her his card so she could contact them if she saw the man or woman again. Barbara scribbled her mobile number on the back.

As they drove away, Alex remarked, 'In any altercation or skirmish, I should be glad to have Miss Beatrice Pitcher on my team.'

'Ditto.'

'Don't suppose she'd want to give up the pleasures of the spinster life now,' Alex mused. Barbara glanced sideways to see if he was joking, but found that she couldn't tell.

Chapter Seven

Reuben walked down the stairs into the bar and was greeted with a smile by Joy Reynolds.

'What can I get you, sir?'

'Reuben,' he reminded her.

'What can I get you, *Reuben*.' Her red-lipsticked mouth rolled his name out as if it were a mildly provocative word like *moist*.

'Pint of best bitter.'

She drew the beer into a straight glass and the journalist watched her graceful arms flex against the power of the pump. She was looking fetching tonight, he thought, in a short black skirt and red sleeveless top, cut low to show a cleavage any woman would be proud of. Bare legs ending in heels that made her stick her bum out as she walked. Not unusual attire for a barmaid but he liked to think it was for his benefit.

'Settling in all right?' she asked.

'Very comfortable, thanks.' He looked round the bar. 'Quiet tonight?'

'Early yet. There'll be a good few in after the evening gallops.'

'Does everyone in this village work with horses?'

She laughed. 'Well, I don't, but otherwise pretty much, yes. Never seen the attraction myself – bloody great smelly creatures.' She slapped Reuben's pint down on the bar and said, 'This one's on the house.'

'Thanks.' He smiled into her eyes, raised his glass in salute, took a long draught of the golden liquid and sighed. 'Ah, that's better.' He might as well launch straight in to his research. 'You don't happen to know a man called Scobie, I suppose? Graham Scobie?'

Joy looked puzzled. 'The name rings a bell but I don't think he's one of our regulars.'

'He's five-eight, bit tubby, thirtyish, thin hair, if you know what I mean – not balding but like there was never much of it to start with, not much colour either, mousy.' Reuben had a good memory for faces and he'd seen Scobie often enough in court. Joy was shaking her head and he concluded, 'Lives quite near here – Eastbury.'

She shrugged. 'Probably drinks at the Plough, then, or the Queen's Arms in East Garston.' She took it for granted that every man had his local since every man she'd met did.

The street door opened and Reuben glanced round to see a lone man enter the pub. Like Scobie, he was about thirty but there the resemblance ended since he was tall and blond and, Reuben thought, not bad looking. He didn't have those brutal, cunning eyes either, the ones that made even a hardened hack like Reuben shudder when he looked at Scobie in the dock. He was wearing casual clothes but didn't look quite at home in them, as if he'd have been more comfortable in a suit. Office man, Reuben thought dismissively.

Joy said, 'Mike! Thanks for coming.'

'I got your message, Joy.' the newcomer said. 'What's up?'

'I got a letter from the tax man this morning I can't make head or tail of.'

'Let's have a look then.'

'Can I get you a drink?'

'Maybe later, when I'm done.'

Joy lifted the bar flap and the man passed through and disappeared behind the bead curtain that separated the private quarters at the back from the public area. She said, 'Give us a shout if you want a refill Mr – *Reuben*,' and followed him.

Reuben ap Morgan went to sit in the corner between the fireplace and the window. It gave him a good view out onto the village street. Apparently he was going to have amuse himself instead of passing a happy hour practising his flirting technique with Joy. It was like tennis, or the violin; you needed regular practise or you got rusty.

After a moment the landlord came in from the back, glanced round the bar and called 'Joy?'

'She's through there,' Reuben ventured when there was no reply, 'something about a letter from the Revenue.'

Eric Reynolds grunted. 'You the new paying guest?'

'Reuben ap Morgan.' He rose to shake hands but the landlord showed no signs of reciprocating the gesture so he sat down again. A lesser man might have felt foolish.

Reuben looked him over for the first time, inclined to criticise. He soared well over six feet and had the physique to match, though what might once have been muscle was turning to flab. Reuben judged his age at forty but his face looked older, florid and weathered. He had brown hair worn collar length and presently caught back in an elastic band, producing not so much a pony tail as a terrier's. He wore filthy jeans, a sleeveless T-shirt stained with cream emulsion and the expression of a man with a grudge against the world.

Perhaps flirting with Mrs Reynolds should be kept low-key, he thought, or abandoned altogether. Pity, as she was a handsome woman who looked as if she might well be up for a bit of extra-curricular activity, especially if this oaf was what was usually on the menu.

Another man came in at that moment: tall, middle-aged, in clothes that gave the impression of being slightly too big for him.

Eric Reynolds moved behind the bar and said, unsmiling, 'What'll it be?'

'Ginger ale please, landlord.'

If Reynolds was surprised by the modesty of this request he showed no sign but snatched up a bottle from under the counter, snapped its top against the bottle opener and handed it across with a wine glass and the words, 'That'll be ninety-five pee then.'

Joy poked her head out from the back and said, 'Oh, I thought I heard voices.'

'And I thought you were looking after the bar,' her husband growled.

'I am! But Mike's here to see about that letter.'

'Oh, Mike!' he said, as that clearly explained everything.

'Do you have to come into the bar dressed in your painting clothes, Eric? It gives a bad impression.'

He ignored the question entirely. 'If anyone wants me, I'll be painting the function room.' And he left.

'Cosying up to your beloved bloody cold store more like,' Joy muttered after him.

'This is a fairly standard letter, Joy,' Patterson said as she rejoined him. 'Nothing to worry about.'

'But do I need to *do* anything?'

'I'll write an equally standard reply for you.'

'Thanks, Mike.' She dropped a light kiss on his temple, a tribute which he seemed not to notice. 'You're a godsend. Only, if it was left up to Eric, we wouldn't be doing the books at all. He seems to think that all that matters is keeping the beer well and that things like income tax and VAT have nothing to do with him. I have to do everything else, including all the work for the paying guests. He thinks the rooms are self-cleaning and that breakfasts cook themselves.'

Mike laughed. 'You're a hard worker, Joy.'

'Only 'cause I got no choice. I'd happily be a lady of leisure, given half a chance. Speaking of paying guests...' She took the five fifty-pound notes from her pocket where she'd kept them since Reuben's arrival, transferring them every time she changed. 'Bloke arrived yesterday, paid a week in advance in cash and I was wondering–'

'Joy, please! If you're going to ask me what I think you're going to ask me then don't. As your auditor I have certain responsibilities and as far as I know every penny you take in this place goes through the books and I can swear to that on oath. Clear?'

'Clear.' She refolded the notes and tucked them back in her pocket.

'Chap staying a whole week?' Mike asked.

'At least!'

123

'That'll be a nice little earner then. What's he here for?'

'Journalist,' Joy said.

'Oh! Looking for racing tips?'

She shrugged. 'God knows, nothing else ever happens in Lambourn.'

'Mind if I join you?' Reuben looked up in surprise but gestured to the shabby man to take the empty seat opposite. He hoped he wasn't about to be propositioned but the newcomer didn't look the type. He did, however, look vaguely familiar, although Reuben was quite unable to think from where.

'Daft to drink alone,' he commented, holding out his hand. 'Alexander Lomax but you can call me Al.'

'Reuben ap Morgan but you can call me ... Reuben.' They shook hands. Lomax took a packet of cigarettes out of his pocket and offered one. 'No thanks,' Reuben said. 'I've given up.'

'Me too. Just one or two of an evening.' Alex lit a cigarette and gulped in the smoke as if it was oxygen and he'd been trapped under water for the past ten minutes. 'Ah! That's better.'

'I'm staying here,' Reuben offered. 'At the pub.'

'Not a local then.'

'Just passing through.'

'I'm new to the district myself. Don't know many people yet which is why I was so forward as to join you. Very un-English, I know.'

'That's all right,' Reuben said, 'I'm Welsh.'

Alex sipped his drink, which would have passed for whisky had Reuben not heard him give his order. 'Reuben ap Morgan,' he repeated. 'I seem to know that name.'

'Fame at last.' Reuben sat back in his chair and lowered the level of his beer by a good two inches. 'I'm a journalist. On the *Daily Outlook.*'

'Ah!'

'But you don't strike me as a typical *Outlook* reader.'

'More of a *Daily Mail* man,' Alex admitted, 'but I like to read widely.'

'And what's your line of work, Al, if I may ask?'

'I'm a salesman,' Alex said.

'Travel in ladies' underwear?'

'Only on my day off.'

Both men laughed, although the old joke wasn't very funny. That wasn't the point.

Alex said, 'You covered the Devon Bliss case?'

'Yes.' Reuben put his glass down, slightly disturbed by the other man's recognition. Readers did not usually remember the journalist's by-line, only the lurid pictures, especially *Outlook* readers, not all of whom

125

could actually read. 'You interested in that case?'

'Very.'

'Might I ask why?'

'Certainly.'

Alex looked away, his eyes fixed on a scene beyond the window that was invisible to his new friend, since it was long ago and far away.

'You see, I knew Devon as a child.'

'When I say I knew her as a child, I meant when *she* was a child,' Alex said.

'I got that.' Reuben had refilled their glasses himself in the absence of any visible Reynoldses and had snuggled down in his chair for the long haul, his feet up on the hearth, nursing his pint in his lap.

'Knew her from birth, in fact. The Blisses lived in the village my mother moved to after my father died, and I would see her being wheeled in her pram as I came home from school each day. Not that I was interested in babies – what boy of sixteen is? But, later, after I'd moved away, started work, I'd come home for a visit – Sunday dinner – and there she'd be, the prettiest little girl you ever saw, blonde and full of life and always dancing and singing and chattering.'

His voice went quiet. 'I loved that innocent kid. I was like a favourite uncle to her.'

'I heard she was a great one for the talent contests.'

'Wanted to be a star, to be famous. A lot of kids do, of course, but she was very determined and she made it. Not that it was all good. I followed her career avidly, as you can imagine. I couldn't help thinking she'd been spoiled by it all – the constant media attention, the men who wanted her only for one thing, who knew nothing of her soul, as I did.' He gulped some ginger ale. 'Innocence dies quickly.'

'She seemed pretty much in control of her life,' Reuben remarked, a little discomforted by the turn the conversation was taking.

Alex spoke on as if he hadn't been interrupted. 'She was so much prettier as a child, in my view – without make-up, tousled in jeans and sweaters; not with dresses slit up to her thigh and necklines slashed to her tits and hair sprayed so it wouldn't move in a force-ten gale.'

'Well that's the way of it if you're on the telly. *Grooming.*'

'And then *he* came along.'

'Who?' Reuben asked provocatively.

'Scobie, of course.'

'But Scobie didn't kill her – the jury said so.'

Alex made a dismissive noise in his throat. 'If you believe that, Mr Reuben *ap* Morgan, then what are you doing here in Lambourn, not two miles from where Scobie has settled?'

'Interesting.' Reuben drained his glass and looked hard at the man on the other side of the table, leaning forward in a manner that was almost threatening although Al showed no sign of feeling threatened. 'I have contacts who can find out that sort of thing for me but you – a travelling salesman – how would you get to know a thing like that?'

Before Alex could reply, if he had been going to reply, Joy came out into the bar with the man called Mike.

'You lads all right in here?' she asked merrily.

'We're fine,' Reuben said, flopping back in his chair, the tension of the moment before broken. 'Though I did take the liberty of helping myself and Al here to another. Just add it to my bill.'

'Mike?'

'Just a half, thanks.'

'Mike's my accountant,' Joy explained. 'My personal treasure.'

Reuben and Alex both examined him with experienced eyes, the eyes of men who remembered faces for a living and summed up characters for a hobby. Both concluded him harmless as he stood at the bar with lowered eyes, his head half turned away, hunching thankfully over the glass of beer Joy pulled for him.

'I must be off.' Alex rose.

Reuben jumped to his feet. 'Hold on!'

'I'll see you again some time, Reuben, now that I know where to find you.' And Alex swept out, pausing only to give a polite nod to the landlady and her treasure. As he left the pub a crowd of people were coming in, stable lads and lasses from the village, talking, laughing and blocking the doorway so that, by the time Reuben got out into the street past them, there was no sign of Al Lomax.

'Damn it!' Reuben murmured. He went back into the pub, ordered a Scotch – 'make it a treble' – and sat down to brood.

After a moment, a man he hadn't previously noticed emerged from a dark corner and came to sit down opposite him. Maybe he should get a more butch haircut. He glanced up and frowned as he'd had enough unsolicited company for one evening.

'Peter Tilsley,' the man said, holding out his hand.

'So?' Reuben did not reciprocate.

'You a copper too then?'

And now he had Reuben's interest.

Chapter Eight

'So, where are we going with this con trick?' Greg asked the next morning, having called Lomax and Barbara into his office for an update. 'What did you call it – the Good Samaritan?'

'We've scanned the sketches Beatrice Pitcher did for us into the computer,' Alex said. 'Correction, *Barbara* has scanned the sketches and we've printed out copies. We've arranged to see all the earlier victims again today, find out if they recognise the woman or boy from the picture or can add anything to it.'

Greg held out his hand and Barbara gave him the pictures. He passed quickly over the boy and examined the woman's face.

'So this is her,' he said.

'One of her incarnations,' Alex replied. 'She's also a brunette and a red-head – more wigs than the Royal Shakespeare Company.'

'And have we passed copies to the *Newbury Weekly News?*' Greg asked.

'I'm holding fire on that,' Alex said.

'May I ask why? Even if we can't find this woman, then we can put potential victims on their guard, maybe get her to move on from our patch.'

'That's just it,' Lomax said. 'They'll move on to the next typical little market town and start again. While they feel safe in Newbury, we've got a chance of catching them and putting a stop to it.'

'But if they go off to – I don't know–' Greg waved his arms frantically, seeking inspiration. '– Bury St Edmunds – then they'll be off our patch and off our crime figures.'

'There's no record of a similar con being worked anywhere in the country,' Barbara reminded them.

'So they're starting here,' Alex said, 'which means that they're local but doesn't mean that they won't move on if we make it too hot for them here and, frankly, I don't think it matters whose crime figures we're talking about. I want to nip this thing in the butt.'

Struggling as he was to evict this image from his mind, seeing the DCI's ferret-like teeth sunk into his fleshy parts, Greg knew that Lomax was right. Honestly. Except that it did matter – crime figures, clear up rate – especially if you were the superintendent. It was all very well for a mere DCI to say that it didn't matter in the bigger scheme of things whose unsolved crimes these were. The clear-up rate in the Thames Valley was now so low that the Chief Constable had recently been ordered, along with half a dozen others, to report directly to a cabinet minister on new initiatives.

This did not make for a happy Chief Constable.

It probably also counted as a street crime and they'd been given specific targets for reducing muggings. He said, 'I'll give you two more days and then I'm releasing these pictures to the press.'

'Right,' Alex said, getting up. 'Then we'll get cracking. Time and motion wait for no man.'

The phone rang. When Greg answered Susan Habib reported that 'a Sir John Hathaway' wished to speak to him.

'Put him through.' He signalled to Alex and Barbara to wait a moment.

'Mr Summers?' Hathaway's urbane tones seemed to flow from the receiver like honey. 'You asked me to contact you the moment anything fresh happened.'

His voice sounded solemn and Greg asked with foreboding, 'How bad is it?'

'Bad enough. It's Indie's racehorse.'

'Ranulf's Daughter?' Greg said, wondering how on earth he could remember a detail like that when half the time he couldn't remember where he'd left his mobile phone. 'What's happened to her?'

'She's been injured, deliberately crippled. She may have to be put down. Indie's distraught.'

'Where are you?' Greg said briskly.

'The stables – Paddy Nash's.'

'I'll be right there. Don't touch anything.' He hung up. Seeing Barbara and Alex's quizzical looks, he explained. 'It looks as if the Hathaway problem is escalating,' he added.

'Do you want us to go over there?' Alex asked.

'No.' Greg remembered the problem of Michael Patterson/Ian Callaghan and the promise he had given to Barkiss. 'I'll deal with this myself. You carry on with your "Good Samaritan".'

'You're handling this on your own?' Barbara said, puzzled.

'No, I'm going with a bloody great SOC team,' Greg snapped, 'see if I can get some forensic to nail this bastard. And I might as well take Whittaker with me,' he added.

Always best to have someone to do the rough work.

'Andy's in the magistrate's court this morning,' Barbara reminded him.

'Oh, well,' Greg said, 'then I suppose it'll have to be Nicolaides.'

'Chief Inspector Lomax.' The desk sergeant called to Alex as he and Barbara headed for the back door and their car. 'There's a gentleman here asking for you by name.'

Alex glanced round and saw Reuben ap

Morgan leaning against the front desk. The reporter grinned and gave him a wave. If Alex was shocked to see him, he gave no sign of it. He said, 'Warm the car up, I'll only be a minute,' to Barbara, grabbed ap Morgan by the arm and steered him into the nearest vacant interview room.

'Come to buy some ladies' knickers?' he asked.

'Surprise!' Reuben said.

'How did you find me?'

'Like I said at the pub, I have way of finding things out. You should never underestimate the resources of a national newspaper.'

'Evidently.'

'So was it true – did you really know Devon as a child?'

Alex perched on the table and folded his arms. 'Perfectly true.'

'Then I think we can do each other some good, Alex.'

Just like always, Lomax realised: Al never stuck. He said, 'So do I, which is why I came looking for you at the pub.'

Reuben was wrong-footed. 'You knew I was there?' he stammered.

'I attended the trial,' Alex explained. 'Camped out night and day in Old Bailey to get a seat in the public gallery. I saw you in the press box, rushing off twice a day to phone in your copy.'

'I knew I'd seen you somewhere before,' Reuben exclaimed. 'We took plenty of pictures of the crowd outside the court each day and your face is on them.'

'When I saw you in the street in Lambourn the other day, it really started me wondering. So I followed you back to the pub. I take it you're here to keep an eye on Scobie.'

'Yes. You?'

'Same. So, I think you're right that we can do each other some good, maybe catch the little weasel before he strikes again.'

'I don't know that I'd go that far,' Reuben protested. 'He was nearly thirty when he killed Devon, *if* he killed her. It could be another ten years and I haven't got that long.'

'Well, I have. Look, I have to go. See you in the pub tonight? Later, when it's busier and we won't be so conspicuous.'

'About nine?'

'See you there.'

'Friend of yours?' Barbara asked as she drove the car out of the station car park and headed for the roundabout.

'Possible informant,' Alex said neutrally.

'Yeah? Have you registered him?'

'Not yet. It's early days. You checking up on me, Sergeant?'

'No, sir!'

Alex wasn't sure why he had confided in ap Morgan. It had certainly not been his intention when he accosted him at the pub; he had been seeking to obtain and not dispense information. Because he needed to talk to someone, he supposed, and he knew nobody in Newbury except his colleagues. The superintendent was a non-starter and, while he liked Barbara, she was so hand in glove with Summers that she would feel obliged to grass him up to the boss if he told her that Graham Scobie had brought him to Berkshire.

Keen to change the subject he said, 'Is it true what I hear that Mr Summers' missus is young enough to be his daughter?'

'Angie? She's twenty-four. They're not married, though.'

'Oh? But she calls herself Mrs Summers?'

'It's a long story,' Barbara said.

'That's okay.' Alex settled comfortably in his seat and closed his eyes. 'I'm not going anywhere.'

'Okay. Angie was married to Mr Summers' son Fred. He died two years ago – leukaemia. He and Angie ... turned to each other for comfort, I suppose.'

'And that's it?'

'That's it. They make a good couple, though.'

'I have noticed,' Alex said, 'that when people say something is a long story, it

136

usually turns out to be nothing of the kind.' He was thoughtful for a moment, then his eyes snapped open. 'Was that his only child?'

'Yes.'

'How old?'

'Twenty-two.'

Alex grimaced. 'Is that why he's so grumpy?'

'You find Mr Summers grumpy?'

'Like he's got a sore bear in his head.' While Barbara deconstructed this, he went on, 'He invited me round to supper the other night. I say supper – it was a Chinese takeaway. I was amusing myself by winding him up – ever so gently – and he didn't get it at all.'

'Hmm. People don't immediately know how to take you, you know, Alex.' Barbara liked Gregory Summers, a lot, but she also liked Lomax. If they were set on a low-grade territory feud then it wasn't her job to bang their heads together.

'Me, I prefer my women a bit more mature,' Alex commented. 'Hovering round the forty mark, been round the block a few times, don't expect too much.'

'Not so choosy?' Barbara suggested.

Alex laughed. 'Not so choosy,' he conceded.

When Reuben was safely back in the driver's

seat of his car he took out his mobile and dialled a number from his address book. It answered on the first ring.

'Keaton.'

'Morgan,' he said.

'Hello, old darling.'

'We all go for Friday?'

'I've even booked my ticket.'

'Good. How do you look?'

'I hardly know myself.'

'Slight change of plan, mind. Or addition to plan, I should say.'

'Oh?'

'There are two men here in Berkshire I'd like you to meet, both of them creepily obsessed with Devon Bliss.'

Chapter Nine

If George Nicolaides was fazed by an invitation to accompany the superintendent on a case, he gave no sign of it.

He had joined Newbury CID only recently after several years with the Metropolitan Police in his native London. Moving to Berkshire had enabled him to put down a deposit on a terraced house – something he could never have afforded in Finsbury Park – and that made up for the general dullness of the provinces, or so he kept telling himself. He couldn't understand why his new colleagues complained about the cost of housing locally since it seemed dirt cheap to him.

It had the added advantage that his mum couldn't keep popping round to see if he was eating properly and if he'd met a nice Greek virgin yet.

Greg had told him to drive and he sped confidently along the B4000 heading for Lambourn. They travelled in silence which Greg was glad of; Nicolaides liked to talk with his hands which didn't make him the world's safest driver. It was barely ten but the London-Greek had a five o'clock shadow and Greg was convinced if he watched closely enough he'd actually be able to see his beard growing.

A few cars behind them, the superintendent could make out the Scenes-of-Crime van he had summoned up with a phone call.

As he signalled right for the turn to the village, Nicolaides spoke for the first time. 'What made you decide to handle this yourself, sir?'

'Sir John Hathaway's a VIP,' Greg said shortly.

'Oh?' The constable took his hands off the wheel to gesture abstractly. 'So it's one law for the posh and one law for the rest of us?'

'It's the same *law* for everyone,' Greg snapped as the car swerved slightly to the right and was corrected. 'Not necessarily the same enforcer.' He conceded mentally that the younger man had a point: would he have been investigating a case of petty vandalism at all if Hathaway hadn't appealed direct to the Chief Super? And a lamed horse, however valuable, was nothing but criminal damage, even it was a sentient creature.

'Belongs to the same lodge as the Chief Constable, does he, this Hathaway?' Nicolaides said cynically.

As they had just slowed down for the 30-mph sign that marked the Eastern boundary of Lambourn, Greg didn't bother to reply.

He didn't mind Nicolaides being a bit full of himself; it made a nice contrast to Andy Whittaker, who seemed to be terrified of him. Instead he said, 'What *is* that awful smell – like 10,000 lilies dead of old age?'

Or, as Alex Lomax would no doubt say, lilies that fluster smell far worse than weeds.

'My new aftershave,' Nicolaides suggested. 'It's called Wild Bull. Supposed to drive the girls crazy but I'm not holding my breath.'

'Well I am,' Greg said.

They found Nash's stables by the simple process of stopping a lad leading a horse and asking. The lad – who must have been forty if he was a day – pointed along the High Street and said in the broadest Berkshire accent Greg had heard in years, 'Just past the church, another twenty yards, then take the left turn and up the hill, half a mile.'

'Thank you,' Greg said. The car didn't move. 'Well?' he demanded.

'Sorry, sir, I didn't understand a word of that.'

Greg repeated it in an accent Nicolaides felt more at home with and they were at the stables in five minutes, making their way up an asphalt drive, past fields of pasture, to the stable yard. They drew up alongside a Range Rover, which the superintendent was sure was India Hathaway's, and a number of similar vehicles. Through the entrance, he could make out an oblong courtyard fringed with what he supposed were called loose boxes, a modern, square, brick house set back behind them.

'Clive Nash,' Nicolaides read out from an engraved metal plaque on the wall. 'Proprietor.' Greg could see why Nash would prefer Paddy to Clive: Clive wasn't a robust, out-of-doors, horsy sort of name; Clive had spectacles and an asthmatic chest.

The gate into the yard was closed and someone had slung a crudely printed notice from the top bar: NO ENTRY. They were taking his instructions about securing the scene seriously. Good.

The SOC van drew up behind his car and two men in overalls got out of the back along with a photographer.

Greg smiled as a petite and pretty woman climbed down from the front passenger seat; Martha Childs had recently transferred from the neighbouring Hampshire constabulary on promotion as senior SOC Officer and he knew already how reliable she was. He thought her well named since, like the Biblical Martha, she was the most efficient of housekeepers – gathering every speck of dust, every hair, every grain of potential evidence from a crime scene.

'Riding shotgun, Mrs Childs?' he said.

142

'Murder scene, Superintendent?' she called cheerfully, hefting her equipment out of the van. He knew better than to offer a hand. Martha was stronger than she looked and asked for and accepted no privileges on the grounds of her sex.

'Not quite,' Greg replied. 'Vandalism of a peculiarly nasty type.'

'Well, I suppose that makes a change.'

She was no more than thirty and had a degree in Applied Biology from Oxford. She lived in Basingstoke with a husband who worked at Heathrow airport in some vague managerial capacity and two infant children. Greg meant some day to find out how she had ended up in such an odd job but the opportunity to ask about it had not yet arisen.

'This is gonna cost,' Nicolaides muttered, then added something about lodges and Chief Constables beneath his breath. Greg decided to let it go. He doubted if Hathaway was a Mason – probably thought it a bit naff – and he knew for a fact that Barkiss wasn't one. It was discouraged in the police force these days.

Greg wouldn't join ... not even if they asked him.

Nicolaides then said something in what Greg assumed was Greek, which was just plain annoying. He turned deliberately away to signal his displeasure, taking Martha on one side, and explained the situation to her. Then he donned a pair of gloves and opened the gate, touching it as little as possible in case he obliterated prints. Nicolaides and the SOC team followed him, not laying a hand on it at all.

As he entered the yard, Greg could hear a woman sobbing. His first thought was that it was India, but he didn't see her as the sobbing kind. The little girl, perhaps, Olivia. That would be understandable.

'Just wait here a minute,' he told his colleagues.

A small group of people stood huddled round the weeper and, as they dispersed, looking round at the new arrivals, Greg saw that it was Grace Rutherford who was making all the noise, lying on the ground in a foetal position, her legs drawn up to her chest, rocking from side to side and howling, apparently oblivious to the mud – and worse – on her clothes and even in her hair.

The huddle consisted of India, her husband and a tall, thin man wearing jodhpurs, a checked Tattersall shirt and a padded Barbour jacket despite the August heat. Olivia Hathaway had her arms round the tall man's waist and her head buried in his abdomen. Greg could see a faint trembling in her shoulders that suggested that she would like to join Grace in her display of grief but had been brought up not to make such a spectacle of herself.

Sir John stepped forward, said, 'Mr Summers, thank you for coming so promptly,' and shook his hand. He jerked his head back at the tableau behind him and lowered his voice. 'She's been carrying on like that for nearly an hour.'

'Does she need an ambulance?'

'The doctor is on his way – held up by a grumbling appendix in Great Shefford, apparently.'

'Just nerves.' Indie joined them and also shook his hand. 'She'll cry herself into exhaustion any minute now. She found Ranulf's, you see, and she's as attached to the mare as I am. She was due to ride her at Windsor next week.'

'Grace was?' he said, surprised.

Hathaway gave him a thin smile. 'Had professional women jockeys for a good twenty years now, Summers.'

'Yes,' he said, feeling foolish, 'I knew that. It didn't occur to me.'

'Easier for them to make the weight,' Indie added drily. Although she would never break down like Grace he could see that her eyes were red and brimming with tears which an ill-chosen word would bring gushing out. He must take care not to choose that word.

He said, 'I'm most awfully sorry, Lady

India. It must be a terrible blow.'

'She's not just a racehorse,' Indie said quietly, 'not just an investment – or an effective way of throwing money away, more like. She was part of the family.'

'And Grace found her?'

'Yes, but she's not going to be in any condition to make a statement any time soon,' Hathaway said.

'I can see that.'

Indie raised her voice above the noise. 'Gnasher?' The tall man gestured helplessly that he could not join them without disturbing Olivia so Greg made his way across to them.

'Superintendent Summers, Paddy Nash,' Indie said, 'and vice versa.'

'This is a bad business,' Nash said, rubbing Olivia's blonde head with his free hand while shaking hands with Greg. He was about fifty, Greg thought, still a handsome man, though weather-beaten like all who worked principally outdoors. He had the same sort of accent as the Hath- aways – belonging to no particular region or class, confident and clear. He glanced down at Grace. 'If she doesn't buck up soon, I'm gonna get the vet to tranquillise her.'

'Gnasher!'

'Only joking, Indie.'

'The vet's here?' Greg asked.

'One thing we're not short of in

Lambourn,' Indie remarked, 'is horse doctors.'

'I suppose I'd better start by taking a look at the horse,' Greg said.

'I'll take you. John, can you...' Nash handed his young burden over to her grandfather for further comfort and he and India escorted Greg into a stable at the end of a row of ten on the left hand side. Above the door the words Ranulf's Daughter were written in chalk.

'Grace was mucking out this morning,' Nash explained. 'She started at the end furthest from the house, as usual, and got to Ranuif's about an hour ago. I was indoors talking to the vet on the phone, as it happened, when I heard her scream. Naturally, I came running. Called the vet straight back and he was here in five minutes.'

'Was the door shut when Grace got here?' Greg asked.

'I can't be sure but I assume so. If it had been open she'd surely have gone to investigate earlier.'

'Okay,' Greg said. 'Let's see the damage.'

When he'd accustomed his eyes to the gloom of the stable, he saw a horse lying on its side. He could hear her panting, almost snorting. A youngish man was running his hands along her flanks, a black leather bag on the straw by his side. India went to her

147

head and crouched down, soothing her with gentle words.

'This is Simon Jakes, the vet,' Nash explained. 'We've called the police in, Si.'

'I'd happily string up anyone who could do this to an innocent creature,' the vet said. He rose to shake hands. 'So anything I can do to help...' He was young, Greg saw, no more than thirty. He was wearing a suit but, sensibly, had covered it with an overall. Bits of straw were sticking to his well worn Timberlands.

His hands were rough and Greg, who knew the sort of places vets regularly put their fingers, half wished he hadn't had to shake hands with him. He said, 'Can you tell me exactly what has been done to her?'

'Someone's taken a hacksaw to both her front legs,' Jakes explained. He kneeled in the straw again and pointed without touching the wounds. Greg flinched. It didn't look like what the newspapers called a frenzied attack but rather as if someone had clinically and carefully set about disabling the horse in the manner of a surgeon. He wasn't over fond of horses – they were too big and sweaty and snorty – but he hated to see a dumb animal made to suffer in this way.

Something brownish-grey with four dainty feet, a tail and a sharp nose darted out of the straw at that moment, running across his left shoe, and he had to restrain himself from squealing. He was prepared to make an exception for dumb rats and mice.

'The tendons are all severed,' Jakes was saying, oblivious to the rodent. 'She's never going to race again. I've given her a sedative to dull the pain but there's not a lot I can do to mend the damage. Time will heal – up to a point.'

The mare whinnied as if she understood and India said, 'There, there, old girl.'

'We need to get her to hospital as fast as possible,' Jakes added. 'I've got an ambulance on its way.' He looked at his watch. 'They should be here any minute. I'll go and see if there's any sign of them.'

This talk of hospitals and ambulances might have sounded odd to Greg had he not seen the big sign – Equine Hospital – pointing up past the church as they drove through the village.

'You ... um ... you put lamed horses down, don't you?' he said.

It was Nash who answered. 'Depends. If the leg's broken then it's usually the quickest and kindest thing, but Ranulf's Daughter will walk again, eventually.' He shrugged. 'It'll be a long and expensive business, though, and it's really up to Indie.'

The vet returned a minute later and said crossly, 'Still no sign. There's not a lot more I can do, Paddy, till I get her out of here.'

149

'Can you let me have a written report?' Greg said. 'Stating the exact nature of the injuries. In case it ever comes to court.'

'Sure. You know where the surgery is?'

'I think I passed it on the way in.'

'Well send one of your men round later and I'll have it ready.'

He went outside again.

'What security measures do you take?' Greg asked.

'We live on the premises,' Nash replied, 'and there's always someone here at night. A lot of the lads sleep here too, in dormitories above the tack room.'

'Including Grace?'

'Including Grace. She's got a boyfriend in the village but she usually comes home each night. The lads have got sharp ears when it comes to their babies. Otherwise we lock up. There are motion-sensitive lights. But you don't expect this sort of pointless attack.'

'But horses do get "nobbled"?'

'Sure, they might get doped before a big race, but that's mostly the champions and, to be frank, Ranulf's wasn't in that league.'

'Don't talk about her as if she were already dead,' Indie snapped.

'Sorry!' Nash turned back to Greg. 'Mostly we're worried about people snooping about, trying to bribe the staff, get inside inform-ation. I've never come across anything like this in thirty years in the business. It seems so ... personal.'

'I fear that's exactly what it was,' Greg said.

The ambulance finally arrived and Greg watched as the mare was hoisted up in the sling that was the equivalent of a human stretcher. She whimpered in pain as her feet left the ground and the superintendent winced in sympathy.

With the injured horse gone, he left the SOC team to do their work in the stable and went back to the yard. Grace was still on the ground, though she seemed calmer now, snivelling rather than screaming. Meanwhile, Olivia and her grandfather were squaring up for a fight.

'She was such a beautiful horse,' Hathaway said.

'She still is. She's not dead.'

'Well...'

'No!' Olivia beat her fists against his chest. 'You can't have her shot. I won't let you.'

'It might be kinder–'

'She can still lead a happy life.' The child's face was twisted in pain and Greg eyed her with compassion and not a little concern.

'Racehorses love to race,' her grandfather said gently. 'It's what they live for.'

Funny that the jockeys always had to whip them then, Greg thought.

'I'll take care of her. I won't let you.

Granny!' She ran off towards the stable and Greg caught her by her wrist.

'Don't go in there just yet, dear,' he said.

'I don't know who you are.' This was not a young woman who would ever allow herself to be abducted in the street. 'Take your hands off me.' She kicked him on the shin. Hard.

Hathaway said, 'Liv!'

'Let go of me!'

'Liv!'

'It's all right.' Greg didn't release his grip. He was used to hanging on to people who were kicking and biting him.

'Olivia.' India returned from seeing the ambulance off, the voice of reason. 'Stop kicking the superintendent. He's here as a friend, to find out who did this terrible thing to Ranulf's.'

'Oh!' The little girl subsided and Greg let her go. 'How could anybody hurt a beautiful horse like Ranulf's?' she demanded, then snivelled and wiped her eyes with the back of her hand.

'I don't know,' Greg said.

'Granny, you won't let them shoot her?'

'No, darling. Nobody's going to be doing any shooting. Now, I want you to apologise to Mr Summers for kicking him. We don't do that, whatever the provocation.'

'That's not necessary,' Greg said.

'Are you related to Buffy the Vampire

152

Slayer?' Liv asked, brightening up a little in her interest.

'I beg your pardon.'

'Only her name's Summers, isn't it?'

'Is it?'

'Yes.'

'Okay. No relation, far as I know.'

'But you fight the bad guys too?' she said hopefully.

'I certainly do ... just not the undead. Not in general.'

He had clearly disappointed the child. Luckily, the doctor arrived at that moment. Within seconds he had coaxed Grace to her feet and supported her as she stumbled towards the house. Greg decided to give them a few minutes. He would need a statement from the 'lad' but hysterical witnesses were not good witnesses and it looked as if the GP knew how to calm her down.

As India took charge of her granddaughter, Greg drew her husband to one side. 'Are you still sure that's it's you and not Lady India who is the target?' he queried in a low voice.

Hathaway stroked a non-existent beard. 'I see what you mean. Laming the horse seems like a clear attack on Indie, and yet the person behind this may not make that distinction. After all...' He grimaced. 'Husband and wife are one flesh.'

Chapter Ten

Greg had Nicolaides drive him over to Eastbury to the address where Graham Scobie was living. A few minutes later they drew up outside a pebble-dashed semi that probably dated from the 1950s. Council, he thought, and lacking the small embellishments that suggested the owner had bought it.

He felt that he had good enough reason to question the man now, without his shouting harassment.

But his landlady told them he was out.

'He's out most days,' she said, having examined his credentials with more than usual care. 'I don't encourage my lodger to hang about the house all day. Usually I don't take anyone who hasn't got a job – stable lads and lasses mostly – but beggars can't be choosers. Not everyone wants to live in the middle of nowhere or, if they do, they want a bijou cottage with honeysuckle round the door. He's looking – or so he says – for a job. Pays his rent on time. He's quiet.' She shrugged. 'He's been a help with the garden. Live and let live.'

Her words were tolerant but her hard

mouth told a different story.

'Mrs..?' Greg said.

'Brakespear, like the brewery.' She looked at him without enthusiasm. 'He promised me there'd be no more bother with the police, that that business was all over.'

'I just need to ask him a few questions, about an unrelated matter.'

She was probably sixty, widowed or divorced, forced to take in a lodger to make ends meet. She clearly didn't spend spare cash on her personal appearance since she was wearing carpet slippers and the sort of wrap-around apron that Greg remembered seeing on women of his mother's generation when he was a boy and which he thought had died out around 1963. He sensed that she had had a hard life and he wanted to pity her but something in her face stopped him.

'May I take a look in his room, Mrs Brakespear?' he asked.

'Have you got a search warrant?' The woman was more wised up than he'd expected: too many cop shows on TV.

'No,' he admitted.

'Then you'd best come back when Mr Scobie's here. Try any time after six.'

She shut the door politely but with determination.

'We'd best do that,' Greg said to Nicolaides.

'I've seen murderers,' Nicolaides remarked,

as they resumed their car, 'a good half dozen of them, but never one like him.'

'He was acquitted,' Greg reminded them both. 'Let's go and see if Grace Rutherford is fit to be questioned.'

'Do I need a solicitor?' was Grace's first – rather odd – question. Now, why did she ask that, Greg wondered, unless she, too, had simply been watching too much television?

She seemed calmer now, sitting on a hard chair in the pseudo-rustic kitchen, sipping a mug of tea. She paused from time to time to run her fingers through her matted hair, dislodging straw and flakes of what Greg hoped was dried mud.

'Has she been sedated?' Greg asked the doctor, leaving the girl's question hanging in the air for the moment. If so, she might still not be up to answering his questions in any useful way.

But the GP shook his head. 'I was firm with her, just as effective.' He was a fatherly man who must be nearing retirement, Greg thought. He exuded an air of tranquillity which probably had a potent placebo effect on his patients.

'I can stay for a bit, if you like,' he added. 'Few minutes.'

Greg crouched down in front of Grace so his face was on a level with hers. He heard his back protest.

'I just want an account of how you found the racehorse, Miss Rutherford. You're a witness, not a suspect so you have no need of a solicitor, although you can have one if you really want.' She shrugged a negative. 'The doctor will stay, if you like, or shall I fetch Mr Nash?'

She nodded. 'Paddy.'

Greg jerked his head at Nicolaides who went off to fetch the trainer. They were back in two minutes. Nash placed a hand on the girl's shoulder and said, 'Bit better now, Grey?'

'Bit better, Gnasher.'

'Is there any more of that tea? I know I could use some.'

'I'll make fresh.'

She went to rise but Nash pressed down on her shoulders and said, 'I'll do it. Superintendent?'

'Won't say no, Mr Nash.'

As Nash filled the kettle, Greg pulled up another chair at the kitchen table and sat opposite Grace. Gently, he said, 'I'd like to hear, in your own words, what happened this morning. What time did you get down to the stable yard?'

'Just after seven, same as usual.'

'But Ranulf's Daughter wasn't your first port of call.'

'No, I was leaving her till last because I wanted to take her out for a run after I'd mucked her out. We're ... we *were* in training for a race at Windsor next week.'

She bit back more tears and Greg said, 'You're doing fine. Thank you.' This last was to Nash who had just placed a strong mug of dark tea on the table in front of him. He waved away a bowl of damp-looking sugar. Nicolaides leaned across him, spooned three heaped helpings of sugar into his mug, downed the beverage in one and wiped his lips on the back of his hand with a sigh of gratitude.

'So, when did you last see the horse uninjured?' Greg asked, pretending not to notice this uncouth behaviour.

'Last thing. I'd been round at my boy-friend's.'

'Mr Patterson's?'

'Yeah. Oh! Yeah, that was you.' She looked at Greg more narrowly, as if wondering why this middle-aged stranger kept stampeding into her life. 'Got back about half eleven. I looked in on her, say goodnight, give her a lump of sugar. She was fine.'

'Well, that gives us a time frame,' Greg said. 'Rather a long one.'

One of the SOCOs came in and asked to take fingerprints from Nash and the girl for elimination purposes. They both complied without demur. Greg said to Nash, 'I'd like your permission to search the place for the weapon – the saw that was used in the attack. I take it you have tools of that type around the place?'

'Quite an assortment of tools at any working stables.' Nash nodded, wiping his inky fingers on a wet sponge. 'Look by all means, but won't he have brought his weapon with him?'

'Maybe, but then he could have discarded it here after use.' He took the SOCO to one side and told him quietly to take a good look at the lads' quarters in case the saw was hidden there.

The man went silently away.

'I don't think there's anything further,' Greg said to Grace, 'although we'll need to get it down in writing.'

She rose. 'I think I'll get a shower, change my clothes.'

'I'd like the ones you're wearing to be preserved for evidence,' he told her.

'What?' She looked dismayed. 'I don't understand.'

'You were the first person on the crime scene,' he explained. 'If the man who did this left any fibres, hair – whatever – they may have been transferred onto your clothes when you came in. That could be crucial in the investigation.'

She looked uncertainly at Nash who said, 'It'll be okay, Grey.'

Greg said, 'You want to find the person who did this and see them punished, don't you, Grace?'

She twisted here fingers together as if forming a cat's cradle with string. ''Course I do.'

'Then I'll send a female SOCO with you to bag up your clothes.'

'I don't think you should get too pally with that man Summers,' Hathaway told his wife. They were still standing in the stable yard, unsure what to do next.

Indie raised her eyebrows. 'I like him.'

'He's a policeman.'

She laughed. 'But I was brought up to believe that the police are on my side, Johnny. Weren't you?'

'Only when I was prosecuting. When I was defending, they were the enemy.'

'But you mostly defended.'

'*Precisément.*'

Greg instructed Nicolaides to drive to the almshouses on the outskirts of Lambourn. 'Wait here for me, George,' he said. 'I won't be long. And for God's sake open a window.'

He rapped once, twice, at the door of the last house and heard noises inside indicating that someone was at home. Patterson pulled the door open an inch or two and looked at him warily.

'Have you got a minute?' Greg asked.

'I suppose, though I'm in the middle of an audit.'

He opened the door wide enough to let Greg in, peering out past him as if alert for danger.

'Anything wrong?' Greg asked.

'Not really.' Patterson stood just inside the door, offering no further hospitality. Greg saw that the dining table at the rear of the room was covered in papers and ledgers. He could see more than on his previous visit, with daylight entering the room from the kitchen window, and he noticed a snapshot of Patterson and Grace Rutherford on the mantelpiece. They were grinning into the camera under a cloudy sky with Windsor Castle behind them.

'What can I do for you, Superintendent?'

'There's been another attack on the Hathaways, during the night.'

'I didn't see or hear anything,' he said quickly.

'It wasn't at the house but at the stables – Paddy Nash's place at the other end of the village.'

'I know it.'

'Of course. Your girlfriend works there.'

'Actually, yes. Is she–' He was suddenly alarmed. 'Has something happened to Grey?'

'Nothing like that,' Greg assured him. 'Lady India's horse was crippled.'

'Oh, my God!' His bland face startled into shock, making him suddenly more human.

'Grey will be devastated. She loves that horse as much as Lady India does.'

'She's certainly upset,' Greg said, recalling the girl's alarming reaction. 'Everyone is.'

He reached for his jacket. 'I'll go round there.'

'There's no point,' Greg said. 'It's all cordoned off as a crime scene at the moment and you won't be allowed in. Besides, Grace was on her way to shower and rest when I left a few minutes ago.'

He laid a hand on Patterson's arm to detain him, then swiftly removed it as if he'd been burned.

The young man stared at him, his pale eyes intense. Greg flinched. Patterson said quietly, 'You know, don't you?'

'...Yes.'

'They said no one would be told.'

'I worked it out for myself.'

'Oh, my God!' The young man was panic stricken. He reeled away and sat down heavily on the sofa. 'This is what I've been afraid of, all these years.' He put his head in his hands and began to sob. Greg knew he should do something, try to comfort him, but he couldn't bring himself to touch him again. He fetched a glass of water from the kitchen and put it down on the table beside the man.

'I *am* a police officer,' he said. 'I'm trained to remember faces.'

162

Patterson picked up the glass of water and drained it in one gulp. He took a deep breath and looked a challenge at Greg.

He said, 'I make your flesh crawl, don't I?'

'... Yes.'

'And do you think it's been easy for me? I think about them all the time – Lily and Rose – what they'd look like, what they'd be doing. They'd be sixteen now, young women doing their A levels and looking forward to adult life, devoted to their big brother. I took that away from them and I more than anyone have to live with that.'

'Was John Hathaway connected with your trial in any way?' Greg asked suddenly.

'Sir John? No.'

'Not even obliquely – someone from his chambers? Has he ever given any indication that he knows who you are?'

'Oh – I see! He prosecuted me sixteen years ago so now I'm vandalising his property and laming his horse to get back at him? Well, I'd never heard of John Hathaway till I came to live in Lambourn. My trial was held in Leeds and the lawyers all came from the North of England. That's all I know.' He concluded with a tinge of self pity, 'I was just a child.'

'Fourteen is not exactly a child,' Greg said. 'Incidentally, when did you last see Miss Rutherford?'

'She was here last night. She's mostly here

in the evenings unless she's working. Why?'

'What time did she leave?'

'Eleven, bit after. Quarter past.'

Which gave her just enough time to get back to Nash's yard at half past and 'say goodnight' to the racehorse.

Since there seemed nothing more to be asked, he left.

He sat brooding as Nicolaides drove them back to Newbury. After a moment, the constable said, 'Sir?'

Greg grunted.

'It's just that nobody calls me George, sir, not even me mum.' Getting no reply, he persevered. 'People call me Nick – short for Nicolaides.'

Greg said something that sounded like, 'Hmm?'

'Good,' Nicolaides said. 'I'm glad we got that cleared up.'

As they drew into the car park behind the police station Greg said, 'Meet me here again at six, George, and we'll have that talk with Graham Scobie.'

Chapter Eleven

Harmless was the word that came into Greg's mind when he looked at Scobie shortly after six-thirty that evening. Ugly, a bit creepy, but essentially harmless. He began to understand how a jury – inclined, whatever the judge's instructions, to make their minds up at first sight of the defendant – had opted for a not guilty verdict.

It was the grim landlady who had opened the door to them and she had called up the stairs. 'Mr Scobie, those two gentlemen from the police are back again, the ones I told you about.'

He moved swiftly and silently down the stairs like a small rodent and Greg half expected him to run across his shoe.

Scobie said, 'Thank you, Mrs Brakespear.'

Odd that they should be so formal when they shared a house, Greg thought; odd, but not unusual. There was also a good chance that they sincerely disliked each other; he certainly wouldn't have fancied living with the woman. He was bearing in mind that Hathaway didn't want Scobie to know of his suspicions, so he adopted a neutral tone, polite and not unfriendly.

'Mr Scobie? I was wondering if I could just ask you a few questions about an incident that occurred in Lambourn last night.'

Since Mrs Brakespear showed no sign of moving out of earshot, Scobie mumbled, 'You'd best come up.'

He took Greg and Nicolaides up to his room at the back of the house, looking out over the garden, which was small but well tended with an abundance of fruit frees. 'Do a bit of gardening for Mrs Brakespear,' Scobie explained, seeing Greg's glance. 'My trade, you might say, and it's something to do on these long empty days.'

He had a high voice; it would easily pass for a woman's over the phone, Greg thought, for no particular reason. People said that women were less superficial than men when it came to choosing their mates but that wasn't Greg's observation, certainly not these days. Scobie would not have to fight them off with a stick.

The room was dark, shabby and averagely untidy. Scobie began to gather things up as Greg sat down on an armchair by the window – a few books into a pile, discarded clothes into a red plastic laundry basket. Nicolaides leaned against the boarded-up fireplace with his arms folded, watching Scobie with the same look that a cat wears when it's stalking a pigeon. Finally, Scobie had finished his displacement activity and sat down on the edge of the single bed, his hands folded neatly in his lap.

'Incident?' he said.

'I think you know Sir John and Lady India Hathaway.'

'I've never had the pleasure of meeting Lady India,' Scobie corrected him. 'Sir John – yes, obviously.'

'And you know that they live in Lambourn?'

'I do now. Bumped into Sir John in the street a few weeks ago. Gave me quite a turn, I can tell you.' He smoothed the counterpane with his small hands. 'Rather too many associations...'

'You didn't know he lived here when you came to settle nearby yourself?'

'How could I? I thought he lived in Holland Park. Big house.' He giggled nervously. 'Worth millions.'

'And what brings you to this part of Berkshire, if I may ask, Mr Scobie? Do you have family here? Friends?'

He shrugged. 'It's a free country. I wanted to get right away. I mean, I walked away from that court without a stain on my character but ... people talk. I couldn't go back to Catford, and certainly not to Blackheath, where poor Devon died so horribly.'

Greg didn't remember the judge saying anything about unstained characters. He did remember that a psychiatrist had described Scobie as being of above average intelligence, which proved that looks could deceive. He also thought it in poor taste to drag Devon Bliss into the conversation like that. He glanced at Nicolaides who was watching Scobie incredulously now, his black eyes narrowed to slits. Greg shot him a warning look and the constable studied the floor.

'So, are you going to tell me what this incident was?' Scobie asked.

'Lady India keeps a horse in training in Lambourn, at Nash's yard.'

'I don't really follow the horses myself. Dogs, more my line. Catford dog track. Dogs don't have a little man aboard holding them back, that's what my old dad used to say.'

Greg had been under the impression from his reading on the case that Scobie had never known his father, but he wasn't sure enough to challenge it. Anyway, an abandoned son was allowed his fantasies of the useful bits of lore that fathers hand down. He said, 'Last night, some time between about midnight and dawn the horse was deliberately lamed. It will never race again.'

'I don't hold with hurting dumb animals!' Scobie said indignantly. 'Even if someone had it in for Sir John, it's not right to attack one of God's creatures that way.'

'I agree,' Greg said mildly. 'May I ask what you were doing last night between those times, sir?'

'Me?'

'We're talking to everyone local who is acquainted with the Hathaways,' Greg said smoothly, 'see if they can shed any light.'

'I see. Let me think. What time is dawn?'

'Half five,' Nicolaides supplied.

'Between midnight and five-thirty I was fast asleep.'

'Here?'

He laughed. 'Of course here.'

'Do you have a car, sir, any sort of vehicle?'

'I've got a rickety old bike,' Scobie offered. 'I take the bus into Newbury once a week to sign on. Otherwise, I walk and cycle everywhere.'

Nicolaides said, 'Excuse me a moment,' and left the room.

Scobie said, 'I'm puzzled, Superintendent. Why would you think that I, of all people, would want to harm Sir John Hathaway?'

'Routine enquiries,' Greg said.

'Yes? That's what they said when they questioned me for hours about poor Devon. Hours? – days more like. Till I was about ready to admit to anything. Only I never, 'cause there was nothing to admit to. Sir John's my saviour.' His piggy eyes were

169

shining. 'There's nothing I wouldn't do for him. Nothing.'

Nicolaides was waiting outside, half sitting on the car bonnet, a French cigarette dangling from his lip. He put it out when he saw Greg coming, grinding it into the asphalt with his shoe.

'Landlady agrees he was here all night, fast asleep.' he said. 'It's not a hotel. He's got a key but she bolts the doors at night when he's safe inside and she's a light sleeper, reckons there's no way he could get out without her hearing.'

'Okay, it was always a bit of a long shot.'

'Can we get his prints?'

'I can think of no possible grounds on which we could ask for them.'

He got into the car. Nicolaides joined him and started the engine. 'What do you make of Scobie, George?' he asked.

Nicolaides said slowly, 'I don't know. I thought I did, but now I don't, if you see what I mean.'

'I see what you mean.'

'I still think he's pretty creepy, whatever that jury said. He's ... clammy.'

'That's right: never let facts get in the way of prejudice,' Greg said. 'You're young, George, and single. Do you think women are less obsessed with physical appearance than men when it comes to choosing a boyfriend?'

'Christ no! They're probably worse. You have to keep yourself in shape, wear the right clothes, have the right hair, the works, or you can forget it. They'll laugh in your face.'

'Not much hope for the Scobies of this world then.'

'None at all. Where to now, guv?'

'Back to HQ, then home.'

'Is supper ready?' Scobie asked, when the two policemen had gone.

'Be another few minutes. I got a bit behind-hand what with the younger policeman asking me all those questions.'

Scobie didn't bother to ask. He had enough experience of the police to know that they'd been checking his alibi. Well, they wouldn't find anything – he'd been tucked up in his bed asleep all night. He said, 'I'll just take a breath of air then, Mrs B. Back in ten minutes.'

He walked down the street to the corner and turned left along the main road to the telephone kiosk. It was one of the old-fashioned red kind and he made sure the door was firmly shut before he dialled.

When the phone was answered, he said, 'I need to see you. Yes, it's important. I've just had a visit from the police. Eleven o'clock? Where? I know it. All right, I'll be there.'

In a side road, Reuben ap Morgan sat at the wheel of his inconspicuous hatchback, hunched down in the driver's seat, watching Scobie through his opaque sunglasses. A map of the area lay unfolded on the passenger seat should rapid camouflage be needed – a motorist who had lost his way and, being a man, refused to ask for help.

When Scobie left the phone box and headed back along the road, Reuben picked up his digital camera, took aim and clicked the button. He edged forward far enough to watch him safely back inside his lodgings, then he drove across to the kiosk and parked beside it.

A few minutes later John Hathaway's telephone rang. He sighed, saved the file on his computer and picked up the handset on his desk.

'John Hathaway... Hello... Hello.'

The phone went dead and the dialling tone came on.

He dialled 1471, listened to the mechanical voice giving him the number of the caller, shrugged and hung up.

Reuben drove past Scobie's lodgings, made a right into a residential road, parked and settled down to wait. He could just make out the front door of the ugly little semi from here. Luckily there was a street lamp outside the house; he would need that when the sun set.

He reached onto the back seat for a carrier bag, took out the brie and tomato baguette he had bought from a garage on the A4 earlier that day and peeled off the cling film. It had gone limp in the heat but Reuben munched it without tasting, needing only to satisfy the rumblings in his belly.

Over the next hour he added two chocolate bars and a can of Pepsi to his diet as no one entered or left the house.

He switched the radio on at nine to hear the news headlines, then remembered with a curse that he had arranged to meet Alex Lomax in the Jolly Fisherman. He hesitated for a moment, then decided. Scobie would keep, but Alex Lomax and his reasons for being here – that could be really interesting.

He threw the litter from his picnic onto the floor in the back, fired up the engine, flicked on his headlights and drove away.

Chapter Twelve

Greg let himself in at his front door shortly after eight, threw his jacket onto the chair in the hall, went into the sitting room and slumped on the sofa. He couldn't summon up the energy to call out, 'I'm home', not sure that he could make himself heard above the noise of *The Moral Maze* coming from the kitchen.

A man with a very sarcastic voice was cross-examining a woman as if he was intent on making her cry. Sometimes Greg wished he was allowed to speak to witnesses that way.

Bellini, the West Highland Terrier, came running into the room, stubby tail wagging, jumped on the sofa beside him and snuggled against his thigh. He scratched behind her ears and she gave a mew of pleasure. He had long since given up telling her she wasn't allowed on the couch as she took not a blind bit of notice and it undermined his authority.

The radio was silenced. So much for Mr Sarcastic, gone at the press of a button.

'Oh, you're home. Good. Supper's nearly ready.' Angie stood in the archway that separated the two rooms. She was of medium height and rather thin build, a dishwater blonde whose average looks were brightened by a big smile of welcome. It was a warm evening and she was wearing a black sun dress with shoestring straps, stark against her pale skin. He could see that she wasn't wearing a bra.

He thought how much he loved her.

She came and stood behind him, her strong hands beginning to massage his shoulders. 'God, you're tense.'

'Ooh, that's nice.' He closed his eyes.

'Gregory ... is something bothering you lately, more than usual?'

'It's ... not anything I can tell you about, my love. Sorry.'

Her hands fell away and he opened his eyes. Looking up at her, he could see that she was hurt at what she saw as his lack of trust. He grabbed her hands and pulled her round so she was sitting on his lap. He put his arms round her, his left hand sliding inside the bodice of her dress, cupping one warm breast.

'Sweetheart, there's nothing I'd like better than to tell you what's bothering me and get your womanly insight into why it bothers me so much, but it's a secret with a capital S. That's just the way things are.'

'So long as it's work and nothing to do with us.'

175

'God, no! You are my rock.'

'What – a hard, lifeless lump?'

'Okay. You are...' He sought inspiration. 'The wind beneath my wings. Better?'

'Better. I suppose it's part of the job,' she said cheerfully. 'It could be worse; you could be in M15.'

'I don't know how the spooks have any sort of private life at all,' he agreed.

'So you could tell me your secret but then you'd have to kill me.'

'Jim Barkiss would kill *me*, more like.'

Angie said, 'Bellini! – off the couch.' The little creature jumped down at once and went to sit in her basket under the bay window.

The oven timer went and she stood up, his hand necessarily falling away. 'Supper! At least you have Barbara to talk to and – what's the new bloke's name? – Alex.'

No, he thought, there was only one person he could talk to about this.

When Reuben got back to the Jolly Fisherman that evening at nine-fifteen, he found Alex already there, sitting at the bar engaged in intimate conversation with Joy.

'Sorry I'm late,' Reuben said.

'No problem, old son. Mrs Reynolds here has been keeping me well entertained.'

'Joy,' she corrected him with a coy smile.

'How apt, since the sight of your bonny

face fills me with the said emotion. What're you drinking, Reuben?'

'Half.'

'Half of bitter please, Joy, and whatever you're having.'

'I'll take a glass of white wine with you, Al, thank you. Soon as I've cleared a few glasses.' She came out through the hatch and brushed against him. 'Oops! Sorry.'

'No problem.' He patted her bottom. 'You can jostle me as much as you like, love.'

They took their drinks over to the same table they had used before and Alex said, 'Nice woman,' as they sat down.

'Shame about the husband,' Reuben said. 'Neanderthal man.'

'Oh, I prefer them married. Stops them getting ideas.'

'What an old cynic you are.'

'That's good, coming from a Fleet Street hack.'

'Fleet Street?' Reuben said derisively. 'Never set foot in the place. That was in another millennium. We're on the Isle of Dogs.'

'Also apt, since you are little terriers snapping at the heels of the Great and the Good.'

'In fifteen years as a journalist, I've met very few Great and almost no Good,' Reuben said.

'You see – you are the cynic, not I.'

Tiring of this banter, Reuben said, 'I hear

your people were questioning Scobie earlier this evening.'

'Is that right?'

'It seems that a horse belonging to John Hathaway's wife was lamed at Nash's stables last night. Lambourn can talk of nothing else. Don't tell me you haven't heard.'

'It rings a bell,' Alex admitted, 'but I am not involved.'

'No, my information is that your superintendent came out to the stables personally. Now why is that? A crippled racehorse may seem like the end of the world in Lambourn but to most sane people it's a minor matter.'

Alex shrugged. 'Mine is not to reason why; mine is but to let sleeping logs lie.'

Reuben wondered whether to comment on this but decided he couldn't be bothered. '*And* he went to talk to the accountant, the one who was here the other night. Remember? Mike, Joy called him.'

'Oh?' Alex sipped at his ginger ale thoughtfully. 'Now, I wonder what that was about.'

'He's the Hathaways' nearest neighbour, of course.'

'Well, there you have it then. Mystery solved... You know a lot.'

'Money opens mouths.'

'Not mine.'

'Odd little man this Michael Patterson,' Reuben said. 'Different. Something about him...'

'It's not a crime, being different.' Alex had been called *odd* himself on more than one occasion.

'Couldn't help thinking I'd seen him before somewhere. Didn't he look familiar to you?'

'Not specially.' Alex drained his glass. 'Your round I think, Taffy.'

Eric Reynolds stuck his nose into the bar to see if he was needed. Not as busy as usual at this time of a weekday evening but no doubt the stables were stepping up security after what had happened to that horse of Nash's last night.

He glanced over at the bar and his features wove themselves into a frown with the ease of long practice. The Welshman with the stupid name: standing at the bar with Joy. As Eric watched, his hand brushed against hers as he took his change and they both laughed.

Then the taffy took her hand and kissed the back of it like some poncey foreigner.

Eric slammed the door and went back to the function room. He picked up his brush and began to slap paint viciously on the walls, regardless of the fact that he'd already painted that portion, between the french windows, and that the first layer of paint wasn't dry yet.

Streaky, he thought. So much for this one-coat, non-drip paint. Joy said they should get a professional in to do it, like he couldn't bung up a coat of paint, like he could afford to pay someone, like he didn't know why she wanted the pub full of sweaty men in overalls.

Ocean sunset? What sort of poncey name was that for a paint? It was a pinkish cream, that's what it was. What did that have to do with bloody oceans? Bloody oceans were bloody blue – unless they were full of blood. He giggled.

Wonder what colour the Welshman's blood was and how it'd look in the waters of the river Lambourn.

She liked to flirt, Joy, always had, claimed it was harmless. But then why do it, he said? To keep my hand in, she said. What's the point of behaving like you want some bloke to bang your brains out if you don't, he said? Oh, shut up, Eric, she said, you miserable killjoy.

Killjoy? Kill Joy. Maybe, one of these days...

Perhaps if they'd had kids, keep her out of mischief, tire her out, but it hadn't happened and she hadn't been bothered enough to try those new things they had for knocking women up – test tubes or whatever it was – and, apparently, it wasn't up to him.

That was one of the reasons he had wanted to leave Greenford, get her away from that Mr Walker at the building society she used to talk about all the time. Mr Colin Poncey Walker, deputy manager. She said there was nothing in it but he'd seen the way they laughed together at the office Christmas party and the way the other staff eyed him as if to say, What are you – stupid?

He had been hurling paint at the walls like Jackson Pollock and now he stopped, breathless, took a clean brush and tried to smooth some of the excess paint away. When the restaurant was open she'd be that busy, too busy to breathe, most likely.

Keep her out of trouble.

Bloody Welshman. How much longer was he staying, anyway? What sort of person dropped in at a bed and breakfast in the middle of nowhere and didn't know how long they were staying? Called himself a journalist. Very likely.

Damned suspicious.

Maybe she meant no harm, Joy, just gave out the wrong signals with her short skirts and tight tops, her hair worn too long and loose for a woman pushing forty. Her ready laugh.

He was hot now. He stripped off his overall and went into the side room, the one that would be the store room for the Fisherman's Rest. He opened the door of his enormous cold store and breathed the chill air into his lungs and felt a bit better.

'Just tell me one thing,' Reuben said. 'What do you intend to do about Scobie?'

'*Do* about him? Not with you, old son.'

'Don't play the innocent, Alex.' Reuben lowered his voice. 'But, all right, I'll spell it out for you. You and I both believe that Scobie got away with murder. For me, it's just work – a good story, if I can prove it. But you, you loved Devon Bliss like a favourite uncle. You told me so. So what's the plan? Some sort of vigilante action? Take the law into your own hands.'

'I'm a police officer,' Alex reminded him. 'Wash your mouth out with soap, Taffy Morgan.'

'Off the record. You can trust me.'

'A bloody journalist?' Alex roared with laughter. 'I don't think so!'

'Only whatever you're planning, I have a better plan, so don't do anything rash.'

'I'm listening.'

'Not now. I'm expecting a friend to join me in a couple of days. I think you'll be very interested to meet her.'

'Is that right?' Alex drained his ginger ale. 'Well, I'm off. Keep in touch. You've got my number?'

'Programmed into here.' Reuben patted the breast pocket of his jacket where he usually kept his mobile phone.

He didn't try to detain Lomax. He gave him long enough to drive away, then went out to his own car and was soon back at his station outside Scobie's house in Eastbury.

'Is that you?'

'Who else would it be?'

The newcomer edged forward, his feet slithering on the evening dew, coming to a halt in front of the other man.

He said, 'I had the police round this evening.'

'So you said.'

'A superintendent, no less. Said there'd been an attack on Lady India's horse. Now why would he be coming to see me about that – what would it have to do with me?'

'I've no idea. Just being thorough would be my guess, checking out anyone local with a criminal record.'

'I haven't got a record!'

'True.'

'Only I'm supposed to be keeping a very low profile and I can't do that with the police camped on my doorstep.'

'You exaggerate. Have you got the gun?'

'A Glock semi-automatic. Fires ten rounds without reloading. Cost me five hundred quid in a pub in Brixton.'

'Are you asking me for more money?'

'... No, it's okay. What you gave me up

front will cover it.' He shuddered. 'Those people are bloody scary, I don't mind telling you.'

'Did they recognise you?'

'I don't think so. They're hardly going to go to the police, in any case. What would they say – "I sold a stolen and highly illegal gun to a man the whole of England believes to be a murderer"?' He shivered and lifted one foot, examining the soles of his cheap shoes. 'I'm covered in mud. Why are we meeting here?'

'No one comes here after dark.'

'I can see why. Have you decided when yet?'

'I'll let you know. Soon.'

'Only we agreed it would look like a random shooting, a break-in gone pear shaped. If the police are sniffing round then I'm gonna bale. I don't need the aggro.'

'You worry too much. That's exactly what it'll look like – a burglary gone horribly wrong.'

'What was that?' He spun round.

'What?'

'Thought I heard something.'

Both men listened for a moment. In the distance a pigeon cooed.

'You're too jumpy.'

'I better get back. The old bag I lodge with is that nosy you'd think she was being paid to do surveillance. Do you know, she makes me leave the house all day, as if I had a job, so I'm tramping the streets of Newbury in all weathers. Says she doesn't usually take unemployed lodgers, like she's doing me a big favour giving me a room in her hovel. Who does she think she is?'

When the other man necessarily made no reply to this, he went on. 'I wouldn't be doing this for anyone but you, John, seeing as I owe you.'

'And don't think I'm not grateful ... Graham.'

Chapter Thirteen

'And what can I do for you?' Chief Superintendent Barkiss asked the following morning.

'If you could spare a few minutes...' Greg pulled up a chair. 'It's about Ian Callaghan.'

'Michael Patterson,' Barkiss said patiently.

'Since you're the only person I can speak to about it.'

'What's on your mind?'

'It bothers me, that's all. I can't stop thinking about it, about those two baby girls, about the sort of person who could do ... *that* to an innocent child. What kind of monster.'

'We've both seen horrible things,' Barkiss said, with the habitually unruffled air which seemed to contradict his words. 'All policemen have.'

'And they just let him out after – what did you say? – twelve years.'

'They wouldn't do that if he was a danger to society.' Barkiss leaned back in his chair and folded his arms across his belly. 'Look, Greg, it's our job to catch criminals and to help the CPS to put them away. After that they're somebody else's problem – the

186

prison service, the parole board, their probation officer.'

'And I suppose that house was bought for him?'

'I daresay he had some financial help, yes.'

'So a double murderer comes out of prison and is living the life of Riley while ordinary, law-abiding people are struggling to pay a mortgage.'

'That's sometimes the way of the world,' Barkiss said.

'I keep thinking about the girlfriend,' Greg admitted. 'She's a lovely girl.' He realised that he had no idea what Grace Rutherford was actually like, other than that she looked beautiful even when she was rolling on the ground, sobbing, but he persevered. 'She has the right to know, in my opinion.'

'But we do not have the right to tell her,' Barkiss pointed out. 'Only Patterson can do that, when the time comes.'

'And if he doesn't? What if they have a child together and he's *jealous* of it?'

'I'm no expert,' Barkiss said, 'but I don't think his probation officer will allow him not to tell her if things reach the point when they want to marry or live together, and if there are children they're going to have Social Services breathing down their necks every step of the way. He won't be able to fart without it goes down in the file. And he's going to have to tell her that too.'

187

There was a brief silence, then the Chief Super said, 'I hear there was an incident with a horse of Lady Hathaway's.'

'Lady India. Yes. Her racehorse was crippled.'

Barkiss winced. 'Racehorse? Valuable?'

'Valuable enough. That's hardly the point, since I assume it was insured.'

'Lot of money spent, I hear – SOCO, photographers.'

'I thought you wanted this case looked into,' Greg said. 'That meant being there to do the forensic this time.'

'All right,' Barkiss said, 'don't spend the whole budget. It's only criminal damage, when all's said and done.'

'Perhaps if you had seen the horse, lying on the floor of the stable in such distress...'

'You haven't been to Patterson's again, I trust.'

'...Yes.'

Patiently, Barkiss said, 'Why?'

'He's the Hathaways' nearest neighbour. He's got a better opportunity than anyone to attack them.'

'But this latest attack wasn't at their house.'

'His girlfriend works at the stables. In fact, she's personally responsible for the horse.' He examined Grace Rutherford's exhibition in his mind, excessive surely. Grief, maybe, but tinged with guilt? 'I had to check that

188

she was telling the truth about her movements that night,' he concluded. 'He was her alibi.'

'Don't get obsessed with Patterson, Gregory,' Barkiss said bluntly. 'In fact, perhaps it would be better if you referred to me before visiting him again at all. Now, is that it?'

'I suppose so.' Greg got up, slightly stunned by this last order. 'Sorry, Jim, but it's been preying on my mind and, like I say, there's no one else I can discuss my fears with.'

Barkiss rose with him and ushered him out of the office. 'My door is always open,' he said, as he closed it.

Michael Patterson was standing outside the general stores in Lambourn High Street reading the notices, when he became aware of someone behind him.

'Hello again.' The voice spoke almost in his ear and he spun round.

'Um...' he said.

'Reuben ap Morgan,' his accoster supplied. 'I'm staying at the Jolly Fisherman.'

'Of course.' He recognised him now, with his dark Celtic good looks. 'The racing journalist.'

'Oh, not racing,' Reuben corrected him. 'General news.'

'Oh!' Reuben was standing closer than was normal for British males and he maintained eye contact in a way that Michael found disconcerting, his own eyes swivelling everywhere in an attempt to avoid the intimacy.

'Busy place, Lambourn,' Reuben remarked, indicating the notice board, crowded with pastel-coloured posters and fliers. 'Weight Watchers, Women's Institute, British Legion.' His face developed a slight but definite sneer. 'Best hanging basket competition, even a carnival. Who says the countryside is boring?'

'Yes, we're quite a little community.' Michael wanted to edge away but the only direction he could go without shoving the Welshman aside was backwards, through the plate glass window.

'Lived here long?' the journalist enquired.

'Three or four years.'

Reuben nodded thoughtfully, as if it was the answer he had been expecting. 'Is that long enough to be accepted as a local?'

Grace Rutherford emerged from the shop before Michael could answer, her arms full of milk, bread, a bag of apples and the village magazine in its bright orange cover. She eyed the Welshman suspiciously and said, 'All right, Mike?'

Reuben took a step backwards under her fierce gaze, releasing the young accountant. His eyes slid lazily and impertinently up and down Grace's body, its pleasing contours visible even in jodhpurs and a polo shirt

190

liberally adorned with horse hair.

'Fine!' Michael took her shopping from her and said 'Nice talking to you again' to Reuben with patent insincerity. They both set off up the road without a backward look.

Reuben watched them go with a smile on his face. What a cracker, he thought. Surely she could do better than a number cruncher who seemed frightened of his own shadow. Maybe she'd like a more exciting boyfriend, like a journalist from the big metropolis.

There were people you expected to be beyond reproach, Reuben mused – not politicians or journalists, obviously, but policemen, lawyers, doctors and account-ants. No, not accountants either, not after recent financial scandals in the States; even doctors, come to that, had been known to administer fatal doses of heroin to elderly patients and write it down as heart failure. And he had done his share of exposing corrupt policemen during his years on the *Outlook,* including one constable with firearms training who had accepted five grand to rid a man of his unfaithful wife.

The *Outlook* had shafted its fair share of politicians over the years – brown envelopes, prostitutes with whips, a fondness for cocaine – but that was never so satisfying to Reuben's mind since the public shrugged its collective shoulders and muttered, What did

191

you expect?

Still, hardened hack though he might be, Reuben still expected certain strata of society to behave better than he would do himself. Perhaps it was a good sign that he could still be disappointed, an indication that his soul was not yet irredeemably corrupt.

This was a big story, probably the biggest of his career. So far. No shoulder shrugging here, but an eager turning over of pages. He had to play it just right – amass his facts and check them meticulously – before he could take it to Jackson Deans.

Or to somebody else, with deeper pockets, and longer arms.

'DCI Lomax would like a word,' Susan Habib said at four o'clock that afternoon.

'Then send him in.'

Alex was right behind her, in fact. He said, 'Thanks, Susie,' and winked at her. This elicited such a big smile from Susan that Greg stared after her departing back; it was unheard of. Was he the only one impervious to the Chief Inspector's charm?

Lomax sat down and said, 'Got a bit of a problem, sir. My niece Toyah just rang.'

'From Taunton?' Greg hazarded.

'Tiverton. My sister's been rushed into hospital with some sort of stomach problem. They're not sure if it's peritonitis or just the aftermath of a particularly bad drinking session but they're going to keep her in for a few days, do some tests.'

'I see.' Greg could guess where this was going.

'Now, our Toyah's only fifteen but she's a sensible girl and well able to take care of herself and the younger ones for a bit but Social Services don't see it that way.'

'I imagine not.'

'So I was wondering if I could nip down for a day or two, make sure they're all right.'

'What about their father?' Greg asked, realising as the words came out of his mouth that it was a stupid question

'Their *fathers* haven't been heard of for years. No, if I don't go, sir, then they'll likely be taken into care and then God knows if Bridget'll ever get them back.' His face took on a pleading look. 'They may not be much, but they're all the family I've got.'

'Well, I don't see why not,' Greg said.

'Thanks. I'm owed a few days and Barbara's very capable. She can handle this con artist.'

'So are you setting off right away?' Greg asked.

'If I may. I've got a few personal errands to run, then I'll drive down tonight after the rush hour's over on the M4/M5.'

'Well, keep in touch and let me know when you'll be back,' Greg said. 'It's not as if anybody's likely to get murdered in Newbury over the next few days.'

Which statement was not, he was to realise little more than thirty-six hours later, going to win him any prizes for prescience.

Chapter Fourteen

Greg was sitting in his office the following morning when Martha Childs arrived to update him on her findings at the stables.

'I thought you'd want an early report, Superintendent,' she said.

He gestured her to a chair. 'Sit down, Mrs Childs.' In his early days in the force, SOCOs had been serving police officers. They had been replaced by civilians for many years now, often career scientists like Martha, and were treated with more respect, since their findings played an increasingly large part in investigations.

'What have you got for me?' he asked.

She grimaced apology, as if admitting to a personal failing. 'Very little, I'm afraid.'

She explained that a meticulous search of Nash's yard had not turned up the weapon which had crippled the mare. There were fingerprints aplenty in the stables; most belonged to the stable lads and lasses but anyone who had visited in recent weeks, including people looking for a new billet for their horse, might have left a paw mark.

'It's not like it's indoors where most people run a duster round occasionally,' she concluded. 'Some of those prints have likely been there years. I'm running the ones we haven't identified through the computer but it's a long shot frankly.'

'I know.' Greg sighed. 'What about the clothing we took from Grace Rutherford – the girl who was first on the crime scene?'

'Straw, mud, manure, horse hair.' She grinned suddenly, looking like a naughty teenager. 'We could maybe prove in court that she'd once set foot in a stable, if that's any help.'

Her grin was infectious and he returned it, despite the bad news. 'Thanks for trying.'

'So we're standing down now at the stables,' she said, serious again. 'Thing is, do you want us to widen the search for the saw? We can scour the back streets and byways of Lambourn for it but it'll be a long and expensive job. He could have chucked it anywhere for miles around.'

'No,' Greg said, remembering Barkiss's warning about the budget. 'We can't justify any more time and money. Take the tape down and re-open the crime scene.' As she rose to leave, he added, 'Thank you anyway, Mrs Childs.'

She corrected him. 'Martha.'

'Martha.'

He decided to pay a courtesy call on the Hathaways to let them know what was happening – i.e. nothing.

The gate to Ascot House was open this morning and he drove straight in. There was no sign of the Range Rover but Hathaway's Aston Martin stood there alongside a Citroen 2CV the colour of a ripe banana, which made Greg smile. A fun car: not the sort of thing a middle-aged policeman could drive.

As he approached the front door it opened and Grace Rutherford came out. She seemed to have recovered from her hysteria of the day before and looked merely weary and plain.

'How are you?' he called out.

She didn't bother to reply – perhaps taking the question for the phatic one it so often was in everyday discourse – but nodded curtly at him, got into the Citroen and drove off with a grinding of old gears. Hathaway stood waiting in the doorway, wearing denim jeans and a black T-shirt, his arms folded.

When he was young, Greg had thought that it was a mistake for men over forty to wears jeans. Then the big four-oh had arrived and he'd shifted the deadline back to fifty. Now, with that birthday in view on the horizon, he was ready to rethink once more. At least both he and Hathaway had kept their boyish figures.

'If you're looking for Indie,' Hathaway

said, 'I'll tell you what I've just told Grey – I've sent her and Liv away to Nethermore Hall, to her brother.'

'Sent her?' Greg queried. It sounded very masterful.

Hathaway let slip a small smile, stepping back to admit Greg to the hall. 'All right,' he amended. 'I suggested they go and she agreed. Given that the grouse-shooting season started on Monday, it didn't actually take much effort on my part.'

'Not a bad idea to get away for a few days.'

'Maybe as much as a month, though Liv kicked up at missing the village carnival since she's supposed to be a carnival princess, so they may drive up just for that day.'

'When is it?'

'The 25th – August Bank Holiday weekend. Then Liv's due back at school at the beginning of September but I trust this business will be resolved by then, one way or another.'

'Where is Nethermore Hall anyway?'

'In Somerset – nice views of the Quantocks. It's not much more than two hours drive.'

'I thought they shot grouse in Scotland.'

'Oh, grouse aren't safe anywhere, poor things! Can I get you some refreshment? There's some quite decent lemonade in the fridge – homemade but not by us, if you get my drift.'

'Er...'

'We got it from the WI sale in town,' Hathaway elucidated, 'along with some "homemade" cakes. I mean, you can't call it a breach of the Trades Descriptions Act.'

'I wouldn't care if you could.'

They drank the excellent lemonade – pithy and not too sweet – seated amicably at the kitchen table. Greg wouldn't have said no to some cake either, since he couldn't remember when he'd last tasted the homemade variety, but it wasn't offered. He thought how glad he was that there were still women in Berkshire who had time to make such things.

He broke the news that they had come up with no useful forensic evidence concerning the attack on Ranulf's Daughter, a fact which his host seemed to accept philosophically. The man seemed to be growing visibly limp, in fact, and as Greg talked he more than once raised his hand to his forehead and stifled a sigh.

'Are you all right?' Greg asked at last.

'One of my migraines coming on. They're rare, fortunately, but crippling. I wonder.' He gestured. 'Pills in the drawer under the kettle. Could you?'

Greg scrabbled in the drawer indicated and found the bottle of white tablets. He removed the child-proof top with some difficulty and fetched the older man a glass of water. Hathaway shook two pills onto his palm and gulped them down.

'I'll leave you to rest,' Greg said.

'Thank you. I'll be fine in a couple–' Hathaway got to his feet, then clutched the table for support.

Greg took him by the arm and said, 'Right, let's get you upstairs.'

Sir John let himself be led docilely to a bedroom at the front of the house. It was spartan, containing little other than a small double bed, the wallpaper a muted stripe and the carpet plain cream. He flopped on the bed and shut his eyes, breathing heavily.

'Shall I close the curtains?' Greg asked and, getting no reply, did so. As an after-thought he opened a window to let in some air.

'I'll be off then and I'll make sure it's locked up downstairs.' He tiptoed out, closing the door behind him.

Across the corridor he could see the open door to a larger and more feminine room, with cabbage roses rambling over the wall-paper. A chaise longue in the bay window was strewn with female clothes, although not of the frilly variety. He realised that husband and wife had separate quarters but that didn't necessarily signify that they were not on intimate terms; it was probably normal in their social circles.

As he drove out onto the lane, it struck him that Hathaway had made an unnecessary point of explaining Grace's presence – that she had stopped by, looking for his wife. He also remembered that Sir John had called her 'extraordinary' the day they had first met. He pondered this for a moment. Indie had mentioned a mid-life crisis in connection with the luxury sports car; retirement for a man like Hathaway – in his prime of strength and health – was an understandable trigger for such a banal episode, but mid-life crises often took a different form.

Was it possible that there was something going on between them, despite the age difference – little greater than that between himself and Angie – despite the presence of Patterson as her official boyfriend, despite the fact that Greg couldn't imagine any sensible man being unfaithful to India?

And what had he meant by 'one way or another'?

'I say we quit while we're ahead.'

Brian, slumped moodily on the sofa, picked up the remote control and started flicking through his cable channels. He had ninety-eight of them so why could he never find anything he wanted to watch?

'Have you shifted your fat arse from that sofa all day?' his mother demanded.

Brian smirked. 'As it happens, I've been

hurtling through space at something like 30,000 miles per hour.'

'But so has the sofa!' Peggy snatched the remote out of his hands and pitched it into the goldfish bowl. The two fish scattered in dismay, their disproportionately large mouths opening and shutting in soundless protest at this abuse. Brian got up, stuck his hand in and retrieved the piece of plastic. He pointed it at the cable box and pressed a button but nothing happened.

'You've bloody messed it up again,' he complained. He was stuck with a tousled blonde woman who was sifting through some earth with a trowel and clearly not wearing a bra.

Could be worse. He sat down.

His mother said through gritted teeth, 'I'm talking.'

'I thought it was me. I said "let's quit while we're ahead", if memory serves. Woah! Charlie! Bend over again.'

Peggy leaned down and pulled out the plug, silencing the television. She stood in front of the screen in her son's line of sight.

'We're good for a few weeks yet.'

'Last time was a close call.'

'Not specially.'

'The old bag rumbled you.'

'She did not! She was just too bloody nice, insisting on paying, but she didn't suspect a thing up till then.'

'Says you.' Brian shifted sideways on the sofa so that he was no longer facing the blank screen and hefted his long legs over the arm. His feet dangled in their expensive trainers. 'It's time to move on. Marlborough.'

'Why?'

'Marlborough, Swindon, Andover, Basingstoke. They're all in the next county – Wiltshire, Hampshire – different police force.'

'Hmm. I thought I was supposed to be the brains of this outfit,' she said grudgingly.

'In your dreams, Ma.'

'The further we get from home the harder it gets. We won't know the area. It'll take longer to find their houses–'

'Good street maps... You're just scared.'

'Maybe I am at that.'

He made chicken noises, putting his hands into his armpits and flapping his elbows up and down.

'It's just that I'm older than you,' she said. 'If you can keep your head when all about you are losing theirs ... then you haven't understood the gravity of the crisis.'

'Very funny. So, we're agreed?'

'No. Give it another couple of weeks. What about Hungerford? Plenty of rich people shop in those antique places – cash in hand and nice pickings from their houses. We'll go tomorrow.'

She sank down on the armchair, suddenly exhausted. 'Or the next day.'

Reuben sat down at the table in his room and lifted the lid on his laptop. His curtains were open and he spent a few minutes staring out towards the centre of Lambourn, watching the play of the early-evening sun on the houses, readying himself.

He opened a new file and pondered his headline. He felt solemn. This was the sort of story that made a journalist's name and won him prizes and he had to get it right.

Half an hour later he was still staring at a blank screen. This was ridiculous. He had to write something, almost anything. He typed *The quick brown fox jumps over a lazy dog* then launched himself into his story. It didn't matter how bad the prose was at this stage; there would be plenty of time to polish it up.

But after half a dozen sentences he stopped and gave an exclamation of annoyance, slamming the lid of the computer down. *This is crap,* he thought. *What's the matter with me?* He was used to deadlines, used to banging out passable copy at a moment's notice, and here he was as useless as he'd been on his first day on the *Aberystwyth Star* when they'd rapidly set him to making the tea.

He reopened the lid and quit the file without saving it. A bit of fresh air, he thought, maybe a couple of pints in the bar. That'd loosen him up and then he'd try again.

No, second thoughts, beer first, walk after. He needed a little flirt with Joy to give him back his confidence.

He thought the landlady subdued. She responded to his gallantry gamely enough but something told him her heart wasn't in it. He stayed sitting at the bar so that he could reclaim her attention each time she returned from serving another customer. After a couple of hours, he'd had three pints and two large whisky chasers and his head didn't feel as clear as he would have liked.

He half hoped that Alex Lomax would come in but, although the door opened every few minutes, it was never to admit the odd, shabby policeman.

Displacement activity, he thought. He'd heard writers talk about it but had never experienced it himself. You cleaned the windows, washed the car, phoned your bookie; anything rather than sit down and stare at that blank screen.

Joy was wearing shorts this warm evening and her shapely legs more than made up for a slight broadness in the beam, not that he objected to that. The fashion for over thinness among women, especially in London, did little to fire his Welsh blood. Not that he would ever date a fat chick as it would do his image no end of harm.

When you were a single man working in a supposedly glamorous job in London, people assumed that you had your pick of women; only a couple of weeks ago one of his colleagues – a recent proud father – had looked sleepily at him in the lift at Outlook House one morning and said, 'How I envy you single blokes – out with a different woman every night.'

If only! Reuben hadn't had a date in three months and he hadn't got laid in ... what was it? Bloody hell, must have been the *Outlook*'s Christmas party, in the stationery cupboard with Jack Deans' slutty secretary Audrey, which made it eight months. In those circumstances a modest width in the hindquarters was no obstacle.

Hindquarters? He'd been in Lambourn too long; he was starting to talk like a racing bore.

Sarah was a game girl; he was looking forward to seeing her again on Friday. What a pity that she batted for the other team. Or maybe not; their friendship wouldn't have lasted all these years if it had been soiled with lust.

'So what do you do for fun, Joy,' he ventured, 'on your night off?'

'Night off?' She snorted derision at the idea. 'It's only *paid* bar staff that gets nights off, Reuben. The owners get the privilege of working every night. Or this owner does. Be nice if Eric lent a hand's turn occasionally, but oh no, he's far too busy.'

She leaned across the bar and smiled into his eyes. 'And when his baby opens – the new restaurant – I shall have to make an appointment for three hours sleep every night.'

'Very overrated, sleep,' he said. 'I can think of better things to do in bed.'

The door from the function room opened and Eric Reynolds peered out. Reuben didn't notice him but Joy did. The look on his face made her step back as if she'd been slapped and Reuben reflected that he was out of practice: too crude, too obvious.

Pathetic.

'Sorry,' he murmured. 'Had a bit too much to drink. Can I buy you one? White wine, isn't it?'

'Not tonight,' she said briskly. 'Why don't you get a breath of air, sir?' And she moved away to deal with two stable lads who had just arrived.

Eric silently closed the door again. At it again, he thought. She didn't learn. Taffy ap Whatsit again. He contemplated his cold store with a ferocious scowl.

What did it bloody take?

He picked up his paintbrush, put it down again, dithered a bit, then left the function room by the back door.

Reuben went out of the Jolly Fisherman and made his way unsteadily down the road towards the centre of Lambourn. This was ridiculous. He knew how to hold his drink. At least Eric Reynolds didn't water his beer.

It was dusk. A war correspondent on the *Outlook* had once told him that was the most dangerous time of day – worse than full dark – when the fading light played tricks on the eyes and you ended up shooting one of your own men.

Lucky his job didn't involve that sort of danger. What sort of person wanted to be a war correspondent anyway, skulking about in flack jackets pretending to be tough? He'd had a few threats over the years from people who didn't like him prying so closely into their affairs, but nothing that caused him to lose sleep.

Better things to do in bed. He wanted to strike his own forehead and shout 'Doh!' like … like … whichever one of the Simpsons it was that did that. Very slick, Reuben. At this rate it'd be next Christmas. Maybe he'd call Audrey when he got back to town, see if she was up for a rematch. Dry times like this he thought it might be almost worth getting married just for regular sex, although tales he'd heard from married men suggested that this was a myth, certainly if there were kids involved.

Fresh air: Joy was right. Fresh air and

exercise. He set off at a steady pace along the lane.

You never knew: he might see something to his advantage. But the sturdy newspaperman didn't wait for fate to fall in his lap, he told himself, a little incoherently. He made the news.

Or, if the price was right, suppressed it.

He reached into his inside pocket, only to find that he had left his mobile in his bedroom. He had looked up a few local phone numbers on the Internet that day – more displacement activity – though he hadn't yet got round to programming them into his mobile. There was a phone box near the church.

He felt in his trouser pocket and brought out a twenty-pence piece. Perfect. He got through and laid out a few succinct facts to the person at the other end of the line.

'I can't tell you what a story like this would be worth to me,' he concluded, 'but I expect you can guess. Mind you, a bird in the hand and all that. If you can come up with enough cash to kill the story, then that's another matter... Where? Okay. See you soon.'

He hung up, a big smile on his drunken face.

Greg went into the back bedroom, the one that had been Fred's nursery when he was a baby and used by him later when he came for his rare weekends after the divorce. Now it was a lumber room, stacked with boxes of books he would never read again or, in some cases, for the first time; clothes he didn't wear but which were too good to throw away; odd bits of furniture that had no natural place.

The walls had been boring magnolia for years but, as he stood there beneath the unshaded bulb which lit up every corner, every crevice, he seemed to see the wallpaper that Sergeant 'Sunshine' Summers had spent a painstaking weekend putting up almost a quarter of a century earlier: ranks of red soldiers marching across a unlikely blue and yellow landscape.

Why soldiers, he wondered? Presumably it had been important to him at the time that his son be 'manly' although, as he recalled, the Action Man he had given Fred for his sixth birthday had spent most of his time not saving the free world but having tea parties with Teddy and Mr Oink, a very fat, very pink toy pig.

He smiled. There had been a time when the misery he felt at his son's early death outweighed any good memories; now happiness and unhappiness were coming a little more into balance. Suddenly, he had an overwhelming sense of Fred's presence in this room but it did not make him flee in terror as it would have only six months ago.

He saw the infant in his cot, waking to reach up his chubby hands to his father, his protector.

He left the room, closing the door quietly behind him as if he feared to wake a sleeping baby with the click.

What sort of man picked up a pillow and stifled a baby as it slept?

What sort of monster?

Reuben laughed. 'What did you imagine – that I wouldn't recognise you?'

He turned away, scuffing his feet against the banks of the stream. He still felt a bit drunk; if anything the fresh air had made him drunker. He felt good; he felt strong, with all the misleading sensations of invincibility that strong liquor brings, of immortality.

He was also, he realised, urgently in need of a pee, all that alcohol working its way through his system. Well, this was as good a place as any, dark and quiet, and his new acquaintance could hardly object. He muttered, ''Scuse me,' and made his way to the very edge of the water, unzipping. Soon he could hear the welcome tinkle of water on water.

Ah! What a relief.

He didn't see the weapon coming in the darkness, although he may have heard a whooshing noise as it careered through the air, striking him on the back of his head, just below the crown, sending him hurtling forward to fall face down in the shallows.

The Lambourn, which gurgled its way happily through the village, was stagnant here and dirty.

As he made to get groggily up, a strong hand was holding his face in the water, a second at the nape of his neck. He thrashed his arms about hopelessly, pressing his palms to the shallow bed of the stream and pushing upwards in vain. Once he got his mouth clear and spluttered for another lungful of air, another couple of minutes of life.

There was a house on the opposite bank but there were no lights on and he had no breath to scream for help.

This was no way for Reuben Morgan to die, he thought, drunk and exposing himself and not having got laid for eight months. He was practically dying a virgin.

Try as he might, he could not get his mouth clear of the river again. When his breath gave out he gulped down a mouthful of cold, stale water, tinged with the acrid taste with his own beery waste, which slid rapidly down to his lungs. A line from an old war film ran, slightly mangled, through his head.

For you, Taffy, the war is over.

He died giggling.

Chapter Fifteen

A Lambourn man out walking his dog found the body just before seven-thirty the following morning. Rather, the dog found it, darting excitedly into the muddy woodland and barking in staccato bursts, ignoring all commands to come, sit, leave or heel, until his owner came to see what the fuss was about. He used his mobile to call 999. A squad car was there within fifteen minutes and Barbara Carey arrived at five past eight.

By the time Greg's car drew up just after eight-thirty the area was cordoned off, a few curious bystanders gathered on the steep, narrow lane beyond the blue and white incident tape, speculating freely and luridly. According to the local gossips the police might have found anything from the remains of Shergar to the bones of Lord Lucan. As a racing community, Lambourn inclined to the former.

The mortuary van stood waiting for the body to be released; a photographer was recording the scene for posterity and a SOC team – once again under the supervision of Martha Childs – were sitting patiently in their van.

He lifted the tape to hunch under it as onlookers loudly discussed who he might be, hearing the words 'Scotland Yard', as if Newbury could not handle its own suspicious deaths. He made his way for a few metres along the polythene pathway that had been laid to protect evidence to where he could see Barbara, clearly visible in a red jacket, as if she had worn it specially as a beacon for him in the arboreal shadows.

Below them, in the water, a doctor he recognised as a Newbury GP was confirming death.

'Where's Dr Chubb?' he asked his sergeant.

'Alaska, according to his office.'

'Alaska,' he echoed incredulously.

'Even pathologists are allowed to go on holiday, boss.'

'That's a nuisance. Means we'll have to get a pathologist from a neighbouring division to do the post mortem.'

'It was very inconsiderate of him to get himself killed during the holiday season,' Barbara agreed.

'Let's not jump the gun. Maybe he'd had a few, went down to the river for a pee, toppled forward, knocked himself out and drowned without any help from anyone.'

'That wouldn't account for the lump on the *back* on his head, I'm afraid,' the doctor called up, overhearing. 'Coming up nicely.

Might have been done by...' He looked round. 'One of these handy tree branches.'

The most recent storm had brought down a tree on the river bank. The council had got round to sawing it up but not to removing it. It was as if they had opted to provide a year's supply of blunt instruments, murderers for the use of.

'Great!' Greg said, 'Have we got an ID?'

'I've got his wallet,' Barbara said. 'Sixty quid in cash–'

'So robbery wasn't a motive.'

'Credit cards, driving licence,' she went on. 'Also an NUJ card.'

'He was a journalist?'

'Apparently. Name of Reuben...' She examined her notebook more carefully, then took a slim torch and let it play upon the page. '*Ap* Morgan. What is that?'

'Welsh, isn't it?' Greg said. 'Means "Son of" like the Irish o-apostrophe or the Scottish Mac.'

'Yeah? New one on me. The driving licence gives an address in East London. Docklands, at a guess.'

'Ties in with his being on a London paper,' Greg said. 'Ring up the dailies, see if any of them have heard of him.'

As Barbara added this to an already long list of things to do, the photographer came scrambling up the bank towards them to stand wiping his hands on his black jeans, his oversized equipment bag lending him a senile stoop. 'As far as I'm concerned, you can move the body now,' he said.

The doctor and a constable turned the drowned man over and Greg and Barbara went for a closer look. He was a young man, Greg saw – well, younger than Greg so that meant *young*. In his prime. Medium height, slim build, dark hair which looked as if it might be curly when dry, though now it was plastered in wet tendrils across his face and neck. It was impossible to tell if he'd been handsome, not like this.

'He's um...' the constable pointed.

'So he is!' Greg said. 'So, I might have been right about him just having a pee... Put him away, will you, Clements.'

'Me, sir?'

'Well I'm not doing it.'

'Me neither,' Barbara said. 'We haven't been formally introduced.'

'Oh, I'll do it!' the doctor said in an irritable tone, bending over to zip Reuben up. 'For God's sake, let's show the man some respect.'

'First time?' Greg asked with sympathy.

'...Yes.'

Greg had seen it before; all doctors thought they were used to dead bodies until they encountered their first murder victim.

'And it still doesn't account for the bump on his head,' the doctor added gamely.

216

'He might have banged it on a low door frame hours earlier,' Greg objected. 'It needn't have anything to do with his death.'

'Only if the frame was made of green wood. There's fresh dirt in his hair at that spot, even a bit of moss.'

'Oh, all right!' Greg knew perfectly well that he was dealing with a murder; he just enjoyed playing devil's advocate.

'I've seen him before somewhere,' Barbara said.

Greg said, 'Where?'

She slowly shook her head. 'I don't know.'

'Think, Babs.'

'It doesn't work like that, sir. Best if I stop thinking about it altogether, then the chances are it'll come to me.'

'His face is pretty bloated,' Greg pointed out. 'Hard to recognise a man's features like that.'

'All the same. It was recent.'

They watched as the body was placed in a bag and stretchered into the back of the mortuary van, which then reversed slowly down the hill. The doctor took a polite farewell and left, no doubt to get his invoice off to the Thames Valley police without delay. The SOC team went into action and Greg and Barbara moved out of their way.

'DCI Lomax picked a bad time to take a few days leave,' Greg commented.

'Want me to call him back?'

217

'No!' Greg said rather too quickly. 'I'll head up the murder enquiry myself, assuming that's what it is.' Barbara hid a grin. 'I'll be needing you,' Greg went on. 'What's the current situation with your Good Samaritan con?'

'All quiet lately,' she said. 'We think the man and woman are lying low for a few days after the last one nearly went wrong on them. They may even have moved on.'

'Well, that's good timing at least,' Greg said. 'Lucky something is.' He hunched his shoulders, feeling cold in the gloom of the woods. He glanced round at the drab, dank woodland where no sunlight penetrated. 'What is this horrible place?'

'According to my map, it's called Lynch Wood,' Barbara replied, 'which seems to fit nicely.'

'It's strangely isolated for somewhere so near the village centre.'

'There's a group of cottages at the bottom of the hill,' Barbara said, pointing, 'and a house on the opposite bank to the crime scene. They're our best bet. I'll get house to house started right away.'

It didn't take them long to ascertain that Reuben ap Morgan had been staying at the Jolly Fisherman for the past week – nosy bystanders had their uses – and Greg decided to set up the incident room there.

Its location on the edge of Lambourn made it as good a place as any.

The function room was the largest space and, despite the smell of wet paint and Eric Reynolds' grumbling, Andy Whittaker was soon installed there with a couple of uniformed constables, taking statements from the landlord and lady, the man who had found the body and anybody else who was prepared to volunteer.

Joy had last seen Reuben in the bar the previous evening and testified readily that he'd been a bit the worse for wear.

'Fact it was me suggested he get a breath of air,' she recalled. She clapped her hand to her mouth. 'Oh, Lord! If I hadn't...'

'No mileage in that,' Greg said brusquely before she could start blaming herself for the whole thing.

She'd been too busy to notice if he'd returned or not and had locked up as usual around midnight on the assumption that he was sleeping it off in his room.

She indicated his car for them, explaining that it had not moved from its usual spot in the corner of the car park since yesterday teatime.

Meanwhile Greg and Barbara took possession of ap Morgan's room and sealed it off for a preliminary search, get to know their man. They donned protective wear and stood gazing round, getting a feel for the place.

'Looks comfortable enough,' Greg said. He opened the wardrobe. 'He's not brought many clothes. Didn't Mrs Reynolds say he was staying indefinitely?'

'It's not as if we're far from London. He could have nipped back any time to get fresh stuff.' Barbara opened his laptop and tried to start it up. 'Password protected,' she said. 'Why are people so untrusting?'

Greg turned over the book that lay upside down on the bedside table – the latest Elmore Leonard paperback. He noticed that the bookmark was at page eight, so ap Morgan would never know how it turned out. Obviously neither an avid reader nor an insomniac.

He opened the drawer underneath and whistled. Barbara came to look. 'Lot of cash,' he said. 'Mostly fifties. Several hundred pounds.'

'Doesn't leave a paper trail,' Barbara said.

'But why would he need to be so furtive if he has legitimate reasons for being here?'

'Force of habit,' she suggested. 'What else?'

In the modern, cashless society a large roll of notes suggested crime, at the very least tax evasion. He said, 'That amount of cash always makes me think of blackmail.'

'I'll check with Mrs Reynolds – see if he paid cash for his room.' She went back to the desk as Greg carefully counted the money. None of it was going missing on his watch.

'There's a mobile phone here,' she called over. 'Wonder why he didn't have it with him.'

'Probably just forgot. I do half the time.'

She picked it up in her gloved hand and pressed the on switch. It asked her for a PIN number. She tutted and put it in an evidence bag.

'Careful man,' Greg commented. 'Normally an admirable trait but I'd have liked a look at his address book.'

'Won't take too long to get access,' Barbara said. 'We can get the PUK number from the service provider.'

'...Okay. Good.'

She went to the door and yelled unceremoniously for DC Nicolaides, then handed him the electronic devices. 'Get our technical people onto getting past the security barriers on those, Nick. Top priority.'

'Sarge!'

'Then get over to the mortuary and attend the postmortem,' Greg called after him.

'Thank you, sir.'

Greg had a poke around in the hope of finding a diary or journal but there was nothing. 'If he kept one, it'd be on the computer, I suppose,' he said.

'There's a digital camera in the desk drawer,' Barbara remarked, removing it carefully. 'Quite a good one. Let's see what he's got on it.' She pressed a few buttons and a series of pictures flashed up in the viewer. 'Eastbury,' she remarked, 'if I'm not mistaken.'

Greg came to look. 'Scobie's lodgings,' he explained.

She clicked up the next shot. 'And here is the man himself, coming out of the front door.'

'Now, what was his interest in Scobie?' Greg wondered.

'I'd like to get these downloaded to a proper computer and printed off. We'll be able to see them more clearly then.'

'Okay, let's get back to HQ, deal with those photos, make a few phone calls and see what we can find out about the deceased.'

Barbara made a series of calls and, after the fourth one, reported that Reuben ap Morgan had been employed by the *Daily Outlook*.

'I suppose it couldn't have been *The Times*,' Greg said. 'Any clue to what he was working on?'

'Yes. He was a crime reporter and he worked extensively on the Devon Bliss case.'

'That again!'

'Seems he was in Lambourn to keep an eye on Graham Scobie. Judging by these photos he was tailing the guy.'

She indicated a sheaf of papers on her desk

and Greg picked them up, leafing quickly through the colour snapshots. Most of them were of Scobie – although invariably from some distance – and Greg recognised many of the locations: several in Newbury, two in Hungerford, one at Combe Gibbet on Inkpen Hill.

'What a lot of violent locations you have here in Berkshire,' Barbara commented when he pointed out the spot to her, 'what with all your gibbets and lynchings.'

'Is this all of them?'

'All still on the camera's sim card. Chances are he downloaded previous batches onto his laptop so hopefully we'll have those soon.'

'Right.'

'The newspaper were also able to give us a next of kin – Tecwyn and Rebecca Morgan of Aberystwyth, his parents. They don't seem to have the "ap", by the way. Andy's on to the local police now.'

'Does it sound hard-hearted to say it's so much easier when breaking the news to the next of kin is someone else's responsibility?' Greg asked.

'Yes.'

'I can live with that.'

'Bloody hell!' was Jackson Deans' reaction to the news of the death of his pet reporter. He sat at his desk to prepare the front page. *Gagged!,* it read a few minutes later, in

223

giant letters with, in smaller type underneath, *Ace* Outlook *reporter silenced in the most final way – has Bliss killer struck again?*

He'd have to run that last bit past the legal team as he had a sneaking suspicion it was libellous, not that a scrote like Scobie could afford fancy libel lawyers. The odd libel action was good publicity, anyway – make up a story about a celebrity, double the circulation for a few days, double the advertising rates, settle out of court.

He printed it off, opened his office door and yelled.

'AUDREY!'

'What? I'm not bloody deaf.' She appeared in the doorway, thirty-five dressed as nineteen, her hands on her hips, her sleeveless dress almost transparent in the shaft of sunlight behind her. The tops of her arms were getting mottled and flabby.

'You should wear a bra,' he said.

'And you should get knotted, hamster face.' Audrey said what she liked; she knew too much ever to be sacked.

He handed her the printout. 'Get this down to Legal soonest. Would you believe it – one of our own reporters murdered out in the back of beyond.'

'Yeah?' Audrey looked at the paper with more interest. 'Who?'

'Young Reuben Morgan.' Deans shook his head sadly.

Audrey said, 'Which one was he?'

'You know. Welsh chap, skinny.'

'O-oh. The two-minute man.'

'Huh?'

'Doesn't matter.'

'He was like a son to me, Aud. I never told him that.'

'Quite right,' she said. 'He might have asked for a raise.'

'John Hathaway.'

'It's me. I'm calling it off.'

'Graham...'

'Some bloke got himself murdered in Lambourn last night.'

'So I hear.'

'Not any bloke, neither – journalist called himself Reuben ap Morgan. He's been hounding me ever since ... hounding me for months, trying to dig up dirt on me, talking to my friends.'

You haven't got any friends, you little weasel, Hathaway thought. Aloud he said, 'There's no need to panic.'

'No? I could get ten years just for having that handgun in my possession. Do you know that? They'd jump at the chance to send me down for that.'

'You've got it well hidden?' Hathaway said in alarm.

''Course I have.'

'Not at your own house?'

'I'm not stupid. I wouldn't leave it there, not with Mrs Brakespear nosing round my room the moment I go out. *Cleaning* it, she calls it. Funny it never looks any cleaner. And I'm expecting another visit from the police any minute. They're probably there now.'

Hathaway brought him back to the point. 'Don't you see, this is precisely the time to act.'

'With Lambourn swarming with filth?'

'Police who are busy with a murder investigation... You don't know anything about that, do you?'

''Course I bloody don't!' Scobie took a deep breath to compose himself. 'God knows, I hated the man but not enough to kill him. Look, if we're gonna do it, John, then it's gotta be soon or I'll be a nervous wreck.'

'Friday night,' Hathaway said.

'Tomorrow?' Scobie sounded both frightened and excited.

'Midnight. Don't call me again.'

He hung up.

Chapter Sixteen

Greg walked excitedly into the CID room just as Barbara was hanging up the telephone. 'Problem?' he asked, seeing her face, his own news temporarily forgotten.

'More of a mystery.'

'Isn't that our speciality?'

'That was Mrs Gladstone – DCI Lomax's landlady,' she added, seeing Greg's blank look. 'Asking if he was here.'

Greg made an exasperated noise. 'Surely he told her he was going to be away for a few days.'

'Oh, yes. He did. But she's just had his niece on the phone looking for him. It seems she was expecting him late Tuesday night but he never showed up.'

'That *is* odd.'

'The niece has been trying his mobile but couldn't get through so this morning, in desperation, she rang his bed and breakfast.' Barbara picked up the phone again. 'Let me try.' She dialled and listened. 'Voice mail,' she said. 'Alex? It's Babs. Can you ring me on my mobile the moment you get this. Thanks.' She hung up.

'We haven't got time to worry about it

now,' Greg said. 'Come and see what ap Morgan was writing in his journal.'

'Technical got in?'

'In minutes. Then we need to get back to Lambourn.'

'Just give me a second. I want to ask someone in the office to ring round hospitals and police stations between here and Devon, make sure they didn't get a John Doe brought in Tuesday night.'

'Okay, but make it quick.'

'This is hot stuff,' Barbara commented, reading quickly through the computer file. 'Almost makes me blush.'

Greg snorted. 'Like I believe that, Miss Shameless.'

'I don't know how much we should make of it, though – it's the sort of thing men write, isn't it? Fantasy, most like.'

'Maybe, but I want a long talk with Mrs Reynolds.'

They had found a file on ap Morgan's laptop in which he indulged in lurid daydreams about Joy Reynolds, descriptions of what she was wearing, speculations about the body beneath, imaginings of what she might say and do to him. The material was meant to be private and Reuben had spared no detail of his onanistic fantasies.

Greg thought how embarrassed he would be if he could see two stolid police officers impassively reading his words, but death – especially murder – deprived you of all privacy and most dignity.

'Kind of adolescent, isn't it,' Barbara said, 'for a man pushing forty?'

'Let's go,' Greg said.

Joy Reynolds had already given her brief statement to Detective Constable Whittaker and was puzzled, even a little alarmed, to be summoned to the presence of the super-intendent, who had commandeered the small office behind the bar for the purpose.

The woman sergeant showed her in then left them to it and she looked at him nervously. He smiled reassurance at her, however, and asked her to sit. She sank down on the opposite side of the table from him and tried to read the piece of paper he had in front of him but upside-down reading was not one of her talents.

'Now, Mrs Reynolds,' he said gently. 'I am Superintendent Gregory Summers and I just wanted a quiet word with you in private. I realise that this is a delicate situation, what with you being a married woman, but this is likely to turn into a murder enquiry so it's very important that you tell me the absolute truth. I promise you that if it has nothing to do with Mr ap Morgan's death then your husband will never hear a syllable of it from me.'

She said, 'I don't know what you're talking about.'

It was a fairly standard response and he let it hang in the air for a moment in case she thought better of it, but either she was a good actress or she was telling the truth.

He pushed the sheet of paper towards her, turning it round to face her. 'We found this material on the dead man's laptop.'

She glanced at him, puzzled, then began to read. After a couple of lines, she let out a gasp of outrage and disbelief. 'He ... the rotten little–' she spluttered, before remembering that he was dead and that she should not therefore speak ill of him. 'How dare he write these things about me. It's disrespectful. And he seemed such a nice young man too.'

If women only knew, Greg reflected, how often men thought of them with disrespect – with craven, furtive lust – they would probably refuse to speak to a member of the male sex ever again. He couldn't even acquit himself, not that he could see Joy Reynolds' charms; she struck him as commonplace and not worth the aggro.

She pushed the paper back to him. 'I won't read another word of this filth, thank you very much. There's not an atom of truth in it.'

Greg sat looking at her for a while as he considered this. She sat staring back, not flinching from his gaze, her full, scarlet-

230

waxed lips set in a grim, offended line that would not have disgraced an elderly nun.

'I believe you,' he said finally, 'but I had to make sure. If there was any kind of illicit relationship between the two of you, then it might give your husband a motive. Do you see?'

To his surprise, Joy's lip began to tremble, and soon she was in tears.

Greg was at a loss for a moment. He didn't know whether to comfort her or caution her. He got up to yell for Babs, then thought better of it. Mrs Reynolds struck him as a 'man's woman' and therefore more likely to open up to him than a member of her own sex. He took out a clean handkerchief and passed it across the table to her.

He said, 'There, there,' rather heavily, at intervals, as she snivelled into it for a couple more minutes.

'Thing is,' she said, drying her eyes and inadvertently smearing blue eyeshadow down her cheek, 'my Eric's that jealous that it hardly mattered what I was up to with Reuben – or not up to, as it happened. Eric was off his head with jealousy either way. I mean–' she raised her red eyes to him coquettishly. '–a barmaid has to be nice to the male customers, doesn't she? Get no custom otherwise.'

'So,' Greg said after a pause for reflection. 'You're saying that, although there was no improper relationship between you and Reuben ap Morgan, your husband believed that there was. Is that it?' She nodded. 'And may have been a threat to ap Morgan as a result.'

'I'm sure he wouldn't ... you know ... *do* anything.'

'Has he ever reacted with violence to a man you flirted with?'

Joy hesitated, remembering the Christmas party at the building society which had ended with Eric pinning Colin Walker up against the wall and threatening to punch his head in. It had taken four men to haul him off and, luckily, Colin had been prepared to laugh it off, put it down to drink, as he'd have been within his rights to call the police and make a complaint of assault. She had never been so embarrassed in her life.

'Mrs Reynolds?' Greg prompted her.

'No! Nothing specific. More bark than bite.'

'I'd better have a word with him next.'

'Can I go?'

'Yes. Go and splash some water on your face – I should.' She held the handkerchief out to him and he waved it away. 'Keep it.'

He got through an awful lot of handkerchiefs in his job, bought them by the dozen from Woolworth's.

It took him a while to find Eric Reynolds but he finally tracked him down in the beer garden, pacing up and down with an inscrutable look on his face, staring at the patchy shrubs as if he hated them.

Greg said, 'A word, Mr Reynolds, if you don't mind.'

'I've given my statement to your boy,' he growled, 'for what it's worth. How long are you going to be using my function room? I want to get ready to open by August bank holiday – pick up some trade from the carnival.'

'We'll be as quick as we can.' Since Reynolds was clearly not in the mood to co-operate, Greg took his arm and steered him to one of the picnic benches that littered the garden. 'I wanted to ask you a few more questions about your relationship with Mr ap Morgan.'

Eric squeezed his hefty thighs in between bench and table with some difficulty and began to drum his fingers rhythmically on the wooden top. 'Didn't have one. He was renting a room here. Joy deals with that side of the business – keeps the rooms clean and collects the rent, cooks the bacon, sausage and egg. I've got enough to do with setting up the Fisherman's Rest.'

He turned to look avidly at the wall of the function room and Greg, following his eye, decided that it needed repointing. The last

233

week in August looked a bit optimistic. 'Are you saying you hadn't spoken to the dead man at all?' he queried.

'Think he introduced himself the day after he arrived. Told that to your boy already. That'd be the extent of our conversation.'

'Your wife's a fine-looking woman,' Greg said slyly.

Reynolds flushed slightly, though whether with anger or pride was hard to tell. He said evenly, 'She's wearing well enough.'

'Customers like a nice, cheerful barmaid. I know I do. Bit of cleavage, laugh and a joke.'

'Bit too much cleavage sometimes,' Reynolds said sourly.

'I'm sure your guests appreciate it too.'

'Look.' Eric leaned heavily forward across the picnic table, supporting himself on his beefy arms. 'I'm not stupid. I know what you're getting at. You think I'd kill a man because he smiled too widely at my missus.'

'It's been known.'

'I never laid a finger on Mr Reuben ap Morgan and that's a fact.' Reynolds got to his feet, almost overturning the table in his haste. 'I wouldn't have soiled my hands.'

Greg watched him walk away until he disappeared into the bar, then made his way back to the office to brood.

'Sir?' Barbara came in as he sat thinking

234

over what Joy and Eric had told him. 'Something you might want to hear–'

He interrupted. 'Sit down, Babs, and give me your views on this.' He told her about his interview with the Reynoldses.

'It's odd,' she said, 'the way women are so quick to the point the finger. Like that time a few years back when we had those three rapes in Newbury and we were knee deep in women claiming their husbands were the perp.'

'It is interesting,' he agreed. 'Especially since, as I recall, one of them was right.'

'But the other five or six were wrong,' she pointed out. 'And people wonder why I'm cynical about marriage. Also, when a witness is quick to tell me they're suspicious of someone, I wonder if they're trying to deflect suspicion from themselves.'

Greg considered this. 'So, Joy Reynolds was having a fling with ap Morgan and he threatened to tell her husband when she ended it, so she silenced him?'

'It's as good a scenario as any.'

'Except that everyone agrees that she was here, in the bar, all evening, whereas he was nowhere to be seen, supposedly painting the function room.'

'So, she arranged to meet ap Morgan in a nice quiet place after closing... Or perhaps they were both in it.'

Greg remembered when a married woman

who committed a crime with her husband could avoid prosecution by claiming spousal duress, it being taken for granted that obedience to the lord and master was part of the job description. The loophole had never applied to murder but he'd more than once watched a woman he knew to be guilty as hell to a very nasty crime slip out of his grasp and walk away, raising two fingers at him in derision, and not always metaphorically.

These days, when a man and woman committed an atrocious crime together, public opinion was inclined to place more and not less blame on the female of the species. A strange reversal. He said, 'Let's leave that tangle for now. What did you come in for, anyway?'

'I've been helping Andy with the donkey work and we've just had a visit from Peter Tilsley. Remember? We brought him in the other day after he had that set-to with Scobie in the Market Place in Newbury.'

'Of course I remember,' Greg snapped. 'I'm not senile. Yet.'

'...Okay He's a regular here – admitted he'd been barred from the pubs in Eastbury and East Garston when I pressed him–'

'Barred for what?'

'Fighting.'

'Charming!'

'And he insists that he saw DCI Lomax drinking in the lounge bar with the victim on two occasions in the past few days.'

'What!'

'Odd, isn't it?'

'It was public spirited of him to come forward,' Greg said, 'after we gave him such a hard time.'

'I got the impression he was hoping to get Alex into trouble.'

'Payback time? Could he be lying?'

'I don't think so,' Barbara said slowly, 'because it reminded me where I saw the deceased before. DCI Lomax and I were going out a few days ago and the front desk told him he had a visitor. He told me to wait in the car but I got a glimpse.'

'Ap Morgan?'

'Uhuh. When I asked him about it he said he was a possible informant, nothing official, and changed the subject.'

'I don't like this,' Greg said. 'Have you been trying his mobile?'

'At regular intervals – voice mail a few times and then it went dead, like the battery had run down. The telephone company can't pinpoint it; they say it's not showing up on their systems.'

'So it's switched off?'

'Or out of range.'

'Which means what – out of the country?'

'Not necessarily,' Barbara said. 'There are parts of Wales and Scotland where there's no coverage.'

'And Wales is not *that* far from his route to the West Country.'

'Which reminds me: I checked back with HQ as well and there've been no reports of unidentified bodies fetching up between here and Devon. I think we need to declare him officially missing, sir.'

'More than that!' Greg said. 'Get his details and photo out to other forces and say he's missing and wanted for questioning in connection with a suspicious death.'

Barbara hesitated. 'What?' Greg said.

'I can't believe I'm such a lousy judge of character, that's all. There must be some simple explanation.'

'Okay, but get on with it. And give them his car number plate.'

She left.

While she was doing that, Greg put through another call to his counterpart in Devon, Superintendent Burnip.

'Haven't seen anything of Alex Lomax, I don't suppose?' he began.

Burnip laughed. 'No, why? Have you lost him? He was always a bit of a law unto himself.'

'He's gone AWOL.'

'Huh?'

'Well, not exactly,' Greg amended. 'He had leave, it's just that he hasn't turned up at his sister's place in Taunton as planned.'

'That would be Tiverton,' Burnip said

evenly, 'and if the wretched Bridget is involved, then nothing would surprise me.'

'Look,' Greg said. 'When I spoke to you before I asked you if Lomax had been ill and I thought you were a bit evasive.'

'You did? I must practise harder.'

'Thing is I have a dead body, a missing officer and a witness says he saw the two of them drinking together a few days before the murder.' Burnip let out a low whistle. 'So, copper to copper and loyalty aside, I need anything you've got.'

'Okay,' Burnip said. 'I consider Alex a personal friend and I'm sure there's a simple explanation but, yes he was ill, in a way, and he told me he was applying for a transfer to make a fresh start.'

'A breakdown?'

'Nothing so dramatic, but he was terribly upset, lost a lot of weight, like you thought. Ever hear of the Devon Bliss case?'

Chapter Seventeen

'DCI Lomax knew Devon Bliss?' Barbara said incredulously.

'Since she was a babe in arms. Took her murder very hard.'

'And it didn't occur to this Superintendent Burnip that his rushing off to Newbury was a bit worrying? Something we needed to know about?'

'Why should it? Burnip isn't Mystic Meg – he didn't know that John Hathaway had moved to Lambourn, or that Scobie was settled a stone's throw away.'

'Good point. You think Alex did?'

'I'm betting on it.'

'He asked you where Scobie lived,' Barbara remembered.

'Bloody hell! So he did. And I told him.'

'But it's not Scobie who's come to harm,' she pointed out, 'nor Sir John Hathaway.'

'But if he knew ap Morgan and if the journalist guessed that he had some plan ... some revenge plot–'

Greg's mobile rang and he answered it.

'It's Nick, sir.'

'Who?'

'DC Nicolaides, sir.'

'Oh. *George.*'

'The PM's finished, sir. Drowning confirmed as the cause of death. Pathologist says late last night is his best guess, though the cold water would have affected body temperature, so any time between, say, ten and four is a possibility.'

'Are we any closer to whether it was murder?'

'Doesn't seem much doubt about it, sir. Apart from the lump on the back of the head, there's bruising developing on the shoulders and neck which the doc says is where he was held face down in the water till he drowned.'

'No other possible explanation?'

'Not that anyone can think of.'

'Me neither.'

'You can see the marks where fingers have dug into his shoulder – quite large, probably a man's.'

'Is it likely that a woman would have the strength to hold him down till he drowned?'

'Well, that's another thing. The blood alcohol level is pretty high. The chances are he was too fuddled to realise what was happening until it was too late.'

Greg wasn't sure if that had made it better or worse for the dead man. 'Good,' he said. 'I want you to take a couple of uniformed constables and get over to Scobie's place at Eastbury. It's time we gave his bedroom a good toss.'

'I'd better pick up a search warrant then, sir. You remember how his landlady was with us?'

'Fine. Let me know what you find as soon as possible.' He decided it was time to bring CS Barkiss up to date, since he was cavalierly making off with large numbers of uniformed officers. Once he'd got past the considerable barrier of Mrs Asquith, he explained the situation succinctly to the Chief.

'Lambourn *again*,' Barkiss said in disbelief. 'It's like a bad joke. I mean, what's the population?'

'Three or four thousand,' Greg guessed wildly, 'not counting horses.'

'Is it something they're putting in the water?'

'Apart from dead journalists?' Greg rejoined swiftly.

'Hah! Good one. All right. Are we expecting a quick arrest?'

'Not necessarily.'

He'd booked the first two weeks in September as holiday. He and Angie were going to the Italian Lakes for ten days before she was due back at Reading University for her second year as a psychology student. Lucky he hadn't bought his Euros yet. Still, murder cases were usually solved quickly or not at all.

'I'll take that as a flat no,' Barkiss was

242

saying. 'Well, keep me informed and, Gregory–'

'I know. Keep Michael Patterson out of it.'

They hung up.

Since they weren't opening the bar today, thanks to the overwhelming police presence, Joy didn't know what to do with herself. In the end she went up to her bedroom on the top floor and sat down on the bed. She flipped on the TV but daytime television was unbearable, even in her dazed state. She muted the sound, leaving the picture for company. There was something soothing in the primary colours of the sets and vapid, smiley faces of the presenters.

She still felt stunned, unable to take in that the young Welshman was dead when he had seemed so full of life, unable to believe that she had pointed the finger of suspicion at her own husband. She didn't know what to think now. Fifteen years she'd been with Eric and had she really believed, however briefly, that his jealousy would lead him to kill?

She had assumed that the superintendent would rush off and arrest Eric but surely she would have been told if that had happened.

The door opened, squeaking slightly on its unoiled hinges, and she glanced up, raising her hand to her throat in fear. The only person who would walk into her bedroom without knocking was Eric.

He wasn't smiling but he didn't look angry either. He said, 'You all right, love?'

'Yes,' she tried to say but her voice wasn't coming out right.

'Bit of a shock, all this.'

'Yes.'

He sat down on the bed beside her and put his arms round her, still trying to come to terms with what he had done. 'It'll be okay,' he said. 'We'll see this thing through together.'

'Eric ... I told the police...'

'I know. Hush. I know. It's all right.'

'I didn't mean ... I never thought. Not really.'

'Didn't you?' He turned her to face him and now he was smiling. 'Think I'd bump off a man you smiled twice at?' His voice was teasing. 'Got a bit of a high opinion of yourself, ain't you?'

'Well!'

He leaned forward and his lips sought hers. She felt a surge of passion such as she hadn't felt for years, not with him. The thought that he might have been a murderer was suddenly exciting.

He slid his hands up inside her T-shirt and pulled it off over her head.

She squealed. 'Eric! The police might come up any minute.'

'Let them.' He unfastened her bra. 'We're

not breaking any laws. So it turns you on, does it, the idea that I would kill for you?'

And she said, 'Maybe.'

Nicolaides turned up looking for Greg towards tea time.

'How you getting on?' Greg asked.

'I've left the guys at work. I thought you ought to see this.' He deposited what looked like a large book on the desk.

'Deluxe cuttings album,' Greg read aloud. 'A scrap book?'

'Press cuttings of the Devon Bliss trial,' Nicolaides said, 'from the time he was arrested to the acquittal.'

'I suppose it was the most exciting thing that ever happened to him.' Greg opened the scrap book at the first page and saw the headline: *Devon – Man Arrested!*. 'Nothing about the murder itself?'

'I imagine if he'd kept a scrap book of that then it would've featured heavily in the trial,' Nicolaides said.

'Good point.'

'Only if you take a look at the clippings from the *Outlook*, you'll see why this could be significant, sir.'

Greg located the first page that bore the *Outlook*'s distinctive typeface. It was essentially a character assassination of Scobie. The by-line had been obliterated in heavy black ink, with scratch marks where the pen had pushed savagely into the flimsy paper.

'Well done, George!'

'Thank you, sir. I'll be getting back then.'

'Is Scobie there?'

'No, the old woman turns him out every day, like she told us. She reckons he was there last night, though, same as when the horse got nobbled. He was in his room reading most of the evening, but she made them both a hot drink and they watched the *News at Ten* together – seems to be part of their routine.'

'The murder may well have taken place later.'

'Again, she's adamant she'd have heard if he'd let himself out of the house in the night. The bolts are old and noisy – I tried them myself.'

'Have you checked the window of his bedroom – see if there's any sign that he climbed out that way?'

'Yes, and there isn't. There's no drainpipe near enough and, although there's a creeper thing growing up the back wall, it's not very sturdy. I wouldn't care to climb down it myself and there's no sign of damage to it. Same with the bathroom. The downstairs windows are all painted shut. I don't reckon the old woman likes fresh air much.'

'Okay, pick him up when he gets home and give me a call. We'll take him in to the station.'

'Will do.'

Nicolaides left as Greg turned back to the scrap book.

He had often been amazed at what newspapers were allowed to get away with, walking a tightrope over contempt of court but so seldom falling off. He could remember cases where a convicted murderer had been released on appeal because the press coverage of the trial had been too prejudicial, but the papers cared nothing for that, only for circulation and the advertising rates that depended on it.

If Scobie had been convicted then these front-page articles could easily have constituted grounds for appeal since they took his guilt for granted and painted him as a dangerous psychopath. True, jurors were told not to read the papers during the trial but they were only human and the temptation was great; and there was no guarantee that they had not read these articles before the trial began, before their names even came up for jury service.

In a high-profile case like this one, it was unrealistic to hope for jurors who were not already familiar with most of the details.

There were interviews with people who knew Scobie although each in turn disclaimed that they had been friends: a neighbour in Catford who had decided that Scobie was a devil worshipper and held black masses in his basement; a woman who had worked with him for a few weeks years earlier when he'd briefly held down a job at a call centre and who described him for no obvious reason as a 'loner and a pervert'; the 'girlfriend' who had been for a drink with him on two or three occasions.

On each of these stories the same censorship of the journalist's by-line had been carried out. It didn't take Sherlock Holmes to identify the author of these pieces as one Reuben ap Morgan, lately deceased.

Nicolaides rang Greg at six-fifteen.

'Scobie got back a few minutes ago, sir, and he's now in custody.'

'I didn't tell you to arrest him,' Greg snapped.

'He didn't give me a choice. When I told him it was about the murder in Lambourn he wouldn't co-operate unless he was arrested so I thought I'd better do that.'

'I see. All right. See you at HQ in half an hour.'

Greg hung up with a sigh. Obviously Scobie had learned a good deal about his rights during his first brush with the police. Arresting him meant that the clock was ticking whereas, if a suspect could be persuaded to attend the police station for questioning voluntarily, there were no real time constraints at all. Greg was glad that the public in general didn't appreciate this anomaly; most people were anxious to avoid the shame of arrest.

He arrived back at the police station half an hour later and found Scobie booked in and waiting in the cell for the duty solicitor to arrive.

'Not less than an hour,' Dick Maybey, the custody sergeant, announced cheerfully.

The two policemen adjourned to the canteen for supper while they waited to start their interview. They sat turning over platefuls of something that went by the name of moussaka, not speaking.

Eventually Greg pushed his plate away half-eaten and sighed. His companion, who had eaten all of his without any actual sign of enjoyment, looked at him in surprise.

Greg said, 'That's supposed to be Greek peasant food, right?'

'I suppose. Don't taste much like me mum's, though.'

'What I don't understand is how some Greek peasant would go to the trouble of separately cooking the mince, aubergine and potato, making a cheese sauce, then putting the lot together and baking it. My partner made it one Saturday night and it took most of our pots and pans and all four gas burners. I was washing up for hours. I mean, after a hard day tending sheep on the hills, or whatever, who would have the energy? Irish stew – *that's* peasant food: shove all the ingredients in a pot and leave it over the fire for a few hours while you're out.'

Nicolaides thought about it, then shrugged. 'I guess we just take our grub more seriously, sir.'

Greg's mobile rang to tell him that the duty solicitor had arrived.

As they left the canteen, Nicolaides said, 'Have you thought of getting a dishwasher?'

Scobie's solicitor took the form of an inexperienced young man called Adrian Flint whom Greg had encountered only once before. More proof that it was the holiday season. His suit looked a little more crumpled than on the last occasion, when it had obviously been new, but the tie knotted beneath his prominent Adam's apple was as loud as ever, with pink door keys dancing against a lime-green background.

Presumably these ties were what Flint had instead of a personality.

He looked startled on being told his client's identity and clearly regarded Scobie as something of a celebrity.

Once the four of them were seated in the interview room and each man had identified himself for the tapes, Greg produced the scrap book and passed it across the table to Scobie.

'You recognise this, Mr Scobie?'

The little man seemed perfectly calm. 'Yes. It's mine.'

'Perhaps you could tell me what it is for the purposes of the recording.'

'Certainly, it's a scrap book. I've kept them all my life. This one contains newspaper cuttings of my recent trial at which–' he raised his voice and spoke directly to the tape recorders '–I was quite rightly acquitted of the murder of Devon Bliss.'

'My men found this book today while carrying out a search of your lodgings at number seven Belfast Place, Eastbury.'

'That would be correct, yes.'

'Now, Mr Scobie, if we look through this scrap book, we see that on a number of occasions the name of the reporter – the journalist – has been scratched out, obliterated.'

'Those are the articles written by Reuben ap Morgan,' Scobie said readily, 'of the *Daily Outlook*.'

'You admit that,' Nicolaides butted in.

'There wouldn't be much point in denying it, Constable.' He turned his attention back to Greg. 'If you've read the articles in question then you'll have seen how vicious they are, how prejudicial. Ap Morgan was appointing himself judge, jury and executioner. I took exception to that, so I took a big black biro to his rather silly name.'

'You are aware that the same Reuben ap Morgan was murdered in Lambourn last night?'

'I was told of it today. Prior to that, I had no idea he was in the neighbourhood.'

'Did you know him by sight?'

'He was pointed out to me in the press box on one occasion. I'm not sure that I would have known him again.'

'Pointed out by whom?' Greg asked.

'Don't remember. One of the court officials, I daresay.'

'Ever been in the Jolly Fisherman at Lambourn?'

'No. I'm not a big drinker, not much of a one for pubs – too noisy and smoky and crowded. If I did fancy a drink there are nearer places.'

'Where were you last night between ten and, say, the early hours?'

'I watched the news with my landlady, as I'm sure she told you. Then I read in my room for an hour or so, then went to sleep.'

'You didn't leave the house again?'

'No.'

'Do you know anything about the death of Mr ap Morgan?'

'Nothing whatsoever.'

Greg was silent for a moment then Adrian Flint spoke. 'My client has answered all your questions satisfactorily, Mr Summers, so if there's nothing else, then I must ask you to release him without further delay.'

He looked, Greg thought, remarkably pleased with this speech which presumably came out of the Duty Solicitor's Handbook, chapter one.

Scobie chipped in, speaking to no one in particular. 'I have great faith in British Justice; it's come up trumps for me once.'

Greg said, 'Very well,' since he could think of no pretext on which to hold him. The connection between him and the dead man was a tenuous one and, as he said, the articles were malicious. Greg had once or twice been on the receiving end of an unscrupulous journalist himself. He could see the temptation in erasing the name of Adam Chaucer, presenter of the local TV news programme, but that didn't mean he would kill the man.

Or only in his dreams.

'That reminds me,' Scobie said as he got to his feet. 'I have been having no success in recovering my scrap books about poor Devon – my own personal property confiscated by the Metropolitan Police as alleged evidence in my trial. Perhaps you could help me with that, Superintendent.'

And perhaps not, Greg thought.

At least he now had Scobie's fingerprints.

Chapter Eighteen

Greg picked up a copy of the *Daily Outlook* on his way into work the next morning, as well as his usual *Times*, attracted by the front page which bore a studio photograph of Reuben ap Morgan under the headline *Gagged* and the truncated subscript, which had eventually been okayed by the legal department, stating simply that one of the paper's most prestigious reporters had been murdered in pursuit of his trade.

When he got to his office Greg settled down with a cup of coffee to read the article which covered the whole of pages two and three. It told him little that Jackson Deans hadn't told his colleagues from the Metropolitan Police who had spoken to him at length the day before, but then that was too much to hope for.

It did dwell, however, on the dead man's connection with the Devon Bliss case, facts which even the lawyers could not deem libellous. It further mentioned that Scobie – 'the man unexpectedly acquitted of this appalling crime' – had gone to live in the Lambourn area, not two miles from the scene of Reuben's death. It reminded readers that the police were not looking for anyone else in connection with the Bliss murder and left them to draw their own inferences.

There was also a mention of the case in Linda Linton's column. If she was to be believed then her dead colleague had been a man of exceptional character and abilities, destined for greatness in the world of newspapers, yes, but never hesitating to take time out to help a blind granny across the street.

He shook his head with a pained smile. The gutter press: were they sexist, racist and half-witted because their readers were or did they make their readers thus? Discuss.

'Big spread,' he remarked to Barbara as she came in. 'Normally a murder like this merits a couple of paragraphs on page six.'

'They look after their own,' Barbara said, 'same as we do.'

Greg turned back to the front page and looked more closely at ap Morgan. Handsome, if he was any judge. He asked Barbara. She took the paper from him and scrutinised it.

'Yeah,' she said, 'wouldn't deck him if he offered to buy me a drink.'

'Alas,' Greg said. 'Too late.'

'You still thinking about Mrs Reynolds?'

'You've seen *Mr* Reynolds.'

'Not the same league,' she agreed. She

shook out the paper and skimmed the article at high speed. 'What about Scobie?' she asked. 'Nick said you had him in for questioning last night.'

'Who?'

'Nicolaides,' she said patiently. 'We call him Nick.'

'Really? Somebody might have told me,' Greg grumbled. He summed up the interview for her. 'The good news is that I now have his prints. The bad news is that they don't match any of the orphans SOCO turned up at the stables, let alone any we've got from the murder scene.'

'So he knows to wear gloves. Who doesn't?' Greg shrugged agreement. It occurred to him to wonder when any police force had last secured a conviction based on fingerprint evidence. 'What's he like, anyway?' Barbara asked. 'I mean, I saw him in the market place that day but we didn't exactly chat.'

'Oddly articulate. Bit wrapped up in his own world, I should say.'

'Classic stalker?'

'Maybe.'

'What did we get from the murder scene?' Barbara asked. 'Not much, I suppose.'

'He definitely died there rather than the corpse being dumped in a quiet location but that's not exactly a blinding revelation. Otherwise there are cigarette butts and sweet wrappers which have probably been there for years.'

'It's almost the perfect murder spot,' Barbara mused, 'just the place you'd lure someone to if you'd decided to dispose of them.'

'Not a spur-of-the-moment thing, you think?'

'I think he was a threat to somebody and that somebody acted quickly and decisively. It also suggests local knowledge.'

'Martha says the place is a jumble of footprints. The foliage is so thick that the ground seldom dries out, even in the hottest weather, so everyone who walks their dog there leaves a trace. They're trying Electrostatic Lifting, see if there are any latents that might prove useful, but I'm not optimistic.'

'What's your instinct on this, guv? I mean, who other than Scobie had reason to fear Reuben ap Morgan poking around Lambourn?'

Ian Callaghan, Greg thought – ap Morgan or any other journalist. Ian Callaghan, who'd lived in Lambourn for four years now and knew the terrain well, knew just the sort of deserted riverbank where he could entice an inquisitive reporter to a cold, dark death.

He was going to have to talk to the man at some stage, despite what Barkiss had said on their last meeting. As a convicted murderer, his fingerprints would be on file.

Trouble was, the chances were they were classified and that even asking for them would raise a red flag somewhere in the Home Office.

He could not do anything that risked exposing Patterson's true identity to a vengeful world. Meanwhile, he had no answer to Barbara's question. 'Have we got the next of kin sorted?' he asked instead.

'They've been informed and have given a statement to the Welsh boys, for what it's worth. Seems he rang up to touch base every couple of weeks and came home for a few days at Christmas, like most single people. He never talked about his work.'

Greg groaned.

'Mr Morgan is on his way to make a formal identification of the body,' Barbara continued. 'Mrs Morgan was too upset to come with him – seems it's only a couple of months since she lost her father.'

'Oh dear. Any word about DCI Lomax?'

'Not a sausage.'

'Then there's really only one thing we can do now,' Greg said, standing up.

'Shall I get a warrant, just in case?'

He nodded. 'Best to do things by the book.'

Mrs Gladstone ran a clean and comfortable house in a quiet suburb of Newbury, with none of the soul-sucking cheerlessness of

Mrs Brakespear's establishment. It wasn't the first time that the local police force had used her to put up an officer moving in from outside the area and feedback was positive, even enthusiastic.

She opened the door to them wiping her hands clean of flour on her apron. 'I'm glad to see you,' she said. 'I've been a bit worried ever since that little Toyah rang, poor lamb. Her mother's in hospital, you know.'

'Yes, I know,' Greg said. 'Thing is, Mrs Gladstone, we're still not sure where DCI Lomax has got to so we thought we'd take a look round his room, if that's okay, see if there's anything there that can shed a light on his whereabouts.'

'First right at the top of the stairs,' she replied, showing no interest in search warrants. 'Can you manage, dear, only I'm baking?'

'We can manage fine,' Barbara assured her.

The room was small, designed for a bachelor. The single divan bed had been made up with a purple and cream duvet in a geometric pattern which matched the curtains. There was a built-in wardrobe in one corner and a pine chest of drawers stood along the adjacent wall with a cream lace runner across the top.

It was very tidy with nothing but a water

glass and a bottle of aspirin on the night-stand to prove that anybody was in residence. Greg picked the bottle up to check that it contained nothing but a harmless painkiller and put it back, satisfied.

'A single man who doesn't drop his clothes on the floor,' Barbara said. 'Now, there's a novelty.'

'Impersonal, isn't it?' Greg commented.

'He still had all his stuff down in Plymouth,' Barbara said, 'as he hadn't completed the sale of his house yet, so I suppose he didn't bring anything he didn't need till he'd got somewhere permanent.'

Greg opened the door of the wardrobe. Four suits were hanging inside, two blue, two grey, all with Burton's labels, nothing flash. There was also the sports jacket in grey herringbone which the DCI had been wearing the night he had come to Greg's house for supper what seemed like a very long time ago.

He counted seven white shirts – one for every day of the week, he surmised, and no expectation of Sundays off. At least Lomax wouldn't have to think very hard about what to put on each morning. Half a dozen ties, all plain or striped, hung on a rail inside the door, along with a black leather belt.

On the floor of the wardrobe stood a pair of brown suede slip-ons, some black lace-ups and one pair of trainers, almost new.

He began to work his way through the pockets of Lomax's suits, jacket and trousers. He even checked the shoes in case anything was concealed in their toes.

The smell of cakes baking was wafting up the stairs, penetrating the closed door easily. His mouth was watering.

Barbara, meanwhile, was rummaging through the chest of drawers, starting with the top one. Had she been a burglar she would have started at the bottom as it saved shutting each drawer after you searched it, but she fully intended to put everything back where she found it.

She had explored plenty of knicker drawers in her years in the police force but it felt oddly intimate to do it in Alex's room. He favoured the stretchy trunk, blue or black, St Michael's label. The elastic was fraying a little at each waist, suggesting that they were replaced only when completely worn out. Probably he had no females to buy him underwear as presents – from what he'd told her of his sister, she wasn't the nurturing type.

Socks were unpatterned, sorted by colour and rolled into neat balls. The words 'anally retentive' suggested themselves to her but she was sure that the man she had been getting to know over the past month was more complex than that.

In the second drawer were T-shirts and

vests. She moved them aside and felt something less flexible, cardboard. She extracted a fat red folder and flipped the lid open, revealing a sheaf of newspaper cuttings.

'Nothing but a three-week-old petrol receipt,' Greg grumbled, 'and some extra strong mints.' He realised that Barbara had gone very quiet. 'You?'

'I think you'd better take look at this, sir.'

She removed the newspaper clippings from the file and spread them out on the bed. Greg recognised some of them – accounts of the Devon Bliss trial which he had seen in Scobie's own scrap book – but there was earlier material too.

'Devon slaughtered,' he read aloud, 'TV newsreader in brutal slaying.' Slaying was a word that appeared only in newspaper headlines, like 'wed', as in 'Pop star to wed'.

'He's got everything here,' Barbara commented, 'from the day her body was found to the end of the trial. Look.' She held up a front page from the *Daily Outlook* with the words 'Not Guilty!' in the largest typeface the paper could muster. Beside it was a fuzzy photograph of Graham Scobie standing on the steps of the court and, at the bottom of the page, another of John Hathaway.

Greg sat down heavily on a spare piece of duvet. 'At least he hasn't blacked out ap Morgan's by-line,' he commented. 'Otherwise this is the same stuff Scobie had in his room.'

'It's not necessarily sinister,' Barbara ventured. 'He knew Devon Bliss so, obviously, he would take a great interest in the case and the subsequent trial. Wouldn't you?'

'I suppose, but it's a bit … obsessive.' Greg pressed his hand against his forehead and sighed. 'We'd better see what else is lurking among his socks.'

In the bottom drawer of the chest they found another folder. This one contained details of Devon Bliss's career while she yet lived. She was resplendent in the gossip pages of the tabloids, decked in high fashion from designers Greg had never heard of, invariably on the arm of a man though seldom the same one twice.

Talk of a whirlwind engagement to pop singer Nathan Hope was mooted and swiftly denied.

'Who's interested in this stuff?' Greg wondered aloud.

'Loads of people. They have whole magazines with nothing but celebrity gossip.'

'I suppose she was a celebrity,' he said, 'but I had barely heard her name when she died and wouldn't have recognised her if I'd bumped into her in the streets of Newbury.' And now she was more famous than she could ever have become while she lived, like

Marilyn Monroe. She had been immortal-
ised.

'You don't really think that Alex might
have something to do with ap Morgan's
death?' Barbara asked, clearly pleading for
the answer No.

'Babs ... I'm starting to ask myself if we
should find out where Alex Lomax was the
night Devon Bliss died.'

'Think about it,' Greg said. 'Lomax was
clearly obsessed with this young woman–'

'He *knew* her,' Barbara insisted. 'They
lived in the same small village in Devon and
were old friends. I daresay her family have
cuttings albums like this one.'

'Maybe she didn't feel as strongly about
their ancient friendship as he did though.
Women like that often move on when they
hit the big time, want their new important
friends and not the old ones.'

'We can't know she was like that, sir.
That's not fair.'

'Okay but bear with me... He felt rejected
by her so he killed her. Scobie was painted
as a stalker but Lomax seems to have had
the same fixation as he did. Scobie was
brought to trial for murder on no more
evidence than–' he gestured at the newspaper clippings. '–*this.*'

'And something Alex said made ap
Morgan suspicious so he had to be disposed
of. Is that it?'

'Something like that. The problem is that, as we both know, policemen make damn good murderers and we have no proof that Lomax left Newbury on Tuesday night.'

Or at all.

Chapter Nineteen

Nicolaides was working his way methodically through the dead man's car – a nondescript little hatchback with a surprisingly large engine.

'Looks customised,' he remarked when Greg came to see how he was getting on. 'Blends into the crowd but you could probably do 120 in it.'

'Not on my patch!' Greg said.

'Looks like it was his own private litter bin,' the constable went on.

Greg peered at the collection of food wrappers, fizzy drink cans and chocolate papers that Nicolaides had dutifully gathered into a transparent bag in case they proved crucial evidence. There was half a tube of Pringles: God's own snack. He had seen cars in this state before, used by undercover police officers who were on surveillance and couldn't leave the vehicle, even for a minute. Chocolate and fizzy drinks provided easy energy and pot bellies.

Nicolaides had just extracted a bottle of yellow liquid from under the back seat and was looking at it doubtfully.

'Lucozade?' Greg suggested, more in hope

than expectation.

The constable unscrewed the top and sniffed gingerly, then recoiled.

''Fraid not!'

'So he spent a lot of time on observation,' Greg said, 'but observing what?' Or whom? The digital photos on his laptop had all been to do with Scobie but that didn't make the little man his only quarry.

'Map,' Nicolaides commented, rifling through the glove compartment. 'Ordnance Survey 174 – Newbury and Wantage.'

'Let's have a look.' Greg held out his hand for the map. He unfolded it, spreading his arms wide to take the big sheet in. It bore no marks except for a thick black cross over the L of Lambourn.

'You're from London, Geo – Nick?' he queried.

'North London,' he admitted.

'How well do you know the east – Docklands?'

'A bit.'

'Well, you're the best we've got. Get up there, take a look at the victim's flat. Bring back his computer and answering machine, his post, any diaries or personal papers–' Nicolaides was looking impatient, with the face of a grandmother being taught to suck eggs, and Greg conceded, 'You know the ropes. Babs has the address and the keys.'

'It'll take me best part of the day,'

Nicolaides said. 'Two hours to get there, minimum, two to come back, what with Friday night traffic leaving town–'

'Then the sooner you leave...' Greg said.

An hour later Greg was back in his office and, within minutes, he got a call from Sergeant Vikram Mistri at the front desk. 'Young lady asking to speak to the officer in charge of the murder investigation,' he reported.

'That would be me,' Greg conceded.

'Says her name's Sarah Keaton.'

'You sound as if you don't believe her,' Greg commented.

The sergeant hesitated audibly, then lowered his voice. 'If I didn't know it was impossible, sir, I'd say she was Devon Bliss.'

Greg saw what he meant as soon as he reached the bottom of the stairs. He stood for a moment covertly watching the woman who was standing reading the notices on the wall, leaning forward slightly to balance on stiletto heels, her face in profile, the sergeant still watching her avidly as though shell shocked.

As he approached her, he saw that the resemblance, though more than superficial, had been cultivated. She was much the same height as the dead newsreader, perhaps a little more muscular in build. Her

268

blonde hair had been cut to hang about her shoulders in the style favoured by Devon and her short-skirted black suit over a cream silk T-shirt was the sort of thing the dead woman had worn for her TV appearances.

'Miss Keaton?' She turned and he saw that her eyes were the same brilliant blue that had looked out from television screens across the country and hooked the viewer to the evening headlines. 'Superintendent Gregory Summers,' he said, offering his hand. 'I believe you have some information about the murder of Reuben ap Morgan.'

'I don't know how much help I can be,' she said, her voice low-pitched and musical, 'but I was coming to Berkshire today to meet Morgan – that's what I always called him. When I'm not working, I like to go cold turkey on news so it wasn't till I got to the airport this morning and saw the front page of the *Outlook* that I learned of his death. I boarded the Heathrow shuttle in a sort of daze and, when I'd collected my thoughts, I decided to come straight here.'

He ushered her into an interview room and offered her coffee, which she declined.

'Very wise,' he said, and drew up a chair for her. At close quarters he could see that she was older than Devon – about ap Morgan's own age of thirty-seven, if he was any judge. She took her jacket off and hung it over the back of the chair, gave Greg a rueful look and said, 'I still can't believe he's dead. We go back a long way, Morgan and I.'

He sat down opposite her. 'May I ask how you came to know him? From your reference to news I assume you're a journalist too.'

'We were colleagues,' she said, 'back in Wales a good fifteen years ago when he was plain Reuben Morgan. I know I don't sound Welsh – got rid of the accent a long time ago so people didn't think I was straight out of the pits. We were trainees together on the *Aberystwyth Star* – cub reporters who could have been rivals but decided to be friends instead, watch each other's backs – only I didn't stay long. Sexism still ruled the roost in local papers in the mid-eighties and I was stuck with flower shows and weddings when I wanted to get my teeth into something stronger, so I quit after a year and moved to Hounslow, made my way up on local papers in West London, then two years on the London *Standard*. I've been deputy editor of *Voice of Scotland* for the last five years.'

'But you kept in touch?'

'Not much at first, with so much distance between us. We'd meet up for a drink when I went home to see my family. But when Morgan moved to London to work on the *Outlook*, he gave me a call and I introduced him to the fleshpots of the capital.'

'Were you and he...?'

'Lovers?' She laughed. 'I'm gay.' Seeing his shock she added, 'We're not all crop-haired dykes in dungarees, Mr Summers.'

'Some of my best friends are gay... Really,' he added, though she had not queried the statement. He cleared his throat. 'So, you were due to meet Mr ap Morgan today.'

'He rang me about ten days ago and asked if I could take some leave and fly down from Edinburgh. He said he had a plan which could make both our names and fortunes. He also told me it might be dangerous, knowing that was a sure way to get my interest. He asked me to dig out a good photograph and make myself look as much like Devon Bliss as possible.'

'You obviously had quite a lot to work with,' Greg said.

'People had commented on a facial resemblance from time to time, despite a difference in colouring. So I bought a blonde wig, which reminds me–' She tore her corn-coloured mane off, startling Greg. Her real hair was short, dark, curly and she was instantly a different woman. 'God, those things make your head hot. I got some blue contact lenses fitted and shopped for the newsreader-totty outfit.' She indicated her suit. 'Have you noticed how all female newsreaders dress the same?'

'As do all male newsreaders,' he said.

'Good point!' She grinned at him. Her

smile was lopsided and very endearing. 'I got some odd looks on the shuttle down this morning.'

'So did Mr ap Morgan explain what his plan was?' he asked.

'He said that he'd fill me in on the details when he met me at Heathrow this morning ... but it seems,' she said slowly, 'that I was to be bait in a trap, for the man Graham Scobie.'

Greg drew in a sharp breath. 'That could be very dangerous!'

'That was what I was promised,' she reminded him. 'Morgan was convinced that Scobie's acquittal was a mistake and that the man was a psychopath. He figured if he was confronted with the ghost of the woman he'd murdered, he'd be pushed over the edge and would either break down and confess or try to kill again.'

'You were going to haunt him?' Greg queried.

'Not literally. I was going to turn up on his doorstep pretending to do some kind of market research – whatever – flick my hair the way Devon always did at the end of the news.' She demonstrated with the wig she was holding. 'Then, whenever he went out, I'd be there, walking by in the distance, popping my head round the door, till he started to wonder if I was real or some ghastly phantom.'

'Sounds like a bad production of *Hamlet*,' Greg commented.

'Ah! "The play's the thing wherein I'll catch the conscience of the king." Very astute, Superintendent.' She paused and sucked in a deep breath. 'Please tell me that it wasn't this crazy plan of Morgan's that got him killed otherwise I shall be wishing till my own dying day that I hadn't agreed to play along.'

'I don't know, Miss Keaton. I wish I did.'

'Oh, and one more thing. Morgan rang me on...' She thought hard. 'It must have been Tuesday, to say there'd been a slight change of plan in that he had two men he wanted to spring me on – two *obsessed* men. Does that make any sense to you?'

'Not at the moment,' Greg lied.

'Well, thank you for coming forward, Miss Keaton,' Greg said as he walked her out of the station. 'Not everyone does.' He was still smiling at the look on Vik Mistri's face when he had emerged from the interview room with a brunette instead of a blonde.

'I cover crime in Edinburgh,' she said with a shrug. 'I know a lot of cops locally and I understand the importance of getting a full picture.' She paused on the front doorstep, her face grim. 'I shall miss Morgan. We were on the same wavelength... It hasn't quite sunk in yet.'

'No. It takes a while.'

'I don't suppose there's a chance of seeing the body?'

'Not at the moment. Perhaps if you come to the funeral...'

'We should have more open caskets in this country,' she remarked. 'In the States everybody expects to get a good look at the deceased. Here we shut them up in a box like a shameful secret.' Her shoulders drooped. 'I must phone Tecwyn and Rebecca ... or maybe I'll write.'

'You're all right to get back to Heathrow?' he asked.

'I hired a car for the day.' She gestured across the roundabout. 'Left it at the supermarket.' She shook hands with him again. 'I'm sorry I didn't get the chance to be the ghost of Devon Bliss but I'll be glad to get out of these high heels and the lenses are starting to make my eyes water. Well, you have my number.'

'I'll be in touch if I have any more questions.'

Interesting, he thought as he walked slowly back up the stairs to his office, but he didn't see what it had to do with the murder. If Reuben had been killed after Sarah Keaton's impersonation of the dead woman, then it might point the finger at Scobie, but the journalist's plan had never got off the ground.

Still, the full picture, as she had said. That was the trouble with murder investigations – you had to sift through so much chaff to find the wheat. Eliminate the impossible and leave only the unlikely.

He rang the *Voice of Scotland* to check that Sarah Keaton was who she said she was.

She was.

'And did she really look like Devon Bliss?' Barbara asked curiously.

'Not up close, maybe, but not a bad impersonation. I suspect a lot of it is how you carry yourself. Women like Devon walk with confidence. They hold their heads high. They expect to be looked at and admired and so, I think, does Sarah Keaton.'

'And Reuben wanted to spring her on *two* obsessed men. There doesn't seem much doubt who the second one was.'

'Lomax. So Reuben was definitely suspicious of him.'

'Enough for Alex to kill him?' Barbara asked.

'I wish I knew. Anything new at your end?'

'The usual leg work,' she said. 'I've got Andy back from Lambourn now we've got all the witness statements and we're working on the dead man's laptop and mobile phone.'

'Then don't let me keep you.'

Sarah Keaton sat in the domestic departure lounge at Heathrow's Terminal One waiting for the Edinburgh shuttle to be called. She had changed into a pair of plimsolls which sat oddly with her suit. She was drinking a large espresso and pretending to read a magazine when her mobile phone rang.

Glancing at the display, she saw the word MORGAN. Trembling she pressed the button to answer.

'Morgan! I knew it must be a mistake. They told me you were DEAD.' The last word came out in a shout as she struggled with her emotions.

'...Sorry, madam. I'm Detective Constable Whittaker of Newbury CID. Your number was programmed into the mobile phone of a Mr Reuben ap Morgan and–'

He talked on but Sarah had stopped listening. She let the handset fall in her lap and closed her eyes to choke back the sobs. Morgan's plan might well have worked, she thought through her anguish: there was nothing like a ghost to shake you up.

The phone in her lap was squawking at her. 'Madam? Are you there?'

She picked it up, composed herself and said, 'I've already made a statement to your superintendent so I suggest you talk to him.' She disconnected and switched the mobile off.

She felt badly shaken. Morgan's death was suddenly real to her. She abandoned her coffee and went in search of the bar.

'That was odd,' Andy said as Barbara came into the CID room.

'What was?'

'Woman in the dead man's address book, under Keaton. She says she's already spoken to the super.'

'Oh, yes. That's right.'

'Well, someone might have told me,' Andy protested. 'I felt stupid and she was clearly upset.'

'I was just going to tell you,' Barbara said. 'Your trouble is that you work too fast and efficiently.' Andy grinned, mollified, and she explained about Sarah Keaton.

'Bizarre,' was his only comment. 'Okay. I've been through all the numbers now but half of them are switched off. I'll keep trying.'

'Nothing useful?'

Andy leaned back and stretched. He yawned widely, then sneezed without warning, making Barbara jump backwards. 'Sorry, Sarge. Family, friends, a few work contacts. Only his mother and one of his sisters even knew he was in Berkshire.'

Barbara leaned over the laptop, scrolling through a list of files, the filenames mostly truncated to the point of being cryptic, like a deeply obscure text message. Like most people, ap Morgan had not been keen on housekeeping and the list included at least ten files that began with 'temp'. One was labelled Scobie, however, and she called over to Andy. 'You read this Scobie file yet?'

'I've printed it out; seems to be some sort of journal only it isn't easy to read. I was going to have a proper go at it as soon as I'd reached the end of his address book.' He handed her a dozen sheets of A4 paper. 'Be my guest.'

Barbara sat down at her desk and began to read, or rather decipher since the reporter used a form of shorthand of his own devising which involved leaving out letters more or less at random. Reuben had been keeping a close eye on his quarry, she deduced, a job made more difficult by the fact that Scobie didn't have transport unless you counted a bike. Given the infrequency of country bus services and the fear of being recognised, Reuben had lost sight of the little man on more than one occasion.

Following him on foot was easier, although once again he had been forced to keep his distance. According to the times and dates listed since Reuben's arrival in Lambourn on August 6th, Scobie had been exploring the Berkshire countryside at his leisure.

'Mon Aug 12,' Barbara read aloud. 'Pol to

S 7pm. 2m. Injrd hrse? Hlf hr. S phn bx. LNR. Intrstng.'

Andy got up and came to read over her shoulder. 'Police to Scobie, obviously,' she said, pointing. '2m ... 2 miles?'

'Two men – the super and Nick.'

'Right! Then he conjectures that they were talking to him about Lady India's horse, which they were. They stayed half an hour–'

'And then Scobie went out to the phone box,' Andy said.

'LNR?'

They looked at each other for a moment, thinking hard. Finally Andy said triumphantly, 'Last number redial!'

Barbara sat up straight. 'Good boy! He did last number redial to see who Scobie had phoned and he found the answer interesting.' She slammed her fist on the desk. 'You're starting to annoy me, Reuben ap Morgan. Why do you have to be so bloody circumspect? Why can't you just tell me who he called? Don't you want me to find your murderer?'

'They're a cagey lot, these journalists.'

'How many phone boxes are there in Eastbury?'

'This is the bit where I say "How the hell should I know?" and you say "Well, bloody well find out", isn't it, Sarge?'

'Yes, though without the unladylike swearing. And then I say, "Get on to Telecom and find out what numbers were called from that box on Monday evening".'

While Andy set about this task Barbara read on. On the same date, Reuben had written, 'Trv Sal JF 9.30. Wldnt tlk.' Jolly Fisherman, that was simple enough, but who had he met there? A travelling salesman? That made little sense; it must be a code name.

'Is there a number in the address book of his mobile for "Travelling Salesman", or some contraction of that?' she asked.

'One for TS. I tried it and it's dead so I assumed it was an old one he'd forgotten to erase.'

'Did you make a note of the number.'

'It's on this list.'

Barbara read it and recognised it. 'Okay.' She put the sheaf of papers in her briefcase and went to consult Gregory Summers.

Chapter Twenty

'The Travelling Salesman is Alex Lomax,' Barbara said.

'Why would he call him that?'

'We'll ask the DCI when we catch up with him, but he's the only person known to have been drinking with Reuben in the Fisherman and his mobile number is programmed into the dead man's phone under TS.'

'So, assuming for a moment you're right, what wouldn't Lomax talk to him about?'

'His reasons for coming here perhaps. Look, sir. The next entry.'

'11,' Greg read. 'Rvr-wds. S mtng. Cntrct. Bglry gn wr.'

'So on Monday, Scobie met someone at night in the woods down by the river, presumably the Lambourn.'

'Cntrct – is that contract?'

'I imagine so.' She scrutinised the next few letters. 'Nope. Leave that for the moment. Could it possibly be Alex that Scobie phoned that evening and Alex he arranged to meet?'

'Who would Lomax want to take out a contract on?'

'Er … Scobie?'

'So he asked Scobie to kill himself for money; that certainly has novelty value. And, even if you allow that Scobie did murder Devon Bliss – and I'm starting to have my doubts about that – there was never any suggestion that he was a professional, a hitman.'

'All right. Leave that for a moment.'

'Maybe it isn't contract.'

'Yes it is, though, because I've just figured out the next bit – it reads "burglary gone wrong".'

'Now I remember why I never send text messages,' Greg grumbled. '...So, ap Morgan followed them and overheard their conversation,' he said slowly, 'in the very place where he subsequently met his death.'

'Whoever Scobie met there used it regularly as a meeting place.'

'Or Scobie did.'

And there had still been no sightings of Alex Lomax.

Ironically, it was Lomax's own press cuttings that allowed Greg to look back over the murder of Devon Bliss and he settled at his desk with a pot of coffee to do just that. The papers were in no particular order and he sorted them by date then located the first report of the murder – the London *Standard* of March 9th in the previous year, an evening paper stealing a march on its morning rivals.

Devon had spent the previous evening at an awards dinner at which she'd been proclaimed news presenter of the year. She'd been photographed arriving, looking ecstatically happy in what were to prove the last hours of her life.

She was wearing a black strapless dress, long but slit up to the thigh on one side. Dizzyingly high heels rendered her a good two inches taller than her escort, identified by the unlikely name of Bailey Todd, aged twenty-two. Greg had never heard of him but it seemed that he was the lead singer for a recently manufactured pop group whose debut single and album had both gone into the charts at number one.

Young, he thought, for Devon Bliss, since the paper mentioned in passing that March 8th was also her thirtieth birthday. He read on. The couple had left the dinner shortly before midnight and Devon's limo had dropped Todd off at his Docklands penthouse before driving the young woman on to Blackheath. The chauffeur was the last man who admitted having seen her alive, saying in his statement to police that he had watched her safely into her house at twelve-thirty before driving home.

It was clear by the next morning's *Telegraph* that neither he nor Todd were serious suspects. In the margin, next to a head-and-shoulders picture of the young singer, Lomax had scrawled 'Faggot'.

Greg assumed this was not his shopping list.

He picked up the phone and rang his own home number. Angie took some time to answer and he was about to give up and try her mobile when she snatched up the receiver, sounding out of breath.

'I was up a ladder,' she explained.

This raised more questions than it answered. Perhaps she was making a start on the outside painting. He said, 'Have you heard of someone called Bailey Todd?'

''Course,' she said. 'He's the lead singer with Jaundice – bit of a teeny-bopper heart-throb for a while.'

Greg refrained from saying that Jaundice was a stupid name for a band in case it made him sound old. Instead he said, 'But not any more?'

'He came out a year or so back. Let me think... Yeah, he'd been escorting some woman newsreader – can't think of her name – and she got herself murdered and people started to whisper that he was involved so his agent put out a press release saying that he was gay and had just been acting as her escort. What *was* her name?'

'Thanks, Angel,' he said.

'*Niente.*' She hung up. She had been practising her Italian for the holiday; if he had to cancel he would spend the rest of his life grovelling. What she had told him explained Lomax's scrawl and the fact that Todd had been rapidly dismissed from the enquiry.

Little more than a year on and Angie couldn't remember Devon's name: *sic transit gloria mundi*. He read on.

The french windows leading from Devon's sitting room into the garden had been open when the police arrived, but there was no sign that they had been forced or that the murderer had entered the house. The pathologist gave the time of death as between midnight and four a.m. so the chances were that she had gone out into the garden of her own accord not long after she got home.

Why would she do that in the middle of the night, he wondered? She might have been hyped up after her triumph at the awards dinner, unable to sleep and gone out for some air. She might have seen an intruder in the garden and gone out to confront him; if so, she had been brave to the point of recklessness, but then her father, speaking from her family home in Bishop's Nympton, described her as 'plucky', a word Greg hadn't heard for decades and which could use a revival.

But what if the man tapping on the french windows hadn't been a stranger? What if it had been an old friend, someone she had known all her life, her 'Uncle Alex' from Bishop's Nympton?

He slammed the file of cuttings shut and went to see Jim Barkiss.

Barkiss sat unhappily twiddling his thumbs together across his belly, as if hoping to discover the secret of perpetual motion.

'There has to be some simple explanation,' he said.

'So people keep telling me,' Greg snapped, 'but what no one can tell me is what it is.'

'I don't like putting out a statement saying we want to interview one of our own officers in connection with a murder. How would it look? Let's issue his photo and say he's missing, possibly amnesiac, and ask for sightings. The chances are he just got deflected on his way down to Devon and will come forward, wondering what all the fuss is about.'

'He may be a killer,' Greg objected. 'He may have killed twice. Are you prepared to take responsibility if he harms a member of the public who accosts him? Because I'm not.'

'Okay!' Barkiss stopped twiddling and leaned forward. 'Give his details to the press. Don't say anything about him being wanted for questioning, just that he's missing, possibly ill. But tell the public not to approach him, to report any sightings to their local police station. Fair enough?'

'I'll get right on it,' Greg said, and went back to his office. By the time he had done the necessary, Barbara had come to find him with some new information.

'Are you sure about this?' Greg asked.

'I'm sure that this is the nearest phone box to Scobie's lodgings,' Barbara said, running her finger down a list of telephone numbers, 'on the main road on the corner of Down's Close. I'm sure that Reuben ap Morgan wrote in his journal that Scobie went out to a phone box after his interview with you on Monday night, say, around seven-thirty or eight o'clock.'

Her finger stopped at a call made at six minutes to eight that evening and another to the same number seven minutes later. 'And I'm sure that this is the number of Ascot House in Lambourn, line rental in the name of India Hathaway. Otherwise, no, not sure at all.'

'You've done a good job, Babs.'

'Andy did the leg work,' she said fairly. When Greg didn't speak, she added, 'Should I pay her a visit, sir?'

'She's away at the moment.' He got up. 'I shall go and speak to her husband.'

'You're keeping this Hathaway business very close to your chest,' she commented, her voice carefully neutral.

He laughed. 'You may come with me, if you like, Babs, to prove that I'm not up to anything sinister.'

He introduced Barbara to Hathaway in the hall at Ascot House half an hour later and the barrister shook her hand vigorously. After both police officers had refused offers of refreshment, Sir John said, 'So, what can I do for you, Mr Summers?'

'I wondered if you'd heard any more from Scobie, Sir John?'

'*Heard?* You don't mean this business with Indie's horse?'

'I was thinking more of phone calls.'

'Oh, no. At least he's not been pestering me that way.'

'Are you sure?' Barbara asked. 'No silent calls, even – you answer and nobody speaks.'

'Oh!' Sir John ran his hand through his silvering hair. 'There are always hang-ups, of course. Some people say it's burglars ringing up to see if you're in but that seems a bit cackhanded to me. I always assume it's a wrong number and the caller's too ill-mannered to apologise.'

'And have you had any such calls lately?' Greg asked. 'Say, Monday evening.'

'Let me think,' Hathaway said. He turned away, his mind moving swiftly. 'Monday... Do you know, I believe I did. I remember because I got two in quick succession but then they do seem to come in clusters.' He wheeled round to face them again. 'Have you noticed that?'

'Actually, yes,' Greg said.

'What time were these calls?' Barbara asked.

'Mid-evening. I don't think I can be more precise than that. Sorry.'

Barbara was nothing if not persevering. 'Say, eightish?'

'Something like that. Is it important?'

'Something and nothing,' Greg said. 'Sorry to disturb you.' He grabbed Barbara's arm and steered her bodily out of the house.

'He's lying!' she said when they were safely back in the car.

'Why would he?'

'How should I know?'

'It all fits perfectly. Creepy little Scobie rang him up, then hung up when he answered. Probably does it all the time. Maybe he was hoping to get Lady India so he could do a bit of heavy breathing.'

Barbara examined her print-out again. 'Well, he did a fair bit of breathing for Sir John then, because the call lasted over two minutes.'

'Let me see.' Barbara passed it over and he saw that she was right. 'The other call lasted literally seconds,' he mused.

'Ap Morgan, doing last number redial to see who Scobie had called then hanging up.

That takes just a few seconds. I think we should go right back in, sir, have another go at him.'

'Leave it.' Greg fastened his seat belt. 'Let him stew for a day or two.'

'Because he's a VIP?'

'Don't you start! No, because he's a highly intelligent man who's not going to be lightly shaken from his story.'

'What if it was him Scobie met that night when ap Morgan tailed him? What if he's employed Scobie for a contract?'

'On whom?'

'His wife?'

'No!'

'Why not?'

'Because ... she's not the sort of wife a man has killed, that's why not.' Not even if he was having an affair with an ethereally beautiful young jockey.

Barbara gave him an odd look. 'As I understand it, she's rich and middle-aged.'

'Yes,' he conceded, 'but–'

'Which is *precisely* the sort of wife a man has killed in my experience, and tomorrow could be too late.'

'Lady India is away at the moment. In Somerset.'

'So he's contracted Scobie to kill her down there. So much the better as he'll be miles away.'

Greg shook his head. 'No way. Look, let

290

him think he's got away with his lie, then we'll steam back in tomorrow.'

'But, sir–'

'That's my last word on the subject, Sergeant.'

'Yes, sir.'

'Sir John Hathaway QC is not going anywhere tonight.'

They drove back to Newbury in silence and Greg realised that she was sulking. He said, 'Trust me on this, Babs.'

'It's just that you've played this Hathaway business very close to your chest from the start, sir, and that looks odd.'

'I know it does, but there are complications I can't tell you about.' He felt a surge of renewed resentment for Patterson and the secrets he generated – secrets that Greg had to keep from the people he trusted most, Angie and Barbara. He said, 'We've worked together for a long time and I hope that you have confidence in me.'

'Of course I do.'

'No way is John Hathaway arranging a hit on his wife. Now, I want you to take the evening off. Call up one of your boyfriends and go dancing–'

'*Dancing?*'

'Out to dinner, whatever. Switch off your mobile. I'll tell uniform to contact me if there's an emergency tonight.'

'Just run it past me one more time,' Barkiss said.

'Ap Morgan was a journalist. Who in Lambourn has most reason to fear being recognised by a news reporter?' When the Chief Super didn't answer Greg supplied, 'Ian Callaghan, that's who.'

'Michael Patterson. Possibly.'

'He got in a blind panic when he realised I knew who he was. You should have seen–'

'You told him!' Barkiss said sharply.

'He realised,' Greg repeated. 'I suppose ... my body language.'

'For God's sake! This isn't like you, Gregory. You're a senior and highly experienced police officer who's dealt with some complete bastards in your time and you're reacting to this boy like a callow rookie. Get a grip.'

Greg felt embarrassed because he valued Jim Barkiss's good opinion and he knew that the Chief Super was right: he had been getting the young man's presence on his patch out of all proportion. He changed the subject. 'You said yourself that if the press started sniffing round Lambourn it could be a disaster.'

'I don't know, Gregory, it's not five minutes since you were trying to tell me that DCI Lomax was behind this murder. We seem to be going eeny-meeny-miney-mo at the moment.'

'The truth is that I don't know yet who committed the crime,' Greg said in mild exasperation. 'If I did then I wouldn't be sitting here arguing with you, Jim. I'd have made an arrest. The fact is that I can't think of anyone with a better motive than Patterson and I need to bring him in for questioning—'

'Oh, no!' Barkiss interrupted. 'If you talk to him at all, it'll be in his own home. Lambourn is crawling with news crews and I will not have them filming Patterson being led off in a police car.'

'All right. I'll see him at home, if only to check his alibi.'

Barkiss was thoughtful. 'Maybe it would be better if I did it.'

Greg raised his eyebrows. 'I can't think of anything more likely to set alarm bells off than the station's Chief Super going out in person to interview suspects. And what will our colleagues make of it? My team aren't stupid – they're going to start putting the same two and two together that I did and getting the same answer.'

'Good point,' Barkiss conceded. 'But keep it low key.'

Patterson was even more wary about opening the door than the last time Greg had called. There was no sign on this occasion that he was working. The television was on with the sound turned low. On the screen, overweight and badly-dressed people were trying to tear each other's hair out, while being held apart by bouncers as the audience whooped and screamed encouragement. A subtitle at the bottom of the screen read 'I had a lesbian affair with my mother-in-law'.

'I daren't go out,' Michael explained, clicking off the TV. 'I've called all my clients and said I'm sick.'

He did indeed look ill and Greg felt a tinge of pity for him until he remembered those two baby girls, sleeping helplessly in their cot in the last few minutes of their lives. 'Where were you Wednesday night?' he asked abruptly, 'between the hours of, say, ten p.m. and four a.m?'

Patterson didn't even think about it. 'Here.'

'Alone?'

'Actually, no.' His putty-coloured face acquired a blush of pink. 'Grey was here.'

'All night?'

'All night.'

'I thought she usually went back to the stables.'

'She does, or did. The attack on Lady India's horse has shaken her badly and she doesn't want to be alone at night.'

'So, if I ask her, she will confirm your alibi?'

Patterson hesitated. 'May I ask exactly what I need an alibi for?'

'You know why all these press people are in Lambourn?'

'Because a man was murdered yesterday. You think I had something to do with it?'

'He was a journalist,' Greg said.

Patterson looked shaken. 'I didn't know that. I don't actually know who he was.'

'His name was Reuben ap Morgan and he was staying at the Jolly Fisherman.'

Patterson took a sharp breath. 'Him!'

'You knew him?'

'We'd met ... at the pub. I do the books there.' He sat down slowly on the sofa. 'I didn't realise it was *him*.'

'So? If I go up to the stables now and talk to Miss Rutherford, will she give you an alibi?'

'Yes, but she will wonder why I – in particular – need one.'

'That's your problem.'

'Yes.' Patterson took a deep breath. 'I suppose it is. You won't find her at the stables tonight, however. She's overnighting at Uttoxeter with one of her horses.'

'Then I'll see what she has to say tomorrow,' Greg said coldly, and left. Back in the car he rang Nash's stables. Mrs Nash confirmed that Paddy and Grace were at an evening meet in Staffordshire, a hundred and twenty-five miles away, and would not return till late tomorrow.

She gave him Nash's mobile number but when he tried it, it was switched off.

Was it possible that Barbara was right? Greg sat brooding at his desk, clicking back and forth the irritating executive toy that his son Fred had given him for his last birthday before the boy's death.

He ran a scenario over in his mind. John Hathaway had become infatuated with Grace Rutherford and had decided to do away with his wife. He would hardly be the first middle-aged man to lose his head over a girl half his age and Greg should know. Yes, divorce was easy these days but it could be expensive.

So a campaign of harassment had begun, directed against India. Clever of Hathaway to claim that he was the target and dismiss the idea that it might be his wife, but then he was clever. And nobody had a better opportunity to cripple Ranulf's Daughter than Grace.

And then Scobie, who might have killed once already and got away with it, who proclaimed loudly that he would do anything for Hathaway, was employed to dispose of India in a 'burglary gone wrong'.

At Ascot House? At Nethermore Hall? The former, surely, since that was where the pattern of harassment had been carefully laid. Which meant that, so long as India stayed in Somerset, then she was in no danger. Didn't it?

No! He slammed the clacking silver balls quiet with his fist. He was sure in his bones that Callaghan was behind this murder; once a killer, always a killer. Only now he was taking a step back, employing a middle man to dispose of somebody he considered a threat. Maybe a policeman who had recently recognised him.

He made a mental note to double check all his doors and windows before he went to bed tonight.

'Here look at this!'

Joy Reynolds sat up straight on the sofa as she watched the early evening news. Her husband looked up and grunted. They had decided to keep the pub shut for another day while they recovered from the strain of the police investigation and, though Eric had gone back to his decorating project, his heart didn't seem to be in it.

'What?' he asked.

'It's that bloke started coming in the pub last week, talking to Reuben. Al his name is.'

She turned the sound up and they both listened in silence as the newsreader asked members of the public to contact the police if they saw the man pictured – a senior police officer named Alexander Lomax who had been missing for three days and might be ill or injured. Details of his car followed, along with the route that he ought to have taken from Newbury to Tiverton.

'What do you make of that?' Joy asked.

'Never said he was a copper. Did you know he was a copper?'

'No.' As her husband got up she said, 'Eric?'

He muttered, ''Nother coat of gloss,' and left the room. She turned the sound down again.

Chapter Twenty-One

John Hathaway was making the most of his unaccustomed bachelor time. Much as he loved Indie and Olivia, for an intelligent man there was nothing to rival the pleasures of solitude, particularly when you had just disposed of two annoyingly tenacious police officers with some polite lies and a lot of juridical charm.

He knew that they had not believed him, or not completely, but it didn't matter. He had postponed further interrogation and in six hours time it would be too late.

He had married young and his cooking skills were basic. He decided to keep it simple that Friday night – a sirloin steak, medium rare with plenty of horseradish, a green salad, some fruit for pudding. Not exactly the condemned man ate a hearty dinner, he thought with a smile, but it was what he fancied.

Since the death penalty had been abolished thirty-five years ago, how rare it was for an Englishman to know the hour and the manner of his passing. He had never prosecuted a murderer knowing that a conviction would mean the gallows and was unsure if he would have been able to, glad that he had been spared that decision.

He went to the cupboard in the dining room where they kept their modest store of wine. This was one final luxury he would allow himself – a bottle of the thirty-five-year-old claret his father-in-law had laid down for them as a wedding present.

'It'll be drinkable only in thirty years time,' the old earl had told him, clapping him on the shoulder. 'See what faith I have in your and Indie's longevity, John.'

The Nethermores had welcomed him into their family, caring nothing for the three-bedroomed semi in a poor part of Manchester where he had his origins; for the fact that, if his ancestors had also come over with William the Conqueror, then no one had bothered to make a note of it. As Indie said so often, stuff like that didn't matter.

They had taken him at his own – very high – valuation and for a moment the memory of old Charlie Nethermore brought a tear to his eye, since he had loved the old man and everything he stood for. He had had a proper wine cellar at the house in Holland Park and Charlie would be turning in his grave to see how they kept his bottles now.

He and Indie had drunk the first bottle on their thirtieth wedding anniversary four years ago, and another each year since. He

300

carefully eased out the cork and poured the purple liquid into an elegant glass decanter, a wedding present they never used. It would need to breathe for a good hour, then he would drink three glasses.

No more, since he must keep his wits about him; no less, in case his courage failed.

He had 'put his affairs in order'. His will was up to date and his share certificates, pension and insurance documents were where they were supposed to be. It shouldn't look as if he had deliberately prepared for tonight, merely as if he was still the sensible and orderly man his family had known for three and a half decades.

Personal papers, including some love letters from India that he had cherished all these years, had been shredded beyond recognition and taken to the municipal tip, buried in a bag of domestic rubbish. He had resisted the temptation to reread the letters, knowing that the pain would outweigh the pleasure.

At seven-thirty he switched on Radio Three to get the live broadcast from the Proms at the Royal Albert Hall. It started with Strauss's *Don Quixote*, not a work with which he was familiar. During the interval he lit the grill and began to pick over the mixed leaves he had washed earlier while it heated up. He grilled steak and tossed salad to a background of Dvorak's *Symphony from the New World,* wishing that the last music he heard on earth might have been something less commonplace, or at least something that didn't remind him of a television advertisement for cheap brown bread.

He took his meal through to the dining room to eat in style. He dug out the good linen napkins and the best cutlery and glassware. Why did they have these things when they never used them?

The concert had ended by the time he had eaten his last dish of raspberries with fresh cream and he clicked off the radio, leaving the house in silence. He left his dirty plates in the kitchen sink, absolving himself of the duty of washing them up, and took his third and final glass of claret into his study. There he plucked a battered copy of *Great Expectations* from the shelf and sat down to read.

When, as a trainee barrister, he had been in the habit of reading aloud to himself each evening, the better to prepare his speaking voice for court, this book had been among his favourites. Family life gave little opportunity for indulging this solitary pleasure as your loved ones merely thought that you were talking to yourself and gave you odd looks. In the early days of their love, he had tried to persuade India that they might read to each other – such an intimate communion, to his mind – but she was a down-to-earth woman who preferred horses and dogs and gardening to literature. Her delivery was hesitant and flat and he had soon given up the fight. Now he gave full voice, letting the vowels and consonants of the opening passage roar forth from his mouth like a rotund army.

My father's family name being Pirrip, and my Christian name Philip, my infant tongue could make of both names nothing longer or more explicit than Pip. So, I called myself Pip, and came to be called Pip.

You couldn't start a book like that any more, he mused, modern readers did not have the patience. You had to jump into the action, preferably with bullets and car chases and explicit sex, and fill in the background as you went along. That must be why he never read contemporary novels.

By half past eleven he had read twenty-seven chapters and laid the book aside without regret. He knew how it ended.

He knew how all lives ended.

He had not drawn the curtains and stood looking out of the sitting room window for a while. No cars passed along the lonely lane. The gate to the drive stood open where Indie had driven out a couple of days ago; he had not bothered to shut it. It was a warm and clear night and he could see the stars displayed against the inky blueness. All those years in London, he thought, where the night sky was barely visible for the streetlights, when he might have been here.

He had satisfied the senses of taste and smell tonight, of sight and hearing. Only touch was absent and he felt a deep seam of misery inside him at the thought that he would never again feel India's soft hands and lips on his body.

'Why me?' he murmured. 'Why me?'

He went out of the back door, wrapped a cheap scarf that he had bought a few days ago round his hand to protect the skin, and smashed a pane of glass just above the lock, hearing the shards tinkle onto the kitchen floor. He stood for a moment listening, in case anyone had heard, but there was nothing but the harsh voice of a rook in the neighbouring paddock. He checked that the door could now be opened from outside and went upstairs, moving slowly since his limbs seemed heavy, holding on to the balustrade.

He debated taking some more of his pills but they wouldn't mix well with alcohol and the headache was tolerable. He bathed and cut his toe nails. He cleaned his teeth, flossing carefully without knowing why he endured this familiar but hateful chore tonight. He changed into his pyjamas, belted his grey cashmere dressing gown tightly around his waist and put on his slippers. He switched out the light – if any car did pass it should look as if he had retired for the night – and sat on the edge of his bed in the darkness.

Waiting, listening. Trying not to think.

The clock in the hall had just struck midnight when he heard the back door open, its hinges left deliberately a little squeaky. Punctuality: a sterling quality. He stood up and inhaled a deep breath, before making his way downstairs.

He did not bother to be stealthy.

In the hall he snapped on the light and Scobie blinked at him owlishly, standing outside the door of his study.

'You're ready for bed,' he remarked.

'That's the theory,' Hathaway said patiently, 'I disturbed a burglar. Remember?'

The Glock pistol hung limply from the younger man's gloved hand. He looked at it without enthusiasm. 'I don't know if I can go through with this, John.'

'Of course you can.'

Scobie held the gun out to him. 'Why don't you just take it, do it yourself. It'll be over in a second.'

'I can't.' Hathaway didn't reach out for the gun but stuck his hands firmly in his pockets. 'If I could then I wouldn't have needed you. I haven't got the guts, Graham, which is why I asked you to do me this one last favour.'

'I don't know that *I* have – got the guts.'

'Don't even look. Point the gun at my chest and pull the trigger.'

'Chest?'

'Head then – whichever, though I'll be grateful if you can make it as clean and painless as possible.'

Scobie looked nervously round the octagonal hall, still putting it off. 'You want to do it here?'

Hathaway shrugged. 'It's as good a place as any.'

'Such a nice room.'

'They're *all* nice rooms.'

'Yes. Yes, I expect they are.'

'And there's no carpet here. It'll be easier to clean up the mess.' Hathaway felt that the conversation was becoming ridiculous, almost surreal. He stretched both arms wide to make a better target, an icon of crucifixion, and closed his eyes.

'Point and shoot, Graham. How hard can it be?'

Scobie took aim at Hathaway's chest since it was the bigger target. He turned the gun sideways in his hand, closed his own eyes, gritted his teeth and tightened his finger on the trigger, his whole body flinching backwards in denial of the act.

Hathaway sought for a final prayer but found none.

The front door creaked, causing both men

to open their eyes in alarm and astonishment. Neither of them had heard the car pull up outside.

Hathaway said, 'Indie!'

His wife stood there in the doorway, a brace of grouse dangling from her left hand, the feathers stiff with dried blood, the eyes staring beadily at the incomprehensible scene. Scobie took his finger off the trigger and began to gibber, a meaningless cacophony of explanation and ingratiation.

India stared at them both for less than a second. She dropped the grouse, removed the broken shotgun which she had slung over her shoulder, reached in the pocket of her breeches for a pellet, loaded it and took aim as the abruptly silenced Scobie stood staring at her, frozen into immobility. Hathaway, finally understanding what she meant to do, yelled, 'Indie! No!'

As the shotgun fired, Scobie crumpled, the pistol falling from his dead fingers and skittering away across the hall.

'No!' Hathaway ran to the flaccid body as it slumped to the floor, spattering blood from what was left of its face. 'Scobie!'

'Scobie!' India exclaimed. 'Is that who it is?'

Hathaway cradled the dead man in his arms, sobbing hysterically.

'So you were right,' India said. 'He *was* threatening you.'

'This wasn't how it was meant to be.'

She took one look at her husband's face and said, 'Johnny, what in God's name have you done?'

Chapter Twenty-Two

'I got the diagnosis on the day the jury acquitted Scobie,' Hathaway began. 'I'd been having headaches since before Christmas, and I never get headaches – any stress goes straight to the stomach, always has.'

Greg, dragged from his bed at one o'clock in the morning, stifled a yawn. He certainly wasn't bored, merely too old for late nights. Groping for the phone by his bed an hour ago with muttered curses, hearing the measured voice of the uniformed inspector reporting a violent death at Ascot House in Lambourn, he had felt for a moment as if his blood had frozen. The immediate assumption – that the victim was India, that he had failed her horribly – had been quickly dispelled, but not quite quickly enough. He had dressed in a daze, aware all the time of the traumatic throbbing of his heart.

India, shocked by the events of the last couple of hours, had been seen by a doctor and told to get a good night's sleep before she answered any questions. She was in a cell downstairs.

Her husband had sought and received no

such postponement. Now he sat in an interview room with Greg and a uniformed sergeant from the night shift who looked stunned at being asked to sit in as second interviewing officer on such a high-profile case and who had spoken only to confirm his name to the tape recorder.

Hathaway had refused the offer of a solicitor. He had forgotten more law than the average duty solicitor had learned and he was being interviewed as a witness, not a suspect. So why did Greg feel as if what he was listening to was a confession? He let the man talk on, choosing his own path to explanation of the night's traumas, however irrelevant it might seem.

'So in late February,' he continued, 'I finally went to my GP and he sent me to a specialist in Weymouth Street, man called Frobisher. He arranged some tests and during the last week of the Bliss trial he'd been leaving increasingly urgent messages on my voice mail asking me to get in touch as soon as possible, but I'd been too wrapped up in work to respond. There was another when I got back to the disrobing room on March 8th. I'd been in court solidly for weeks and at that moment I just wanted to get away from the Bailey, so instead of ringing him, I hopped in a cab.

'He didn't keep me waiting about – that should have forewarned me, I suppose, but somehow it didn't. What he told me came as a complete and utter shock, the second I'd had that day. It was a brain tumour. It was inoperable. I was going to die within months. He wasn't quite that blunt, of course, he broke it gently, but the bomb was still the same however pretty the wrapping paper.

'I walked the streets of London for hours in a sort of daze, gradually making my way back to my chambers in Middle Temple. It was raining, I remember, though not heavily. I looked at everything with new eyes – the colourful window displays in the shops, the endless array of people in all different shapes, sizes and colours, beautiful and ugly, old and young – trying to get the concept of death into my mind, the nothingness of it, the absence of ... of *me* from the scene.'

He paused and Greg admired his eloquence. He had never witnessed Hathaway in action in court but he could see now how he had mesmerised the judge and jury.

'By the time I got to Chapel Court, I'd made my decision. No one was to know of my illness, not even Indie.' He laughed. 'I've just remembered a funny thing: I got a crank phone call – "Tell John Hathaway he's a dead man" – and I thought *How can he know?* I told my partner I was retiring – made out that it was something I'd resolved on months beforehand, not a spur-of-the-moment thing. I said my house in London

311

was up for sale and that we were moving permanently to Lambourn and by the next day that was true.'

'Didn't Lady India find all this a bit sudden?' Greg asked.

'Hmm?' Greg realised that Hathaway had forgotten he was there, absorbed in his own memories, in the simple flow of his words. 'Oh, she'd been urging me to take it easy for ages. She was thrilled to bits at the idea of seeing Ranulf's Daughter every day.' His face clouded over. 'Ranulf's Daughter. That was the hardest thing.'

There would be time to ask about that later. Greg needed to keep him going on a linear course. He prodded. 'So you determined on retiring to Lambourn?'

'Yes, because it was when I knew that I was dying that I knew what my course of action must be, how I must put Graham Scobie in prison, where he belonged, for a very long time.'

'I don't understand,' Greg said, feeling the sergeant stiffen with shock next to him. 'He was your client and you'd just used your best efforts to get him off. Why the sudden change of heart?'

Hathaway grimaced. 'I know how to mar a curious tale in the telling, as the Bard says. I've started too far in. I need to go back to that morning, to explain how all this came about.'

It dawned on Greg that he had not cautioned Hathaway since he'd been treating him as a witness, but if he did it now there was a danger that he would interrupt the flow and remind the man of the wisdom of silence. He kept quiet and let him talk on.

If the worst came to the worst he could argue that the barrister knew his rights as well as Greg did. At the moment, maintaining his limited right to silence seemed the last thing on his mind as he talked on.

'The jury had been out for days but the judge had told them late on Wednesday afternoon that he would take a majority verdict, so I was optimistic of a result that day. There's not much for a barrister to do while we're waiting for the jury to come back. Nor the defendant, come to that; he sits in his cell and frets. I went to visit Scobie at about half past ten. He seemed agitated. He's oddly passive, as a rule.

'He asked me if we would get a verdict that day and I said I thought we would. He said would it be the right verdict, and I told him that I was cautiously optimistic but that, if it went against us, we would launch an immediate appeal. I can see him so clearly in my mind's eye at that moment, hear his common little voice. He said, "She had to die, Sir John. She was too beautiful". I froze. I knew what I was hearing and I knew that I should walk out of the room before it was too late, but my legs wouldn't obey me.'

'He was confessing?'

Hathaway nodded. 'He said, "It was her thirtieth birthday last spring, Sir John, March 8th, a year ago today." That was true – I checked – I suppose it was the anniversary that set him off like that, *reminiscing*. I can remember his words exactly; they're etched on my brain. "I sent her a card, as usual, but I knew that it must be her last, that she must be preserved the way she was, in her prime – not the callowness of youth but the full bloom of womanhood."'

'Jesus!' Greg got up and opened a window. It was tiny, high up in the wall and it had bars across it but it was better than nothing on that sultry August night. Hathaway seemed to be speaking now with Scobie's flat London voice, as if the creepy little man possessed him. The sergeant shifted uncomfortably in his seat, then took out a handkerchief and wiped his forehead.

'He said, "She mustn't be allowed to decay, to wilt, to grow old. That would be wrong. It would be evil. She is like a rose that blooms for one perfect day, then dies." He said, "I saved her. You do understand, don't you, Sir John? I saved her."'

He resumed his own voice, to Greg's relief. 'I felt sick. I think I had to sit down and one of the warders fetched me a glass of

314

water and then someone came running to say the jury was back. I gathered my wits and made my way to the courtroom, praying to whatever God I believe in that the jury would find him guilty, but knowing in my heart that I had done too good a job, that I'd got him off with my silver tongue.'

He gave himself all the credit, Greg noticed, although, to be fair, the Crown had not made out a particularly good case for the prosecution. 'Surely when a client confesses guilt to a barrister, the barrister has to withdraw,' he said.

'Normally, yes – at the start of a trial, even half way through. If I'd known in the beginning I would have told him to find another lawyer, but it was too late. The trial was over, bar the shouting, and there was plenty of that over the next few days.'

'There was certainly a lot of bad feeling,' Greg said woodenly.

'It seems I was the only person fool enough to believe that Scobie was an innocent patsy, somebody the police had fixed on as a plausible fall guy for a high-profile case in need of a quick solution.'

'We don't do that!' Greg said angrily.

'No? Maybe *you* don't, Summers, but I've been a barrister a long time and I've lost any illusions I might once have had. I had no idea what to do. Then I saw Frobisher and suddenly it was all very clear to me: I had a

315

few months left and I had to right the terrible wrong I had done. And if I could put a premature end to my own suffering at the same time, then so much the better.'

'So you *invited* Scobie down to Lambourn?' Greg asked.

'Sure. I gave him money, lots of it, in cash, so he'd have something to live on. I told him I was dying. I was completely honest with him about that – he was the only one who knew, the only one I could talk to about it, a bloody psychopath! I had to make like he was my friend when all the time he made my flesh creep. He told me that he'd do anything for me after the service I'd done him and I asked him to kill me, to get hold of a gun and put me down like a rabid dog.'

'Why should he take that risk?'

'I made it sound as risk-free as possible: an isolated house, a break-in gone wrong, everything carefully planned, no forensic, nothing to point the finger at him.'

'Except that there would be.'

'When you examine my computer you will find reams of journal about how I'm scared of Scobie, convinced that he intends to kill me. That is what my "memoirs" consist of. I got hold of his fingerprints too – had a drink with him one night before we left London and walked out with his glass in my pocket. I transferred them to the back door of the house tonight before he came. Smudged, perhaps, but identifiable.'

'Clever.'

'It wasn't hard. He trusted me completely. It's my belief that he had no memory of having confessed to me that day. He may even have believed in his own innocence most of the time.'

Greg remembered a recent conversation about fingerprints with Barbara, about how modern criminals knew better than to leave them. What would his reaction have been to Scobie's 'carelessness' when he investigated the murder of John Hathaway? Would such a handy clue have aroused his suspicions? Realistically, he admitted to himself, he would have seized on the evidence with delight, ascribing it to the legendary stupidity of the criminal mind.

He said, 'Why didn't you simply kill Scobie yourself?'

'I thought about it, but I wanted him to be tried and convicted as a murderer, as he should have been, and serve the sentence he deserved for killing Devon. I do not support the death penalty, even for men like him. Also I wasn't sanguine of getting away with it and I didn't fancy spending my last few months in a prison cell. Besides, it solved my own dilemma – two birds, one stone.'

'Suicide was always an option,' Greg pointed out.

'I am a physical coward. I wasn't lying

tonight when I told Scobie that I couldn't bring myself to put the gun in my mouth and pull the trigger. And my insurance policies wouldn't have paid out on suicide and – God knows – they've cost me enough.'

'Weren't you taking a risk in telling me that Scobie was behind the attacks on you?'

'I had to sow the seed in your mind, but then I back pedalled, as you will recall. Actually, it bothered me a little, when you turned up on my doorstep that day. It never occurred to me that Barkiss would send someone so senior, so experienced, and I could see that you were a shrewd operator and that Indie instinctively trusted you.'

'Flattery,' Greg said. 'Don't think it's not appreciated.'

'And, when I called you about Ranulf's, I assumed you would pass the whole little mess over to someone more junior...'

'There were reasons,' Greg said, 'reasons you can't imagine.'

'Reasons my barrister will delve into–'

'Oh no he won't! And my *juniors* weren't fooled by you, Hathaway.'

'Ah, the charming Sergeant Carey! Yes, she saw right through me, didn't she?'

'To her credit.'

'It was risky, yes,' Hathaway conceded, 'but the whole plan actually had a beautiful simplicity about it and a rightness. Can you imagine the public reaction, Summers, the *glee* at the news that Graham Scobie had murdered John Hathaway, that the smart-arse lawyer had got his just deserts?'

'If only it hadn't gone disastrously wrong,' Greg pointed out. 'If only your wife hadn't come home unexpectedly and killed Scobie. If only she wasn't now facing a possible murder charge.'

Hathaway buried his head in his hands. 'You can see that it was all my fault. I've confessed. There's no need to bring Indie into this.'

'It was her finger pulled the trigger. I can't keep her out.'

'But murder? She came home in the middle of the night to find a known criminal pointing a gun at her husband. She happened to be holding a gun herself and she shot him. It counts as self defence – manslaughter, at the very worst, with a non-custodial sentence.'

'That's not up to me,' Greg said, 'as you well know. The CPS will decide what charges she faces, and Scobie was not a "known criminal", thanks to you. So who did carry out those attacks on you? I take it that it wasn't Scobie.'

'It was me,' Hathaway said simply. 'I did it, and that was the hardest thing of all. You will find the hacksaw in the garden shed – with traces of Ranulf's blood still on it, no doubt.'

'Your wife's racehorse,' Greg said in disgust. 'Olivia's beloved puppy.'

'That ugly, stupid mongrel? Oh, please!'

'You saw how they suffered.'

'It was for the higher good. Somehow, when you're dying it puts things into perspective. So, I had laid all my plans, prepared myself, got rid of Indie and Olivia for a month, but I was hesitating over the timing. The headaches were tolerable. You tell yourself you can have another week – another fortnight – of life if only you don't put it off too long. But Scobie was getting cold feet. It wouldn't have taken much to send him scuttling back to London, so I knew it was last night or never.'

'And what if the plan hadn't worked? What if some clever-bastard barrister had got Scobie off again?'

'The only barrister clever enough to get him off would be dead.'

'You bloody arrogant swine,' Greg shouted.

Hathaway looked at him in genuine surprise, then got heavily to his feet. 'Well, if that's all, Superintendent, then I need to get off and get some rest. I assume my home is off limits so I'll check into a hotel.'

'You're not going anywhere,' Greg said in disbelief. The uniformed sergeant rose automatically and his fingers went to the handcuffs at his belt. Greg laid a hand on his arm and sat him gently down again.

Hathaway looked at them both with contempt and his voice was cold.

'Since I'm not under arrest, I beg to differ. As you just pointed out so helpfully, it was not my finger that pulled the trigger. I'll be back in the morning to give you my written statement and see about Indie's case.'

He picked up his jacket and smiled glacially. 'I suppose you could arrest me for conspiracy to murder myself; that should give the magistrates a good laugh.' The smile disappeared and he said, as if confiding in his best friend, 'I feel so tired, Summers, tired and disappointed. I should have been dead a good two hours by now.'

Greg rubbed his sleepy eyes. Exhausted as he was, everything was now very clear to him. He stood up. 'John Hathaway, I'm arresting you on suspicion of the murder of Reuben ap Morgan.'

Hathaway sighed and resumed his seat as Greg recited the caution. When it was finished he said, 'Prove it.' His eyes were laughing, as if he would enjoy the sparring match. 'Just bloody prove it.'

'All right.' Greg sat and began to enumerate on his fingers. 'One: Reuben ap Morgan kept a journal of his stay in Lambourn–'

'How very juvenile of him.'

'–in which he records the night he watched Scobie ring you from a call box in Eastbury and, himself, did a last-number-redial to

321

check who was being called and hung up when you answered.'

'I told you I got a couple of hang-ups that night.'

'Except that Scobie's call lasted more than two minutes – too long for a hang-up. Two: ap Morgan followed Scobie later that night and witnessed the meeting between the two of you in Lynch Wood in which you planned last night's little fiasco. It's there in black and white – *a burglary gone wrong.*'

'If that's true then why didn't you arrest me earlier?'

Greg went on. 'Three–'

'Answer my question! If ap Morgan named the person Scobie met then why the delay? Because he didn't, did he? You're just blowing smoke.'

'*Three:* my Scenes of Crime Officers are lifting footprints from Lynch Wood – where ap Morgan died, as you well know.'

'I walked Pizza there once or twice,' Hathaway said, 'there's no way that terrain would take a useful footprint.'

'Guess again. My people have the technology now to lift "invisible footprints" from hostile terrain. Electrostatic Lifting Equipment – I'm surprised you haven't come across it in court.'

'Even if that's true, then it's mere circumstance,' Hathaway said. 'You have nothing. I just told you I've been there.'

322

'Yes, you did. I noticed that you made a point of it.' He didn't underestimate his adversary and he expected the same courtesy in return but Hathaway clearly had no respect for him, despite the flattery, and that might prove a mistake.

He went on. 'But the place where you stood to strike ap Morgan down with a tree branch will be easy to determine and why would you stand in that exact spot while walking a dog? Four: I bet if I take a close look at that log store in the garden at Ascot House I shall find the murder weapon, cleverly concealed in plain sight among a pile of other logs.'

Hathaway made no answer, suddenly mute, and Greg nodded in satisfaction. 'Collect enough *circumstantial* evidence and it makes a case – you know that; you've argued enough of them in court – a case that'll keep you in prison, on remand, until...'

He ground to a halt, remembering that the man before him was already under sentence of death.

'Yes... You will have to bring me to trial quickly, Summers, or you'll be too late.'

'You admit it then.'

Hathaway looked from Greg to his passive colleague and back again. 'Oh, I'm too damn proud to deny it any longer, much as I doubt your "evidence". In the end, what difference can it make? My fate is sealed, my sentence passed by the judge with the black cap against whom there is no appeal. The Welshman was a shabby little blackmailer.' Hathaway laughed without mirth. 'Do you know, he actually thought I was employing Scobie to kill Indie. Can you imagine?'

'It's an easy mistake to make,' Greg said. 'You don't expect a man to arrange his own murder.'

'True. But Indie! The banality of it. I was insulted.'

'I daresay ap Morgan hadn't had the privilege of meeting Lady India.'

'Mind you, for a tabloid hack, he wasn't a bad prose stylist.'

It was an epitaph of sorts. Greg had heard worse.

He left the uniformed sergeant to put Hathaway through the arrest process – booking him in, emptying his pockets, removing anything he might use as a weapon against himself or others – then he resumed his questioning.

He had once heard a commander from the Metropolitan Police – one of the senior officers of the Catholic Police Guild – put forward the theory that the policeman is not the murderer's nemesis, but his redeemer. He had yet to meet a murderer who was grateful for that redemption.

He snatched two or three hours sleep in his office and at eight a.m. had the custody sergeant unlock the door of India Hathaway's cell for him, telling the man to wait outside.

India sat sipping tea from a mug, outwardly composed, her heavy-lidded eyes suggesting that she had slept as little as he had. She looked odd in a white paper overall, the clothes she had been wearing at the moment of Scobie's death confiscated as evidence. She looked like a space traveller, a visitor from another world. Beside her was a plate with a slice of buttered toast on it, one neat bite taken from a corner.

She glanced up as he came in but did not speak.

He sat down. 'I have some bad news, I'm afraid, Lady India. Were you aware that, while you were away in Somerset, a journalist was murdered in Lambourn?'

'Johnny mentioned something about it on the phone the other night.'

'A few hours ago I charged your husband with that murder.'

She didn't protest the impossibility of this as he might have expected. She took another sip of tea and said, 'After last night, I don't think anything can surprise me again. What now?'

'He'll be up before a magistrate this morning for remand. Then he'll be taken to the nearest prison that has room for him.'

He would spend his final weeks in jail, as he had feared.

She said, 'Can I see him?'

'Not at present.'

She picked up the plate and bit into another corner of toast, the buttery crumbs sticking to her full lips. She chewed for a moment then spoke with her head lowered, as if addressing the plate.

'So now it's my turn, I suppose.'

'Will you take a word of advice, Lady India?'

She glanced up. 'From you?...Yes.'

'Ask for a solicitor called Deirdre Washowski to represent you.'

'Oh, but my husband will know... No. Okay. My brother...'

'I'm sure Lord Nethermore has a good lawyer,' he said, 'but he's probably not an expert in criminal law. I've been a detective for twenty-five years and, believe me, Deirdre Washowski is the best. May I call her for you?'

'...Yes. Thank you.'

'It'll take maybe an hour.' He looked at her plate. 'Are you sure you don't want a better breakfast – a poached egg, bacon sandwich – keep your strength up?'

She shook her head. 'Thanks, but I can only manage a slice of toast.'

Greg left the room and told the custody

sergeant, 'She wants Dee Washowski to represent her.'

Dick Maybey tutted. 'Bad luck, sir! I was sure she'd send for some posh twat from London – expert in estate duties but can't tell his *habeas corpus* from his *mens rea*.'

'Well, you win some, you lose some,' Greg said. 'Just call her, will you?' He glanced at his watch. 'I'm going to get another forty winks in my office. Ring me when they're ready for interview.'

As he made for the stairs he collided with Nicolaides who was coming in at the front door. The constable was encumbered with a large cardboard box in which Greg could make out, among other things, an answering machine and half a dozen typewritten envelopes.

'Got it, sir,' he said.

'Eh?'

'All the stuff from Morgan's flat you sent me for yesterday. Didn't get home till gone two so I left it till this morning.' He jerked his head back. 'Computer's in the car. Where d'you want it?'

'Ah!'

Greg felt uncomfortable by lunchtime. After the way Hathaway had behaved, he felt a tinge of guilt about his attitude towards Michael Patterson. Patterson had been a kid, acting on the spur of the moment, whereas the calculation in Hathaway's plan had been spine-chilling.

Barkiss had been right and he, Gregory Summers, had been making a fool of himself.

Deirdre Washowski, comprehending in two seconds flat why Greg had recommended her, had dealt swiftly with India's interview and got her charged and remanded on bail as he had intended. What he needed now was to go home and get a few hours more sleep; instead, he got into his car and drove to Lambourn.

Patterson took some time answering the door. When he did he growled, 'Oh, you again,' and turned away. He had left the door open so Greg took that as an invitation and went in. He could smell drink on the young man's breath and a bottle of whisky stood half empty on the coffee table, no glass.

Greg glanced involuntarily at his watch as it was early in the day for strong liquor.

Patterson seemed to have abandoned his carefully cultivated persona as an accountant, standing now in an open-necked shirt and jeans that were ripped at one knee. He was barefoot and his feet were not clean.

The room looked subtly different too: as if the life had gone out of it, been drained away. Glancing round, seeking the source of the change, Greg noticed that the photograph of Michael and his girlfriend had disappeared.

'Grace?' he asked.

'Gone.' He spat out the word. 'I told her and she left me. Of course she did! What sane woman would do otherwise?'

'I'm sorry,' Greg said inadequately.

'I knew I'd have to tell her some day. They made that clear to me – that if I wanted to marry, or live with someone, I'd have to tell her.' He picked up the bottle and took another swig of whisky, swallowing it with a gulp. 'I mean, what if we had a baby and it was taken into care?'

He waved the bottle at Greg. 'The psychiatrist in the secure unit, he told me that if I had a kid I might harm it because I'd be jealous. Jealous! They think I killed the twins out of *jealousy?*'

Greg felt uncomfortable, out of his depth. He wasn't a therapist and this wasn't his field. He said, 'You know, I think you've had enough.' He reached out a hand for the bottle. 'Let me put that away and make you a pot of coffee.'

'Sod you!' Patterson held the bottle out of reach. 'I haven't had enough, nowhere bloody near enough.' He swigged again.

'She might come back, you know, when she's had time to think it over.'

Michael shook his head. 'Maybe if I'd been able to tell her in my own good time, when she knew me better and had come to trust me, but I had to tell her before I was ready, before she was, before somebody else did.'

'She wouldn't have heard it from me,' Greg said. 'No one will.'

'But there were too many people sniffing around.' Patterson sat down on the sofa, the bottle hanging limp from his hand. 'It was like Lambourn was suddenly the centre of the universe. That bloody reporter – they can smell a story, men like that.'

'Reuben ap Morgan?'

He nodded. 'After you told me you recognised me that day, I got to thinking that he might have too. He was staring at me hard enough when I ran into him in the street the other day asking personal questions.'

'There's no indication that he did.' Or that he had even heard of Ian Callaghan.

'And now he's been murdered and the place is swarming with reporters, TV as well as newspapers. I haven't dared stick my nose out of the house since they got here in case I get a camera thrust in my face and find my picture all over the evening news. So! You can ask Grey for my alibi now, see that I was telling the truth.'

'No need, since we've charged a man with the murder,' Greg said. 'The press are packing up to leave. No more story.'

Patterson was too far gone to ask for details, too wrapped up in his own sorrows. 'And then there was that other copper,

330

always hanging round the Fisherman – like you say, you're trained to recognise faces and he looked me over hard enough the other night.'

'What other copper do you mean?' Greg asked, despite having a pretty good idea.

'Al, she called him.'

'She?'

The young man glanced up and sneered. 'Joy Reynolds. Who else? She was getting pretty pally with him Tuesday night – flirting across the bar, *accidentally* brushing hands, giggling and whispering – but then she'd go for anything in trousers. Why don't you ask her about it?'

'Perhaps I will. Are you sure it was Tuesday?'

Patterson didn't reply but stared into the golden depths of his bottle.

If it had been Tuesday night, Greg thought, then it was after Lomax had asked for leave to go to Devon, making Joy Reynolds possibly the last person to see him before he vanished.

There seemed no point in another attempt at taking the bottle from Michael. There was nothing Greg could do to stop a man from getting paralytic in his own home. He said a goodbye that Patterson didn't bother to acknowledge and let himself out.

Somehow, now that he knew Alex Lomax wasn't a murderer, it seemed more and not less imperative to find him.

He decided to leave his car outside and walk to the Jolly Fisherman. It would take less than ten minutes and he felt as if he could do with a bit of air and sunshine after his recent encounters, a little normality. It might help wake him up.

For the first two minutes, as he strode along the deserted road, he thought about Michael Patterson and the way his life had turned out.

Then he ran back to the almshouses as fast as he could. He arrived panting and almost resolved upon joining a gym.

He hammered on the door. No response. He pushed open the letter box and tried to see into the dark interior but there was a wooden box on the inside. It had been fifteen years since Greg had kicked in a door but this one didn't look foot-breakingly sturdy. He stepped back, cocked his right leg up and slammed it with full force into the panelling just below the lock.

It splintered. He tried again and the lock gave way, the door falling in before him so that he had to grab onto the frame to keep his balance.

Patterson was hanging from the banister by what looked like a leather thong, his face beetroot-red, his legs still flailing only inches from the floor, a kitchen stool kicked away in front of him. Greg dived beneath him, standing up to support his weight as if he were giving the man a piggy back. He was heavier than he'd expected.

Panting, Greg reached up to tear the loosened rope from the boy's neck. He found himself holding a leading rein for a horse and flung it from him. He set Patterson down on the sofa, checked that he was still breathing and used his mobile to call for an ambulance. He hovered over the young man while he waited, hoping that he wouldn't stop breathing, that he wouldn't be obliged to give him the kiss of life.

When the ambulance had left, he rang a carpenter of his acquaintance to come and secure the door. The man had to come from Newbury but said he'd be there within the hour. Waiting for him to arrive, Greg made a desultory search of the house. He had no right to do so and no reason either but he was mildly interested to see what this baby-murderer's home looked like.

The layout was much as he had conjectured, with the bedroom at the front, a narrow double, the duvet in a rumpled heap in the middle. On the bedside table a single photo of a woman looked unsmilingly at him. She was in her forties and looked intelligent, elegant in a yellow blouse, not unhandsome, something unforgiving about the eyes.

Mrs Callaghan, he thought, or whatever

she called herself now.

There was a cold bathroom at the back, few toiletries and those the cheapest brands, the soap worn to a sliver. There were no luxuries in prison and ex-cons either went all out for indulgence on their release or maintained the habits of frugality they had learned.

The fridge was similarly unexciting – milk, butter, eggs, a pair of lamb chops – and Greg sat down, his nosiness satisfied, to muse on his recent actions.

Why had he saved Patterson's life when part of him thought that he deserved to be dead for what he had done? Greg was more equivocal about the death penalty than many of his colleagues – most of whom supported it whole-heartedly, having seen at first-hand the consequences of brutal crimes – but no reasonable person thought it should apply to minors, and Ian Callaghan had been fourteen when he had killed.

But no, he had not thought of that. He had not thought at all. He had acted on instinct, a policeman's instinct.

Chapter Twenty-Three

Once he was satisfied that Patterson's house was secure, Greg set off once more for the Jolly Fisherman. He went by car as he had wasted enough time. The pub had now reopened and, as he walked in the door, he noticed for the first time a plaque on the wall which read: *Time spent fishing is not deducted from your life span.*

Greg had been persuaded to go fishing one afternoon in his teens and it had indeed proved a foretaste of eternity.

He found a rather subdued Joy Reynolds in the bar. She did not look pleased to see him but asked, 'What'll it be, sir?'

'Business, I'm afraid, Mrs Reynolds, not pleasure.'

It was early and the only occupants of the bar were a pair of exhausted-looking walkers, probably a married couple, who were drinking beer and arguing over which of them had forgotten to pack the sunblock and was therefore responsible for the peeling red patches on their faces and necks.

He said, 'Can we go through to the back?'

Joy led him silently into the office and stood with her arms folded waiting to see what he wanted, not offering him a seat.

He said, 'I believe you made the acquaintance of one of my officers recently, a man named Alexander Lomax. Tall man,' he clarified, as she made no reply, 'mid-forties, thinnish, bit shabby.'

'I know who he is – saw the thing on the news last night.' She paused and he thought that she blushed, although it wasn't easy to tell under the generous make-up. 'Bit of a charmer, was Al. I didn't realise he was one of your lot till last night.'

'Al?'

'That was what he said to call him.'

'Can you tell me when you saw him last?'

She thought about it. 'He came by Tuesday evening.'

'You're sure it was Tuesday?' She nodded. 'What time?'

'Early, 'bout seven-thirty.'

'And how long did he stay?'

'Maybe an hour.'

'You know that Alex Lomax has gone missing?' he said brusquely.

'Well, yeah, like I said, I saw the TV appeal. He told me that night he was driving down to Devon for a few days. Some problem with his sister.'

'He never arrived in Devon,' Greg said.

'So I gather but I can't help you. He was here about an hour, like I said, then I got called away to the phone and when I got back, he'd gone, so I assumed he'd set off for his sister's place. Thought it was a bit rude – him not saying goodbye like that.'

There was no mistaking the blush this time. Greg said, 'How well did you know Alex Lomax, Mrs Reynolds.'

Her body language shouted defensive. 'Hardly at all. He'd been in maybe twice before Tuesday night. Come to think of it, both times he was in here before, he ended up talking to Reuben, all quiet like in the corner by the fireplace.' She was gaining confidence, relaxing under the impression that she was diverting the course of the interview. 'The second time, I reckon they'd arranged to meet 'cause when Reuben come in he said something about being late.'

'And did you ever talk to "Al" by yourself, one to one?'

The defensive stance was back as she realised that Greg had no interest in Al's relationship with Reuben, knew all about it. 'Might have done. I think he bought me a drink one time.'

'Only once?'

'Or twice. Lots of people buy me drinks. It's normal in a pub, in case you didn't know. Men have a few ... get generous.'

'A few ginger ales?'

'Sorry?'

'Alex Lomax didn't drink alcohol.'

'...No, that's right, come to think of it. He

never. So what?' She swelled her chest out indignantly, switching instantly from defence to attack. 'I dunno what you're getting at. First you accuse me of having an affair with Reuben, now it's this Al. What sort of a woman do you take me for? You can't go round making insinuations. It's libellous.'

'It's not even slanderous,' Greg corrected her. 'Not without witnesses. I repeat, Mrs Reynolds, how well did you know Alex Lomax?'

'Yes.' Eric Reynolds' voice behind him made him spin round. It seemed they had a witness after all and he was damned light on his feet for such a big man. 'Tell the superintendent, Joy. Tell him how well you knew the *defective* Chief Inspector.'

Joy pressed her hand to her mouth in dismay. 'Eric! How long you been there?'

'Long enough.'

Greg took an aggressive step towards the landlord, pulling himself up to his full height which still only brought him up to Reynolds's eyeline. He had it from the man's own wife that he could be violent when his jealousy was roused. 'What do you know about the disappearance of Chief Inspector Lomax, Mr Reynolds?'

'Never knew he was a copper,' the man muttered. 'Couldn't *smell* it on him.' He looked down at Greg, wrinkled his nose and

338

laughed. 'I thought he was just some randy little punter who needed to cool his ardour for a bit.'

'Oh my God!' Joy squealed. 'Cool his... Not the cold store. Eric! You didn't...'

'The cold store?' Greg queried.

'Off the new restaurant,' Joy said faintly.

Greg looked from husband to wife for a moment in disbelief, then he ran out of the office heading for the function room. As he ran, he fumbled for his mobile and called Barbara, ordering her breathlessly to get a squad car and an ambulance over to Lambourn and to detain both the Reynoldses when she got there.

'Can't explain now,' he panted and disconnected.

He braced himself as he dragged open the door of the cold store, but DCI Lomax looked remarkably peaceful, sitting with his back to the wall, his knees bent up, his arms clasped round them. But his torn and ragged fingernails told Greg a different story, a story of how he must have scrabbled, desperately trying to force the door open from the inside, before realising the futility of it, accepting the inevitable and making himself comfortable while he waited for death.

He was white from hair to toes, frosted over like a joint of pork left too long in the supermarket meat cabinet. In one hand he

339

was still clutching his mobile phone – no hope of a signal inside these sealed metal walls, this tomb. On the ground around him lay the butts of a dozen final cigarettes.

'Oh dear,' Greg sighed.

Bending over him without touching him, he noticed that a notebook and pen lay on the floor, half hidden under his right thigh. In breach of all procedure, he prised them out. In capital letters Lomax had written, 'This murder was committed by Eric Reynolds.'

If only they were all that simple.

'Just wanted to cool his ardour,' Reynolds repeated bovinely, standing in the doorway, reluctant to approach, 'and when I came back a few hours later he was dead.'

'Well, of course he was, you moron,' Greg snapped. He was already shivering himself – slapping his arms against his torso to keep warm – and he was wearing a jacket, unlike Lomax who was dressed in chinos and a short-sleeved shirt.

'Didn't know what to do,' Eric said hopelessly, 'so I just left him. Thought it might turn out to be all a bad dream.'

'I never...' Joy said. 'I flirted with him. We had a laugh. I would never have taken it any further. You might have known that, Eric.'

The landlord's face darkened. 'He had his hands all over you. I saw him. Patting your bum, brushing up against you every chance he got, and you were loving it.'

'That's not true!'

'I saw you.'

'Eric–'

'I SAW YOU!'

'It was nothing. I didn't encourage him.'

Eric looked like a huge sulky child, his lip trembling. 'When you thought I might have done for the Welshman you said it turned you on that I would kill for you.'

'Not literally, you big soft ... Eric?'

But he was gone. Greg didn't think there was much point in chasing after him. Reynolds was younger than he was and a lot bigger and stronger. Even if he could catch him, he doubted he could subdue him alone. He wouldn't get far; the wail of sirens was already audible in the distance and he had nowhere to run.

Joy said eagerly, 'It's not true, Mr Summers.' She didn't even look at Lomax, bent over on the floor. She had no pity to spare for him, interested only in her own skin. 'I never flirted with Al, or Reuben, well just a little bit, and I never said I wanted him to kill for me. That's–'

Greg said, 'Just shut the hell up, you stupid slapper.'

'Oh! You can't talk to me that way.'

'No? Who's going to stop me?' He crouched down so his face was level with the dead man's and murmured 'I'm sorry,

Alex' in his ear, although he wasn't sure what for. For thinking that he had killed Reuben ap Morgan, perhaps, or Devon Bliss.

Or simply for not liking him more.

'It was a cream pashonnel,' Reynolds said.

'You what?' Barbara said incredulously.

'Crime of passion,' Eric translated helpfully, 'like in France. You catch a bloke shafting your missus and you blow his brains out. They can't touch you for it.'

'It was nothing like a crime of passion,' Greg said firmly. 'That's when you catch them in the act and just happen to have a gun in your hand at the time. And this isn't France, in case you hadn't noticed, and we most certainly can "touch you for it".'

Eric growled something incomprehensible.

'I want to know exactly what happened,' Greg said. 'You won't help yourself by holding back now.'

'Saw him in the bar Tuesday evening,' Eric said reluctantly, 'and he was all over her and she was liking it too. I saw the look in his eyes – bastard – and with another man's wife. No respect. Then she went to answer the phone and he drank up and went outside so I followed him. He was going to get into his car but then he decided he wanted a fag so he lit up and walked round into the beer garden. It was a nice evening.'

He paused and Greg said, 'Go on.'

'He was leaning against the wall of the new restaurant smoking and I came up behind him from inside, real quiet like, and grabbed him by the throat and wrestled him into the cold store. I'd opened the door ready. It was just to teach him a lesson, make him show some respect. I wouldn't have done it if I'd known he was a copper.' He looked from Greg to Barbara and back again. 'Honest.'

'Oh well, that makes all the difference!' Barbara snapped.

'It was an accident. That's all. A simple accident.'

'It was murder,' Barbara said through gritted teeth.

'He was only in there a few hours. I didn't know...'

'You should have known.' Barbara was almost shouting now. 'It's bleeding obvious to anyone with half a brain that a human being can't survive long at that temperature.'

Greg laid a hand on her arm to calm her. He could feel her trembling. He said, 'What did you do with DCI Lomax's car?'

'Waited till after closing,' Reynolds muttered, 'then sneaked out and dumped it in them woods round Ashdown.'

By the time Greg had charged Reynolds and put a call through to Plymouth, Superintendent Burnip had gone home for the day. A modicum of bullying secured his private number and Greg broke the news about Alex Lomax to him after making sure that he was sitting down.

Just as well, since his Devonian counterpart sounded shattered by what he had heard.

He took Greg's number, said, 'I need a drink, call you back,' and hung up without further ceremony. It was fifteen minutes before he rang back and Greg hoped he hadn't had too much since he wanted him to go and break the news in person to the sister and her children.

'Tell me all of it,' he commanded, 'exact details.'

'It's an odd business,' Greg said, 'and we may never know the whole of it now that DCI Lomax is dead, but it seems that he came to Berkshire specially in search of Devon Bliss's murderer.'

'You mean Scobie?' Burnip queried. 'But he was acquitted.'

'Technically, but it seems that he did indeed kill her and, since he too is dead–'

'Please tell me Alex wasn't responsible for that.'

'No ... it's too long a story and you'll read most of it in the paper tomorrow. Look, Alex was hanging round Lambourn, got flirting with the barmaid of–'

'Always was a ladies' man,' Burnip said sadly. 'I could never figure out what they saw in him personally.'

'No, anyway the husband took umbrage and, in a moment of madness, killed him.' He explained the circumstances. 'I hardly know if it was deliberate or not. He insists not but the charge is still murder.'

'Bloody CPS'll likely downgrade it to manslaughter,' Burnip said.

'Not if I have any say in the matter... Although the fact that he made no attempt to hide the body, or move it, might be seen as proof that he was as horrified by what he'd done as the rest of us.'

'They say hypothermia is quite a painless way to go,' Burnip commented after a pause.

'They do.' It seemed like no time since Greg had had the same conversation with Lomax himself. What was it – a fortnight ago?

'But I call it a damn shabby death,' Burnip added.

Another epitaph, Greg thought, the second he had heard that day, not such a good one.

'What's happening about the funeral?' Burnip asked.

'Damned if I know. The family...'

'Oh! If you leave it up to Bridget, she'll

probably stick him in a skip to save money. Look, would you be offended if we handled it at this end? He was with us for twenty years...'

'Be my guest!' He asked Burnip if he would take responsibility for informing the next of kin.

'I'm on my way,' Burnip grunted, 'and I know what her first question will be: How much was he worth?'

He hung up.

Chapter Twenty-Four

Beatrice Pitcher had spent a happy hour browsing the antique shops of Hungerford Arcade. She had little spare cash but an eye for a bargain. She glanced at her watch and decided she would treat herself to some coffee and maybe a cake while she decided whether she could afford that Barbara Pym first edition and, if not, whether she could bear to be without it. She headed for the counter of the small café on the first floor, pleased to see that there was no queue this morning. Then something made her stop dead so that a woman moving purposefully in the same direction behind her cannoned into the back of her, then bypassed her triumphantly to go to the head of the line.

Beatrice shrank back into the shadows.

It was those broad shoulders that clinched it, despite the brunette wig, facing away from her, luckily, in a blue blouse, rather old-fashioned, no doubt to reassure. She had a clearer view of the other woman: about her own age, looking shaken, almost ill.

She was filled with fury. Did it never occur to that woman that she might kill one her elderly victims, give her a heart attack or stroke?

She backed away, turning into the nearest booth in the arcade where a middle-aged man in good clothes was examining a china ornament. She grabbed him by the arm and dragged him a few yards further away, out of earshot of the café.

'Quick,' she snapped in her best school-mistress tones. 'Give me your mobile phone.' She knew he would have one. Men like him always did.

If the man thought he was being mugged by a pensioner he showed no sign of it. He reached into his inside pocket without comment, took out the mobile and pressed a couple of buttons to unlock the keypad.

She dialled nine twice, then thought better of it. She felt in her purse for the card DCI Lomax had given her and rang his mobile number but the line seemed dead. She cursed mildly, then tried the number the woman sergeant had scrawled on the back of the card. It was answered at once.

'Sergeant Carey.'

'It's Beatrice Pitcher,' she said in a shrill whisper. 'I'm in the Hungerford Arcade and *that* woman is here, with her latest victim, in the café.'

'I'll have someone there within ten minutes,' Barbara said. 'I won't be long myself. I'm only in Lambourn.'

'Hurry. I'll wait for your people out front.'

'Don't do anything stup–' Beatrice ended the call and handed the phone back to the man. If she had to do something stupid, like tackling the bitch herself, then she would.

The man stood there looking at her with mild interest.

'You can go now,' she said.

'What, and miss the show?'

The owner of the stall came over and said, 'Can I help anyone at all?'

'No!' they said in chorus.

She looked at the man in exasperation, then said, 'Well, if you're hanging around you might as well make yourself useful.' She drew him carefully back to where they had an oblique view of the café. 'You see that woman – second table from the counter against the wall, with her back to us?'

'The one in the blue blouse?'

'If she tries to leave before the police get here then we shall have to stop her.'

'Fine.' He asked no questions but looked as if he hadn't had so much fun in years. They sneaked away and down the stairs to the pavement outside. 'Is there a back exit?' the man asked.

'Good question. Go and look,' she commanded.

He returned in two minutes, shaking his head. '"These doors are alarmed,"' he announced. 'I always think that's quite a funny sign, don't you?'

Beatrice stared at him in disbelief. 'Get a grip!' she snapped.

She began to pace up and down on the pavement until a marked police car pulled silently into an empty parking space a few yards down the hill. She rushed over and wrenched the passenger door open.

'Miss Pitcher?' asked a startled Constable Jill Christie.

'Yes! She's still in there.'

Jill got out of the car and put her hat on. PC Sharon Moore got out of the driving seat and did likewise.

'Sergeant Carey's on her way,' she remarked. 'We'll wait.'

'Look out!' The man with the mobile hissed a warning. Beatrice spun round and saw the woman leaving the Arcade, her victim still pathetically thanking her for her help. Then she caught sight of Beatrice and the two police women and her face shifted into panic.

Barbara Carey's car drew up at the kerb at that moment, with Andy Whittaker at the wheel. Peggy bolted. Her victim called 'Dorothy?' after her in bewilderment. 'What is it? What's the matter?'

'Check your bag,' Beatrice snapped at her and the woman began to rummage in her handbag, soon emitting squeals of dismay.

Sharon and Jill were right behind Peggy as

she headed down the hill and round the corner into Church Street. They were younger and faster than she was but, as they gained on her, she was making for the blue Ford Cortina which was waiting on a double yellow line just outside the municipal car park. Seeing her predicament, the car driver swung out and drove straight past her without stopping, turning right at the junction. Peggy stopped and stared after him in disbelief.

'You little bastard—'

The two constables grabbed her simultaneously and not very gently by each upper arm, as the Cortina accelerated away up the High Street.

'That's him!' Beatrice shouted as he approached. 'That's the boy she works with.' They all watched as the Cortina roared past, in need of a new exhaust. Barbara began reciting the number plate and description into her radio at high speed, as Sharon and Jill returned with their struggling quarry.

'It's all his fault,' Peggy shrieked. 'My son. Brian O'Connor, of fourteen Aspen Road Newbury.' She added under her breath. 'Think you can run off and leave me to carry the can, do you, Brian?'

Barbara repeated the address into her radio, raising her voice to be heard over Peggy's ranting.

351

'He knocks me about if I don't do what he says. I'm just an innocent victim here.' She noticed Beatrice again. 'You – you old bitch. You've been nothing but trouble from–'

Beatrice stepped forward and, before anyone could stop her, slapped the woman very hard across the face, shocking her into silence.

Though not for long.

'Assault!' she yelped. 'That was an assault.'

'I didn't see anything,' Barbara said. 'Did you, Constable Whittaker?'

'No, ma'am.'

Soon Peggy was safely bundled in the back of the marked police car which moved off towards Newbury while Andy was comforting the latest victim and getting her details. Barbara turned to Beatrice and her new ally. 'Thank you very much, Miss Pitcher. And you are...?'

'William Harrison,' he said, handing her a business card. 'Technical support and general back-up to this good lady.'

'It says stockbroker here,' she pointed out.

'Ah, that's just my day job. Show me a phone booth and I'll change into my super-hero costume.'

Barbara raised her eyes briefly to the heavens and pocketed his card. 'Someone will be in touch to take a statement, Mr Harrison, and from you, Miss Pitcher. You've done a good day's work here. Andy, let's get this lady to the station.'

She had been supervising the murder scene at the Jolly Fisherman all morning and was glad of an excuse to get away for an hour or two. She'd been at plenty of murder scenes but never one where the victim was a colleague she had been starting to think of as a friend. There were moments when the memory of Alex's pathetic collection of socks and underpants made her want to howl like a wolf.

She inserted the old lady gently into her car.

'May I buy you a cup of coffee, Miss ... is it Pitcher?' Harrison said as the police officers drove away.

'I think we both deserve one, Mr Harrison.'

Ten minutes later they were William and Beatrice to each other and she had told him the full story of the Good Samaritan con.

'Extraordinary the way she turned on her accomplice,' William commented. 'Did you hear that?'

'Indeed I did. Most distasteful.'

'Mother denouncing son, putting all the blame on him. Telling them where to find him even. What sort of woman betrays her own son like that? ... I would never let my kids down, no matter what they did. Hmmm? You listening, Beattie?'

'Beatrice,' she corrected him automatically,

her thoughts quite elsewhere. 'I was a schoolteacher all my working life – nearly all – and these last few years it seems to me that parents are far too indulgent of their children's faults. I've seen colleagues threatened with physical violence for attempting to discipline an unruly pupil.'

'Well, that's going a bit far,' he admitted.

'Children must have clear boundaries, understand right from wrong. Give them good principles and then they are responsible for their own actions.'

'But if they don't have those boundaries,' William said, 'if they don't understand, then it's *our* fault, the parents – not the teachers, not society, only us. Do you have children?'

'...No.'

'Then you can't know what it's like. I would do anything for Imogen and Rosalind.'

She snapped, 'Giving your daughters Shakespearean names doesn't impress people, you know,' then, seeing his crushed look, she relented. 'Maybe if you'd called them Goneril and Regan.'

'So, even though Lomax stayed away from the bottle all his life, he still ended up freezing to death,' Greg said, 'just like his father. If I believed in anything at all, I'd say his fate was pre-ordained and he couldn't escape it. Lucky I don't.'

He and Angie were curled up together on the sofa, keeping each other warm, no danger of hypothermia here. A bottle of Savemore's best Rioja was open on the table in front of them. He had just finished catching her up on the last couple of days. It had taken a long time.

'But why did this Alex Lomax come to Newbury?' Angie asked. 'Did he intend to kill Scobie, or Sir John?'

'We shall never know. Perhaps he didn't know himself, hadn't reached a decision yet. I like to think that something in his policeman's training would have steered him away from vigilante action when it came to the crunch.'

'If I were in danger,' Angie said, 'and you hadn't enough evidence to put the person who was threatening me away, what would happen to your policeman's training then?'

'Oh... Let's not go there.'

There was a comfortable lull in conversation until she said, 'So, can you tell me your Secret now?'

'No, darling. That's one secret I shall probably have to take to my grave.'

'Okay.'

'And if it's any help, I've behaved like a hysterical adolescent about the whole thing.'

'Ooh! I spy a man in need of counselling. When I qualify, in a few years time, you can tell me all about it and patient confidentiality will apply. Deal?'

'Deal!' he said, confident that by the time she qualified as a counsellor the subject would have been long forgotten. He had called the hospital this afternoon to check on Patterson and been told that he'd made a good recovery and been sent home. Didn't the Chinese believe that if you saved someone's life you were thereafter responsible for them? Troubling thought.

He tucked it away in the back of his mind, leaned forward and refilled their glasses. They twined their arms together to drink a loving cup and managed to spill wine over themselves and the upholstery.

'Oops!' they chorused and laughed.

Bellini came bounding up beside them and began to lap at the red pools on the sofa.

On Sunday evening, Beatrice Pitcher sat in her armchair and gazed into space for a long time, running over her conversation with William that morning in her mind, about how parents betrayed their children.

Her only son had been, if she was honest, a disappointment to her: a shy, furtive boy, only averagely bright and given to emotional outbursts and anxiety attacks, even before his father's departure. Besides, she had dreamed of a daughter throughout her difficult pregnancy, a civilised child with a gift for music and painting, gentle yet spirited. Even so, it had pained her to cast him off, to deny his existence, though it had seemed the right – the only – thing to do at the time.

And then there had been her own guilt – the surge of exhilaration she had felt on hearing the news of the babies' deaths, savouring the devastation wrought on her greatest enemies, her ex-husband and his floozy.

So long ago; was there anything sadder than stale emotion?

She had kept herself busy all day since the excitement in Hungerford – an invitation to lunch from a neighbour, gardening in the afternoon, six o'clock evensong – but now she was alone with her thoughts and could not scare them away any longer. She went into the kitchen, took a bottle of white wine from the fridge, prised out the cork and poured herself a large glass.

If she had so finally cast Ian off then what had made her buy this house in Berkshire on her retirement, less than ten miles from his? As his official next of kin, she was one of only half a dozen people who knew his present identity and whereabouts and she had moved two hundred miles away from everybody and everything she knew to be near him.

So what had she been waiting for?

When the bottle was empty, she pulled the telephone onto her lap. She looked at it for a long time, then picked up the receiver and dialled a number she had memorised before she moved to Berkshire.

'Michael? ... I am speaking to Michael Patterson? My name is Beatrice Pitcher – but that won't mean anything to you. You will know me better by the name I went by sixteen years ago. In those days I was Bea Callaghan.'

She felt something wet drop on her hand and stared at it in amazement. Then the tears she had not been able to shed for sixteen years were falling freely.

'...Michael? Are you there?

'...Ian?

'Yes, it's me, darling. It's Mummy.'

She gulped back the tears as she stammered, 'Forgive me.'

Epilogue

Greg decided to go to John Hathaway's funeral on a drizzly Saturday morning in early December, when the beakerful of the warm south that had been the shores of Lake Garda seemed a lifetime past. He wasn't working that day so it was in his own time and the alternative seemed to be going Christmas shopping with Angie in Oxford.

Hathaway had been in a prison hospital since his arrest but had been allowed out for the last two weeks on compassionate grounds to die. He had spent the time in a hospice in Reading, being kept as comfortable as possible during this last trial.

Greg put on his grey overcoat over his best suit, white shirt and black tie. He polished his black shoes and arrived two minutes before the ceremony was due to start.

He slipped in silently and stayed at the back.

The huddle at the front of the crematorium chapel was a small one: he could see India, Olivia, a tall distinguished-looking man of about sixty whom he guessed to be India's brother, the eighth Earl of Nethermore, and a younger – but also distinguished-looking –

man who had his arm round Olivia and who had to be her father, Richard, home from Moscow for a few days for a family funeral.

Or perhaps permanently, since having a murderer for a father did not go down well in the diplomatic corps. It did not inspire confidence, even in Moscow.

Next to Richard was a tall woman with honey-coloured hair who looked, even in full mourning, like a fashion model, balancing on legs so thin that Greg feared they might snap at any minute. He tried to remember the name of Olivia's mother, but couldn't.

Paddy Nash came rushing in after the ceremony had started and took a place across the aisle from Greg, his head bowed, his hands folded in front. If he saw Greg then he did not acknowledge him.

It was a brief and unsentimental few minutes, almost impersonal, before the curtains swung back and the coffin lurched its way to the furnace. By the time they all gave the little sigh of relief that always seemed to end a cremation, Nash had slipped out as quietly as he had come and Greg was left wondering why he did not do likewise.

He assumed that India would not want to speak to him but, when she turned away at the end and caught sight of him for the first time, she made purposefully toward him and he stayed for her like a rabbit caught in a car's headlights. She was wearing a dark trouser suit and a black headscarf over her blonde hair. He thought he could see wisps of grey escaping, a natural response to all she had been through.

Her voice was as gentle and self-controlled as ever. 'Mr Summers, thank you for coming.' He bowed his head. She did not introduce her family but told them to wait for her outside. They left, giving him curious looks. She said, 'You will forgive me if I don't invite you to the wake. My family wouldn't understand. It'll be a dismal affair, in any case. They are ashamed.'

He said, 'How are you, Lady India?'

'Not too bad.' She grimaced. 'Now, why do I say that when, actually, I'm scared to death? Reggie Westfield – John's old partner in the Temple; he's acting for me – says the trial won't take place till next summer at the earliest.'

Greg knew that there had been much debate in the CPS over going ahead with the prosecution at all, public sympathy being greatly with her. The *Daily Outlook* had started a 'Free Lady India' campaign, demanding the right for householders to kill in self defence, or what they perceived to be self defence. Greg suspected that the paper's more cerebrally-challenged readers had somehow gained the impression that India

Hathaway had shot the man responsible for the death of the lately beatified Reuben ap Morgan.

Ironically, her privileged position had counted against her; it had been decided that failing to test the case in court might be construed as the establishment protecting one of its own. So being an earl's daughter wasn't all roses after all.

The charge against India was manslaughter. Even if the jury convicted her the judge would have a dozen reasons not to jail her, but there were no guarantees. Eric Reynolds, on the other hand, was in prison awaiting trial for murder and he was looking at a life sentence. The jury might let him off with manslaughter on the grounds of total stupidity, but he'd still serve many years. The last time Greg had driven past the Jolly Fisherman it had been closed and boarded up.

'At least you're out and about,' he said.

'Yes. Thank you for not opposing bail.'

'That would have been absurd since you're obviously not a danger to society.'

'And thank you for recommending Deirdre Washowski. She's been a tower of strength.'

'I see that Ascot House is up for sale.'

'I can't live there again. For me, it will always smell of Scobie's blood and John's deceit. I had to put it on at quite a low asking price; the estate agent said tactfully that not everyone wanted to live in a house where a brutal death had occurred.' She gestured back at the closed curtains where her husband had vanished forever. 'The idea was always that John and I should be buried together in the family plot at Nethermore Hall, but somehow that doesn't seem appropriate now.'

'I'm sorry,' he said, meaning it.

'I can't quite forgive him for what he did to Ranulf's Daughter and Pizza, you see.'

'And to you.'

'Ah, that was different. That was an accident and not part of the plan. That, I can forgive.'

He wondered if she would feel the same if she ended up doing time. He said indignantly, 'And I notice he made a point of vandalising *your* car and not his precious Aston Martin, of attacking *your* racehorse and Olivia's puppy and nothing that belonged to him.'

'I got a good price for the Aston, at least – notoriety value. People who don't want a haunted house are happy to swan around in a murderer's car, it seems. It'll help to pay my legal fees.' She shook her head. 'You never knew John Hathaway, Mr Summers. You never met him. By the time you came knocking on our door that day in early August, the real John Hathaway had already gone, his body inhabited by ... some sort of demon.'

'I know that he was once a great man,' Greg conceded.

'The man I married was no murderer.'

Tell that to Reuben ap Morgan, Greg thought, destroyed in the prime of life, to the parents and sisters in Wales who mourned him, to lifelong friends like Sarah Keaton.

'I like to think that it was the tumour that led him to act as he did,' India went on. 'So out of character. I've been reading up on it and it can change your personality completely.'

He merely nodded, which she took as assent. He hoped she was right. It was true that he hadn't met Hathaway until the cancer had begun its deadly work, but there had been an arrogance about the man which made him nervous and he had met too many barristers who placed Justice – their Justice – above the law.

'That last fortnight,' she said, 'in the hospice, he didn't know who I was.' Her eyes misted over. 'We were so happy and for such a long time. I won't let these last four months destroy that.'

He patted her arm in sympathy. 'You need not.'

The young-but-distinguished man poked his head round the door.

'Mother?'

'I'm coming, darling.' She held out her hand to Greg.

'You're staying at Nethermore Hall?' he asked.

'Yes, one of the conditions of bail. The next time we meet will be at my trial, Mr Summers.'

He shook hands warmly. 'And I wish you the very best of luck.'

He knew the two words he wanted to hear at the end of that trial:

Not guilty.

The publishers hope that this book has given you enjoyable reading. Large Print Books are especially designed to be as easy to see and hold as possible. If you wish a complete list of our books please ask at your local library or write directly to:

Magna Large Print Books
Magna House, Long Preston,
Skipton, North Yorkshire.
BD23 4ND